More Books from The Sager Group

The Swamp: Deceit and Corruption in the CIA
An Elizabeth Petrov Thriller (Book 1)
by Jeff Grant

Chains of Nobility: Brotherhood of the Mamluks (Book 1-3)
by Brad Graft

Meeting Mozart: A Novel Drawn from the Secret Diaries of Lorenzo Da Ponte
by Howard Jay Smith

Death Came Swiftly: Novel About the Tay Bridge Disaster of 1879 by Bill Abrams

A Boy and His Dog in Hell: And Other Stories
by Mike Sager

Miss Havilland: A Novel
by Gay Daly

The Orphan's Daughter: A Novel
by Jan Cherubin

Lifeboat No. 8: Surviving the Titanic
by Elizabeth Kaye

Into the River of Angels: A Novel by George R. Wolfe

See our entire library at TheSagerGroup.net

Secrets *of* Ash

JOSH GREEN

Secrets of Ash: A Novel

Copyright © 2023 Josh Green

All rights reserved.

Published in the United States of America.

Cover and Interior Designed by Siori Kitajima, PatternBased.com

Cataloging-in-Publication data for this book is available from the Library of Congress

ISBN-13
eBook: 978-1-958861-21-9
Paperback: 978-1-958861-22-6

Published by The Sager Group LLC
(TheSagerGroup.net)

Secrets *of* Ash

JOSH GREEN

THE SAGER GROUP

Artifex Te Adiuva

"Nothing weighs on us so heavily as a secret."

– Jean de La Fontaine

For Mom and Marley

Part I

1

From the outset, Chase Lumpkin couldn't shake the feeling he was under investigation in Cherokee. His suspicions were confirmed his third night in town when he found the Lonesome Cub, a quaint dive bar on the downtown square. Chase was watching the Braves on televisions above the bar, drinking lite beer and saying nothing, when the county sheriff stood against a high-backed stool next to him and laid his hat on the bar. Darkened at the wide brim with waves of sweat, the hat was inscribed with the Ash County emblem, a bear and bounding deer on opposite sides of a forested oval, with three cursive Latin words. The sheriff smelled tangy, like a Southern man who works outdoors in summer.

Chase turned his big shoulders and nodded, surprised by the genuine kindness on the sheriff's red face, the smiling eyes. "I'm really sorry," Chase said. "Not up for talking this evening."

The sheriff spun the stool around and sat down, as though he hadn't heard Chase, leaving one empty seat between them, inspired by the challenge. "I try to welcome all my new residents," the sheriff said. "So just a quick introduction, and I'll be gone."

Chase nudged his beer to his right and abandoned his seat, moving two spaces down, next to a logger who smelled better, like cedar chips and gasoline. "Don't blame you," the logger whispered. "Nosy fuck."

The sheriff grabbed his hat, tossed it over, and ordered a ginger ale and bowl of boiled peanuts. He limped behind two seats, took the third, and said, "You're out of running room, son. Just speak to me a moment. We have things in common."

"Sir," Chase said, sighing. "What do you want to hear?"

The sheriff clutched his ginger ale and nodded to the bartender, a young woman he found inexcusably attractive, which he'd hesitated to acknowledge because he'd known her since girlhood, since the day drug-running lowlifes shot her father dead in the high country. Nonetheless, the sheriff had been drafting vague plans in his mind to court this pretty bartender, Carrie, despite their age difference and his upcoming thirtieth anniversary, for which his giddy wife was planning grand Alaskan escapades on well-appointed boats. "Let's start with your full name, son." The sheriff spoke so slowly it sounded condescending to Chase.

"I'm not a kid."

"I know that, of course."

"I don't need parenting."

"I know that, too."

"Then please don't talk down to me, sir."

The sheriff leaned back. "Easy," he said. "I apologize, soldier. We speak like this up here. Like we mean it."

Nothing about Cherokee was turning out how Chase had planned. Back in Atlanta, while walking the streets of Cabbagetown one hot night, pictures in a Realtor's storefront caught Chase's eye, and he stopped for a moment, ogling colorful advertisements with many exclamation points. He saw a multitude of North Georgia residential properties—wide lots with mountain vistas, extravagant cabins, and simple rustic shacks—taped in long rows against the Realtor's window. With his disability checks and serviceable credit score, Chase knew he could afford the more modest ones and execute a quick escape. The possibility of leaving the city made the veins in his neck surge, and he walked the streets dizzy, romanticizing mountain life, convinced he stood at the precipice of great change. A week later, he broke his apartment lease despite the $200 fine and fled the neighborhood, bound for the most isolated but functional mountain town he'd read about. His whole life fit in the back of a four-door Honda. Old clothes and lamps and a beaten footlocker lay in clumsy heaps. Seeing this cargo packed, all bound for somewhere else, Chase felt optimistic, almost buoyant. For once he was in control. For a brief time he felt revived, unencumbered by the horrors of war. In his mind he saw a simple, wonderful existence in the mountains: a city boy cooking slab bacon over axe-split hickory, stealing brown trout from icy streams. He foresaw a simple, earnest wife, too: a woman bored by things like artisanal brass jewelry and restaurants in gritty-chic neighborhoods. A woman who would rub his back and sing hymns from her Bible. And so, driving north, Chase watched Atlanta's exurbs wash out into pastures, and he let loose a wild and joyful scream. He screamed until he feared his throat would bleed. Free of the urban cacophony, his mind filled with baseless ideations of the place he was going: a town where sins were cleansed and secrets quarantined, where people were sparse, kind, and forgiving. "Quainter it is," he'd said to himself that day, exaggerating hillbilly dialect, "the better it is." He envisioned an ice cream parlor on a cobbled public square, a faux Western saloon, and a sleepy Bible college—a perfectly boring haven. The real estate literature had promised all of that in Ash County, in the town of Cherokee.

Instead, Chase found himself alone again, drinking with vicious purpose, and now saddled with this inquisitive old lawman. He knew exactly where their conversation was going. He lifted his glass and gulped until the beer was gone.

"Now, about a proper greeting." The sheriff relaxed, resting his elbows on the bar. "I'm Monte Gaylord. Been sheriff of Ash since 1998, after *my* army service, two deployments to Iraq in Operation Desert Storm." He paused to gauge Chase's reaction. He studied the aching eyes, green and handsome as early spring, and the muscled jaw, but he saw nothing. "Some sand flea with a kitchen grenade sent me home with this busted hip," said the sheriff. "It hampers me to this day, obviously, but I ain't bitter."

In one fluid glance Chase sized up the sheriff from boots to gray hair, which fell in a perfect Kentucky Waterfall. "Just don't," Chase said, nodding for another beer. "You know my name, and you know a lot more. My Realtor is the nephew of your mayor, your good friend. You probably think I'm too dense to know that."

"Speaking of," said the sheriff, "how's the house up there? You get a deal?"

"It'll do."

"Good to hear, real good," the sheriff said. "They used to cook a whole lot of meth up there. But the old tenants won't be around for at least twelve years, thanks to me and a few top lieutenants. I'm sure it was thoroughly cleaned, though. And I'm sure you got the deal of the century on that place—"

"I don't need a babysitter, okay?" Chase said. "I just need to clear my head, sir. All I want is fresh air and silence. And beer, I guess. It was starting to get—I don't know—claustrophobic in Atlanta. This seemed like a good destination, but maybe I made a mistake."

"Bobcat," the sheriff said. "That's what you remind me of."

"Just leave me alone, sir."

"Why so *mean*?" the sheriff said. "Feisty like a bobcat."

"With all due respect, sir, you're being a gnat."

"Holy hell!" the sheriff said, leaning back. "Damn! You always been like this?"

"I guess so," said Chase, rocking his shoulders to loosen the hard, thick neck. "I'm proof that pharmaceuticals aren't magic, like Mom said. And that anyone can ruin a nice upbringing."

The sheriff chuckled in a slow, worried way, sipped his drink, and watched the Braves' reliever toss two strikes. "It don't have to be like this, Bobcat."

Chase's next beer arrived, and he drank it angrily, hissing with the burn of carbonation. "Do taxpayers know you're here, killing time?"

"Look," said the sheriff, "I know you boys saw some shit overseas. Understand that I appreciate you for going, and I appreciate your friends for dying. Just know that I'm here to listen, when you're ready to talk. That's all—a peace offering. We're finished."

The sheriff stood up and felt satisfied with himself, with the progress he'd made in the introduction, confident this kid wasn't apt to blow the town apart or start knifing tourists, despite the rumors. "Until next time," he said, with what he thought was both warmth and authority. "Just mind your manners." The sheriff exited the Lonesome Cub, his stuttered boot steps knocking on the old heart pine, and the door slammed so hard Chase nearly dropped his glass. Beside him, the logger shook his head, convinced he was sharing the bar with some sort of outlaw.

The logger reached out a big hand to pat Chase's back but retracted before contact. "He won't leave you alone," the logger said. "Everyone knows our crippled old sheriff gets his man."

Chase managed a half-smile and patted the logger's immense back, slowly releasing an emphatic, brotherly, troubled sigh. He watched the bartender as she sliced limes and stole shy glimpses at him.

***

Residue.

That's the word Sheriff Gaylord used the second time they met, near the toy museum on the town square. Chase was walking from a parking lot to the Lonesome Cub, his jittery hands plunged in jean pockets, when the sheriff spotted him and yelled, "Hey, Bobcat, sit down!"

Chase stopped, allowing the sheriff to catch up and stand beside him.

"Let's sit a moment, on this bench," the sheriff said.

"I'm good."

"Okay, we'll stand."

"No offense, but I wish you'd go away, sir."

"No you don't, believe me," said the sheriff. "But I understand. Your little revolts are to be expected. It's just part of the process."

Chase dropped his head. "I appreciate the welcome. I really do. It's great to know people care up here. It's the opposite of what I always heard about Nam you know. But it's kind of suffocating, too. I was just hoping to blend into the backdrop, to kind of vanish, and when strangers try to help me, especially after a few drinks, I have a tendency to push back. I've always had the tendency to push back."

The sheriff took a quick, unsteady step away from Chase, eyeing his waist for the outline of a weapon. "I'm going to be honest with you," said the sheriff. "That weight in your guts gets lighter, but it sticks. And if you don't talk, it gets metastatic. A few years back now, I organized group sessions at the VFW, and I've seen this in everyone coming back home. Every single one. If you don't open up to somebody, like me or the shrinks, at least clue your family in. What are they like, if I can ask?"

At this question Chase simultaneously bristled and laughed. "Why's that matter?" he said. "I'm grown."

"That's true, clearly," said the sheriff. "I'm just curious why you'd leave them behind. At a time when you'll need 'em."

Again Chase found what looked like focused, unselfish compassion in the sheriff's eyes. "Well, my brother's on the radio in Atlanta, about to be famous," Chase said. "He's a little older, a hotshot in sports-talk radio. I'm proud of him, though, not jealous. You may know the name Jack Lumpkin?"

"Can't say I do."

In the shadows of blossoming crepe myrtles—trees so explosively pink they looked like giant tufts of cotton candy, assaulted and ripped apart by children, lining Cherokee's streets—they stared at each other for a moment. "I guess the radio signal doesn't reach up here," Chase finally said. "But otherwise, my family hasn't been much help, though they try. My grandfather's retired army. My mom's there, too, worried sick about her baby boy, fighting her own fight with social anxiety, or something like that. We're normal folks but totally abnormal at the same time. Basically your typical American shitshow." Checking his watch, Chase feigned a pressing appointment, and he took a step toward the tavern. "Okay, I'm gonna get going."

"Just give me another minute."

"Just *don't*," said Chase.

"Relax."

"Stop it."

"Just breathe, son."

"*Stop*."

"Hands down, to your hips," the sheriff said, cowering. "Unclench 'em and give me a listen."

"I can't take this pressure, sir." Chase shivered in the public square, a nervous defect set ablaze by the high-altitude sunshine, crisp and hot. "I can't breathe with you pressing down on me."

The sheriff launched into a spiel about postwar residue, the stress of coming back alone, and something about the danger of private firearms within reach at home. Chase rubbed his eyes and walked away, too fast for a hobbling man, which only made the sheriff more resolute to save Chase— and Chase more determined to avoid him. He learned the sheriff's work schedule and stayed home, in the hills, for the most part, during his shifts.

***

In those early Cherokee days, there was a woman one morning in Chase's arms, a gorgeous but stern apparition in his living room. She was asking a hundred questions as the sun came up across the Amicalola Valley. He hadn't a clue how they'd come to be there, but he could vaguely recall them kissing. He recognized her long-sleeved flannel and the glint of her serious eyes before realizing he knew her as the Lonesome Cub bartender, Carrie. Once this registered, Chase gently backed away, bashful as always, and in doing so, her voice permeated his blurred consciousness, like soft music through a passing storm. The questions began to register, too. Carrie was asking why his hands trembled above the bar top, even when he was adequately inebriated, and why he couldn't stop clashing with law enforcement. She called him reckless. She called him a rebel. And life, she said, never ends well for mountain rebels.

"I don't know," is all Chase said.

"Come on," Carrie pried, "open up a little."

"Not sure why I'm like this," Chase said, his heart racing. He tried to smile, to deflect, but he felt too cornered, ashamed. "I know your overserving me doesn't help, though."

"Get serious," said Carrie, in her unblinking way.

Her face tightened toward her small nose, to the point it looked like she was making a plea, or desperately praying, straining to exorcise frustrations that felt foreign to her. She was used to having her way with Cherokee's men, and the stubbornness of this tall, hawkish, thick-chested enigma was pissing her off. "It's concerning," she said, "because you're too young to fall apart."

Chase nodded, gave in. "Look, I just keep blacking out and doing stupid shit," he said. "Pissing in the street and getting arrested, sowing wild oats. But it's all minor charges. Just fines so far. If I was back in college, I'd be doing the same things, but you'd laugh it off as normal frat-boy bullshit."

"It's not normal."

"Why are you here?" he said. "And sorry, but how'd we *get* here?"

"Good God," Carrie said, tossing her arms. "You can't hold your liquor for shit."

"I'm serious. No clue."

"We agreed to come talk, man. Over coffee. After closing time. So let's talk."

"We just did."

Carrie dropped her arms, slapping hands against tight jeans, eyeing the front door. "I don't want to like you," she said, "if I can't understand you a bit more."

"Why would you like me?"

That sentiment struck Carrie as whipped-dog pathetic, yet somehow endearing. She wanted to call him a pussy but caught the word in her mouth, fearing the potential cracks it might cause in such a fragile psyche. She stepped closer. "This is a little town," she said. "You don't know it, but you're a big deal, at least for the girls who aren't married. Guys who look like you don't usually stick around."

"So you're hungry for options?"

"I'm hungry," she smiled, making silly claws of her hands, "for fresh meat."

Chase noticed the coffee mug beside him and swigged the remaining half-cup. "Jesus, girl," he said.

Carrie demurred, stepped away. "Just tell me this," she said. "What are you looking for, down in the tavern? What are you trying to fix, or hide from?"

Chase exhaled, wheezy and sinking, a limp raft in his living room. He stepped back until his legs were pressed against the couch behind him. He couldn't retreat any farther without being rude. He felt the tension creeping in and decided to combat that with a confession, a purge. "I'm just trying not to drink by myself."

"Why, though?"

"Because all it takes is like five minutes by myself, and I start to let my mind wander, and I start thinking about overseas. If I start thinking about overseas, I start thinking about the lives that were lost. If I start thinking about the lives that were lost, I pull out my laptop here, and next thing you know, I'm looking at pictures and crying for a while, until I leave or just cry myself to sleep. Nobody understands. Don't tell me you do, either. It's like the walls are closing in. There's no place to go and get myself back. And it's even worse when I *don't* drink—"

"Stop," Carrie interrupted, lifting open palms. "That shit's bringing me down."

"I'm sorry," said Chase. "Didn't mean to alarm you."

"I like messes," she said. "But this is a disaster."

"Being here is probably a mistake."

"You invited me."

"I don't deserve this."

"I thought we might have something."

"I don't deserve you—"

"*Enough*," she said, hustling to the door, waving him off. "Sleep it off, Chase. Go take your pitiful ass to bed. And then go see somebody or something. You're a good boy, and God don't we all have demons. But you are way out on that edge, man. And I don't see me being able to reach you."

From his picture window Chase watched her taillights dim a mile down the highway. He collapsed into a pile on his ratty carpet and burrowed within his T-shirt to hide from the rising sun, from another furiously mundane day. Carrie's words echoed, softened, and then lifted Chase like a benediction: *Go see somebody. Go see somebody.*

***

The final meeting between Chase and the sheriff came two years later, before dawn, on the highway that led to Chase's cabin. It was sometime in late September, the oaks showing first hints of gold.

That morning, Chase wobbled up the highway, his white shirt smeared with wet Georgia clay, a mud the color of rare meat. Four drivers called 911 to report him; two recognized Chase, and they thought he was bleeding.

Responding alone, the sheriff told dispatchers he could quell the situation himself, eager to finally lure Chase into his patrol car for a meaningful conversation. He reached for the switch to engage the sirens but instead put down the windows and eased the cruiser up next to Chase.

"Fine morning for a walk," the sheriff said.

Chase whipped his face to the left, his drunken eyes distant and pink.

"Just hop in," the sheriff said. "Let me lay some towels out first, cover these seats, and I'll get you home. Dispatch said you been making threats all morning, but I'm willing to call it even, to let you sleep this off."

"Just go on," Chase slurred. "Almost there. Down this hill, up another."

"What the hell's happened to you, Bobcat?"

"Lost my keys, your honor. Had to walk."

"And your clothes? Been mud-wrestling?"

Chase halted, as if shocked. "Some fucker tripped me, for no reason," he said. "I think he was me."

"Happens," the sheriff said. "Get in."

"Swear to God I'm not going to jail."

The sheriff laughed. "I swear."

"I was telling you," Chase said, "not asking."

The sheriff flipped on the reds-and-blues and parked his cruiser. He walked around the front of the car, raised a hand, and stopped Chase. "Now I'm telling *you*," he said. "Get in."

Chase turned around, opened the rear passenger door, and surrendered, flopping down the length of the seat and groaning, "I got the spinnies, your honor."

The sheriff sped up the road, ignoring Chase's pleas to slow down. "You're not passing out on me, and I'm not carrying you in." They roared around a bend, up another hill, and onto Chase's driveway. The sheriff examined the cabin, washed in first morning hues. Back and forth, up and down, he scanned the property, searching for some outward sign—a busted window, a firearm in the yard, a noose—that Chase could be a hazard to himself or neighbors. He turned off his radio and peeked back through the wire mesh.

"Let me out now, please." Chase sat up and yanked the door latch, then crawled across the seat to open the other door. The cruiser was locked; Chase tensed his shoulders. "You've got no grounds to cage me."

The sheriff smiled. "We're kindred spirits. Calm down. I know what it is to be discharged—"

"Ah, no," Chase said. "Not this."

"If you don't believe me, pop in my office for coffee this week. I've got proof on my walls. I think it's time we talked about getting you sober—when you're sober—because this ain't going no place but hell."

Chase grabbed the door handle and pulled and pushed, budging only his body.

"You come from good stock, son. Who taught you to act like this?"

With his palms Chase pounded the cage.

"For the last time," the sheriff said, "I'm here to help you, because I can see you were a good kid, and because I feel a little bit responsible for y'all. Don't ask me why."

Chase dropped his hands and leaned back in the seat, the dried mud now flaking off his shirt. "Don't make me kick your windows out."

The sheriff turned the cruiser off, pulled his keys from the ignition. "I'll let you walk, like I said, but in exchange, we need to talk, right now."

"You wanna hear me whine? Is *that* it?" said Chase. "You have no idea what I've gone through, what I've done, or what it's like right now."

"What do you *mean*, 'What I've done?' Tell me what you're hinting at, son. It wants to come out, and you know it."

"Forget it."

"No," said the sheriff, "I won't forget. I won't back off. That's not my MO. But remember that I'm your ally, okay? Whatever you say in here remains in confidence." He switched to a quieter, consoling tone. "I know, to an extent, where you're coming from. War is ugly as hell. Sometimes we're called to do horrendous things. I don't like what all I did, either. But it's what situations demanded, and in those situations, we use our training and react—"

"I'm not talking about hero bullshit," Chase said. "I mean something you'd be duty bound to report back to the government—the big government. The feds. Something unforgivable."

The sheriff twisted around, looked back, and stared into Chase, deeper than flesh. "I don't know you well, but it sounds like you're overreacting."

"You have no idea. And you need to let me go, right now."

"But I *want* to know," said the sheriff. "Go ahead and tell me, Lumpkin. Tell me *something*. Let it breathe."

"All right," Chase said, keeled over. "I'll bitch, if that's what you want."

"Go on, son."

"Look," Chase said, "I have nightmares, all the time, constantly. About what happened to me, what happened to my brothers. Every single night. Every time I take a nap. At Walmart I think everyone's staring at me. It makes no sense because my scars are concealed. I treat everything like a war zone. If I hear a bang outside, I'm going to grab a gun. If I hear little steps on the front porch, I'll grab a gun. It's insane, but I keep thinking it's necessary. What's that old quote by General Mattis? You know it? Something like, 'When you go into a room, be polite to everybody, but always have a plan to kill them all.' That's me now. That's where my head is. It's fucked!"

"It's okay," the sheriff said, proud of the inroad he was making, trying to sound soothing. "There's no shame in this."

"No, wrong," said Chase. "It's shameful."

"Listen," the sheriff said. "You're dealing with an enormous amount of guilt, and we have to get to the root. Is there a specific event, or events, that triggered all this? Something you can't shake out? I'm trained at reading people, and I can see on your face there's something you aren't telling anybody. I can see in your eyes that maybe you weren't bluffing a minute ago."

For a while Chase said nothing. He huffed beer-breath around the cruiser, lost in thought and pain. Then he flinched. "How would you feel," Chase said, "if I told you I killed one of our own?"

Again the sheriff twisted around, looking Chase in his face. "What do you mean, exactly?"

"I mean a platoon mate."

"Well," the sheriff said, "I wouldn't feel much different, I guess."

"How can you say that?"

"I can say that because it happens—friendly fire happens. Throughout military history, back to Stonewall Jackson's death and surely much further back. It's a horrible thing, but it's no reason to ruin your life."

"But how would you feel," Chase said, "if I did it on purpose?"

"Come again?"

"You heard me."

"No," the sheriff said. "Say that again for me."

"You heard me, sir."

"I guess, in that case ..." said the sheriff, sounding angrier and perhaps more frightened than he'd meant to, before relaxing his tone again. "I guess that would make me feel different."

"I was afraid of that."

"Why would you do that, Chase?"

From the backseat, no reply.

"*How* could you do that?" the sheriff asked. "Say something, son."

"Because I thought it was right, for the good of everyone else."

The sheriff looked forward, toward Chase's cabin, both hands on the wheel, feeling exasperated, dizzy, disappointed. "I won't report you," he said. "That sounds like an international mess I can't begin to get involved with. And I can see you're paying your own price now. But I need you to tell me exactly what happened. And I need to hear it now."

With that directive Chase felt violated. He hung his head, as if studying his muddy boots, and he shoved two fingers deep into this throat. The orange vomit came quick and sour, speckling the floorboard and seat.

"You little dick!" said the sheriff, his sympathy dissolving. He hustled out of his seat, unlocked the cruiser, and flung open the back—"Out!" When Chase didn't move he looked down at the mess and spun around in an infuriated circle. "This is what you're going to do," he shouted. "Get inside, find some towels, a bucket, and a big bottle of dish soap. I'll give you five minutes to wipe this shit from my car, every bit of it."

Rolling his head, Chase moaned and slowly budged out of the passenger's side, opposite the sheriff. He lumbered around the car and clearly, to the sheriff, had no plans of following the law's directive.

The sheriff latched ahold of Chase's left wrist, put a palm in his back, and applied his weight, trying to budge the larger man up the driveway. The grip infuriated Chase, and the hand on his spine was intolerable. He spun away, freeing his wrist, but he lost his balance and planted his shoulder in the sheriff's chest, knocking the man against his car, his head whipping back. Now they were facing each other, Chase a head taller and twice as broad. By instinct the sheriff dropped a hand to his asp baton, but he thought better of it; instead he raised the index finger of his right hand into Chase's face, letting it hover at his nose. Before the sheriff could scold him, Chase slapped the hand away, and the sheriff countered with a solid punch to Chase's chin, chipping away skin with the gold of his wedding ring.

The sheriff stepped back in retreat, reaching for the nine-millimeter in his holster, but Chase leapt forward and latched ahold of his neck. The old brown eyes spread open, the astonished face wrinkled. They fell into the grass, and Chase straddled the sheriff, squeezing his throat until the cheeks and forehead purpled. The sheriff cackled and choked and spat foamy mucus across his lips. He let go of Chase's hands, reached to his hip, and unholstered his gun. He slung the weapon upward, but Chase wrested it away with the crook of his elbow, his left hand still tight on the sheriff's neck. Chase disengaged the gun's safety button and pointed it down into the sheriff's face.

"Mouth," he said.

The sheriff only wheezed.

Chase loosened his grip. "*Mouth!*"

The sheriff struggled to draw breath, and then he screamed for help, but the plea was weak, and there was no help. He turned his focus to Chase, whose eyes were gone, and he knew he'd best comply. Slowly the sheriff parted his lips and held them open.

Chase nudged the nose of the gun between the sheriff's lips and ran the metal across the teeth, forcing the weapon in deeper. The sheriff mumbled and gagged, tears streaking down, helpless against the weight of Chase.

For a moment Chase said nothing, only marveled at the awful turn of events, the reallocation of power. The situation seemed external from him, as though he was dreaming this, above this. The sheriff stuck his hands up the legs of Chase's pants and clawed and pinched hard. A pain like wasp stings made Chase briefly cognizant again. He removed the gun from the sheriff's mouth, flung it across the yard, and fell into the grass, onto his back, watching a red-tailed hawk cut the mountain mist.

The sheriff scurried on hands and knees to his weapon, spitting out metallic dust. He clutched the trigger and drew a bead on Chase. "You wanna *die?*" the sheriff said, frantic, still panting.

Chase lay still in the grass, his arms outstretched beside him.

"I have every right to shoot you in the chest, right now!" The sheriff was standing over Chase, blocking daylight and the bird.

"I'm sorry, sir."

The sheriff holstered his gun, stepped aside, and kicked Chase hard in his ribs. He cocked his leg to kick again, but Chase curled, gripping his ribs and rolling away.

"Tell me what you have in the house—what guns."

Chase gasped, still rolling. "Jesus, I'm sorry."

"There's no helping you," the sheriff said. "Stay the hell out of my town. You are banned. You *hear* me?"

Lying on his stomach, his head on the meat of his forearm, Chase closed his eyes.

"In one month you'd better be gone—for good. *One* month. Get out of this house, get out of this county, and don't return so long as I'm alive. I'm going to expedite a warrant, and we're coming back today to confiscate your weapons. All of 'em. You hear what I'm sayin', Chase?"

Wincing at the sheriff's screams, his eyes closed, Chase nodded on the ground.

"Whatever you did overseas isn't my concern, and that damn sure ain't my jurisdiction," the sheriff said. "But it's no excuse, either. You're not fit to be a civilian. You're a waste of good training. You're a lost cause."

The sheriff walked to his car, opened the door. "I'll be back real soon to take your guns, Lumpkin," he said. "I won't be alone, and if you think of drawing on me again, we'll kill you. You hear me?"

But Chase had passed out.

He was still asleep in the grass, splayed out and sweating, when the deputies swept through that afternoon and took all of his weapons, except the nine-millimeter he'd buried in a shoebox in the woods.

2

Three weeks later, on the day he would die, Chase walked out the door of his cabin and saw the valley in a bright October sheen. He squinted, his combat grimace. The day seemed too perfect, the sky too crisp. Chase could not cope with the strain of perfection. His saliva dried out. His heart raced for no reason but for fear it would race more. He clenched his jaws, performed the breathing exercises the doctors had prescribed, and then he thought about the valley. The Amicalola range lumped off in blue distance, and dying leaves smeared the foothills yellow and red. There was no violence up here, not today, save two gray squirrels in his front yard grappling for nuts. The yard sloped down to the highway, where every night the logging trucks would heave and bitch.

Chase liked to drink his morning coffee in the open air. Languidly he paced his wide splintered porch, as if guarding a place too valueless to raid. In summer he'd wear only his white underwear, sunning his long tight muscles and freckled back. But come October he liked to wear fatigues. Nobody saw him on the porch, not usually, one way or another. He loved the solitude though he didn't fully trust it. Sometimes the peacefulness could buffer Chase from himself. Sometimes it put him at odds with his own mind.

After two years on the mountain, and now facing the sheriff's orders to leave within one more week, Chase had lost the will to salvage himself, and his thoughts were huge and tangled. In the midst of his anxiety he had become obsessed with time—the impermanence of time. Each morning felt to him like a collapsing chance, and he'd concluded that his life, like every life before his, was a pointless trek, a howl on the wind. He would not go down a hero. In fact, he thought, he had devolved into a grotesque antihero. Despite his efforts, or because of them, there would be no Chase Lumpkin monument. His greatest ambitions had been products of his teenage military fantasies, and few of them happened; the rest would never happen now. Chase knew he had overestimated the therapy of high altitude. Clean wind and whistling brown thrashers were no ointment for the internal gash. As with the big city's streets, he now felt caged by limitless open space. He knew no other place to go.

Chase set his empty mug on the deck railing and inhaled piney air, a whiff of grandpa gin. The parade of last things was finally here, and he knew it: the last bird-chirp sunrise, last coffee, last hours of what he'd been calling the Highcountry Mindfuck Hellride. But first he had to beat back the panic attack, this thing provoked by nothing. The tension spread out from his chest and circled back inward, a constricting snake around his arms, lungs, and neck.

Doctors' instructions: Exhale—"*Whooooh.*" Bring it back—"*Huuuuh.*" Hold for two seconds. Exhale again. Now focus on nature. Feel the tranquility. See the mountains. Repeat until outwardly normal.

On clear days like this, as the old yokels swore, anyone with decent vision could see the spires of Atlanta, due south, jutting over God's Knuckles, a series of distant ridges. Chase never did see the city. And though he put no stock in what the mountain codgers told him, he squinted once more in hopes of seeing skyscrapers, those landmarks from the capital, birthplace of his failed potential. Again he saw nothing, though, and that pained him. He lifted his hand, shielding the sun, and dropped it hard against his chest, frustrated. "To hell with that shithole anyway," he said. "Godspeed to those idiots."

**

The Excellor Building jutted above its peers in Buckhead like an up-pointed modernist thumb, an overt gesture signaling to the rest of Atlanta that life at Excellor was magnificent. Sixty stories of chic blue glass and impossibly large balconies—all in the shape of a thumb—represented the complacency of its residents, as if to say, "We are just dandy in here, plebes!" At the building's 2006 christening, heralded architects and design critics had gathered in a ballroom, holstering their contempt for each other just long enough to hoist champagne. Unanimously, they anointed Excellor the grandest condominium tower in metropolitan Atlanta, a wonder of technology and metaphor.

From afar the building shone like a twisting prism, a skyward icicle, with a gargantuan blue fin affixed to its torso. The tower's rooftop was shaped like a pond, and the liquid theme carried down to the saline swimming pools of the lounge level, and then into the lobby, with its cylindrical shark aquarium, forty-foot ceilings, polished bamboo floors, wrap-around couches of cerulean leather, and televisions thin as cardboard. Business chatter in this room soared. Sunlight swam through it. From the lobby, four darkened hallways led to the core of Excellor. Deep within them, the walls shone with lighted art installations, each by a Parisian whiz kid billed as the technological Cézanne. The pieces pulsed with fiber-optic pomp. Each was a long rectangular palette of wondrous things: storm clouds, galloping Colorado horses, cresting Maui waves, and the City of Atlanta itself, morphing within the frame from brilliant sunrise to sparkling midnight cityscape. In these hallways hidden German speakers dropped a low techno pulse. The corridors hinted at sex, and each had been designed to make visitors feel pleasantly, willingly seduced. The elevators themselves, clad in lacquered sea-blue panels, were the city's fastest. They shot like hurried prayers into the great tower's heart.

The private elevator, meanwhile, was reserved for Excellor's biggest fish. A space capsule of riveted stainless steel, it was operated by specialized electronic keys. With the most exclusive key of all, the elevator climbed to the penthouse, which was the personal Shangri-La of Jack Lumpkin, the debauched wild man of national sports radio.

On the FM airwaves, and at every public place, they called him Bachelor Jack, and each aspect of his residence reflected this attitude. Once it had reached the Penthouse Suite Level, Jack's elevator played ethereal chimes and opened to reveal a lighted BJ on his door. Facing this huge teak slab, guests typically would pause, wondering whether to knock, marvel, or assign crude meanings to the acronym. The nickname had become Jack's alter ego and brand, his two-word manifesto, and he projected an obnoxious sort of pride in embodying perpetual bachelorhood. Besides, as he often said on air, his given name lacked radio poetry. A name like Jack Lumpkin, to him, was better suited for has-been boxers and hillbillies.

On the morning Chase gulped coffee and planned to die, his famous brother was enjoying what his radio colleagues would call an enviable vantage. Her name was Maddy. She was young, ambitious, penniless, and ferocious.

***

Chase tried to come to terms with another troubling thought: October 19th would be the bookend date on his tombstone. There was nothing tidy or ceremonious about the nineteenth day of any month, and he was sorry he hadn't more thoroughly planned this. Couldn't he have died on October 1st or the 15th—some number that made sense?

Dying on Halloween would be too gothic. Holding off any longer, into the holidays, would be selfish, as if the act itself wasn't selfish enough. In its irrelevance, he thought, maybe this day was perfect. Or maybe he was overthinking trivial things again.

Beside him lay a calligraphy pen and the only sheet of paper he'd found in the cabin. The paper was thick and almond-colored, meant for resumes. For the past year, Chase had communicated from this mountain outpost with hand-written letters. Writing by hand forced him to take his time, craft the ink into the pulp, and imbue the messages with heart, often for several pages. He wrote so many letters, all to his mother and brother, the 500 sheets of white paper in his bedroom had been depleted. So it was ironic: He'd have to pen his suicide note on paper he'd bought to sell himself to employers—to aspire. The irony would continue in the handwriting itself, how a cussing former grunt like Chase could strike graceful, dancing lines on paper. He'd brought all the necessary pens for a proper note because he still had them in case it came to this. The pens were relics of a Bible study art class he'd taken in eighth grade. He liked that class but never admitted it, because a knack for art seemed indicative of weakness. Somehow, he hoped, the calligraphy would help atone for today's act, the sin, the last of too many.

For as far as he'd fallen, Chase's motivations had initially been innocent and honorable. He was just fourteen years old, a lanky and curious sponge of a boy, when the towers fell. He'd been waylaid that morning by late-summer fever, unable to attend middle school, so his mother called his paternal grandfather, retired army Lt. Col. Henry Lumpkin, to pick him up and watch him. They went back to his grand-father's house and talked for a while about fishing—until news footage shattered the morning talk shows. Immediately they feared for the towers of Atlanta, filled with family and friends, and when the second building collapsed, Henry left the living room and came back with a loaded pistol. He sat down and held the weapon between his knees for hours, until they couldn't stand to watch the screaming any longer, until Chase's mind spun with paranoid confusion. They walked to the river on a bright blue afternoon. The water and the pines had a purifying, natural grace. Some other people came, but no one spoke. No one smiled. They tossed rocks until Chase started to cry, and then his grandfather drove him home, the boy's fate all but sealed. That night Chase read about the army, his grandfather's great love, on the internet. Later he listened to every word the school recruiters would say. The way he saw it, army recruits could choose from airborne school, Ranger school, sniper school, scuba school, para rig school—a million schools. He could rank up quickly in the army, distinguishing himself from the fellow enlisted by virtue of his fearlessness and sniper's aim. It sounded like an adventure: basic and then airborne school, unlimited skydiving for free—and then, revenge. He hassled his grandfather to take him to shooting ranges. He jogged in August heat and pretended it was Iraq. Such was the good benign start that, by Chase's Cherokee days, was so far gone it felt like a faded mirage, a lie he'd only been telling himself.

A logging truck climbed the highway, hugging the bend around Chase's yard. A redheaded woodpecker flitted from one pine to another. It was late morning, and it was time. Chase slugged the last of his coffee and began to write his note. His hands trembled but the lines were right, with proper branching and powerful down strokes. Tears dripped off his jaw. He was careful not to speckle the ink, to give no indication he'd been afraid. For months each word of this message had knocked around his head, jagged at first like a sticker burr but refined now into a clear, eerie whale song of thought.

Finished, Chase blew the note dry and looked across the mountains, their sharp crests beaten down by time. For two centuries these forests had kept the secrets of forgotten cemeteries, silently digesting the dead. How much difference, Chase thought, could one more dead sob make? He went inside to eat something, to fuel himself for the hike.

***

In Jack's circular love bed, an ocean of black Egyptian silk, Maddy was stretched on hands and knees, joyful and stiff. A constellation of freckles dotted her flexing back. Jack reached to touch the freckles and nearly toppled over. It was seven in the morning, and neither of them had slept, on a Tuesday—a workday—no less. Now a thrusting, sweaty, beer-bellied Jack looked to his left and squinted. Daylight broke west across wavy treetops, over midrise apartments, and through Jack's floor-to-ceiling bedroom windows, igniting Maddy's hair into a glowing amber mane. With regional fame and Atlanta's most seductive residence at his disposal, these dalliances had become shockingly easy for Jack, almost boring, and he yearned for fresh approaches to meaningless intercourse, because meaning seemed unachievable. He'd bought costumes for every role he could imagine (one favorite: bus driver and cranky passenger) and invented a game of blindfolded, sexual hide-and-seek that was perfect for such a cavernous condo. If it weren't for Jack's endearing playfulness, his dates would've been repulsed by the retropubescent sleaziness of it all; but not even the jangly leather swing he'd installed in a guest bedroom was too much for adoring fans. Still, the process had gone stale, the courtships hollow, and each sick morning revealed the same empty pit in Jack. Something about Maddy, however, seemed different. They had chemistry for sure, and her bedroom daringness had seemed genius to Jack in the celestial predawn. Now, as Maddy flipped Jack over and rode him again, all glistening sweat in bright sunshine, she squeezed his plump face and demanded that he bark for her.

"*Bark?*" Jack cried on his back. "Are you serious?"

"Do it!"

"What breed?"

"Uh, Rottweiler!"

"Ah, right." Jack gasped, inflating his lungs, deepening his voice. "I'm a big kinky dog—ruff."

"*Louder!*" Maddy shouted. "Bark dirty!"

Jack paused, inhaling again, forcing down his smile into an animalistic sneer: "*Grrrrrr*-ruff!"

Laughing at himself, Jack hopped up to his knees and folded himself behind Maddy, forcing her face and chest toward the pillows, though as gently as possible. Last thing he wanted was to fuck an intern to death. For a moment he was exhausted, panting and old, but then he felt inspired again, so he kissed her hair, beat his chest, and cried, "Wahoo!"

"Yes!" she replied, into the sheets. "Wahoo!"

Now Jack was clapping, applauding her feistiness. "You're too damn much," he said. "I can't keep up with you."

She reached back and clawed his stubbly cheeks. "You're out of your goddamn gourd, Bachelor Jack!"

***

In its respect for others, there was nobility in Chase's plan, the last of many he had considered. He nodded now in thinking this final course was right.

The first plan, without question, had been ridiculous: It went that he would sit at home and drink himself blind on Evan Williams; at the last second, before whiskey comatose, he'd toss a struck match onto gasoline-soaked carpet. The cabin would be his casket inferno. That plan was flawed in almost every respect. Knowing he burned to death would haunt his mother forever; the destroyed cabin would be worthless to his family; and Cherokee's ragtag legion of volunteer firefighters would be pulled from families and jobs to hose his selfish corpse.

After the inferno plan came the daredevil plan, the one that could be masked as an accident for anyone who hadn't known Chase. Riding a dirt bike, he would tear through the forest and launch himself off Leaper's Cliff, a high ledge famously used by the daughter of a Cherokee City Councilman a century before. According to legend, this rebellious daughter had fallen for the son of a liberated slave, and together they leapt into history, by way of bone-splitting boulders. The slight chance that the fall would not immediately kill Chase dissuaded him, as he couldn't stomach the thought of anguishing in a twisted heap. And besides, the cliff was too far away, in the wrong direction, across the most populated regions of the valley, where any old man raking leaves could spot him and help search teams piece together his whereabouts. The mountain face directly behind his home was inhospitable and virgin, with plenty of little plateaus where a resolute depressive could take his time. Up there, in the absolute wild, Chase could make a more common exit.

He mulled the noose, the aspirin, and the knife-split arterial veins. But ultimately, he thought it best to be simple: a painless procedure, quick as a whipcrack, the explosion muffled by high-altitude winds, a bullet through the meat of his brain.

Chase sat on his couch and choked down a microwaved platter of sprouts, corn, and beef Stroganoff. He ate heartily despite the day's dire task, his eyes wandering. It all felt like the cusp of another bad mission, like the night his platoon had come to war in a lumbering cargo jet with a red-lit interior and cockpit, a fat black target in the midnight sky. Chase clamored that night at the cabin windows, trying to glimpse the alien landscape he would call home for a twelve-month deployment. He peeked out and saw the iridescent patchwork of a bona fide city: scattered lights that could have been pieces of Portland, Detroit, Phoenix, anywhere. When vast black patches broke apart the city, he saw a long thermometer of light. The landing was smooth, but Chase felt a jolt—something internal, something final, a mix of wonder and dread. He hated the smell of Afghanistan from his first in-country breath. Among the runway chemicals and gasoline, he caught a whiff of beach. It was sandy but not in a way that evoked palmettos. Sandy like a desert, like despair, like hell.

Chase's cabin was sparsely decorated. The faux wood paneling bore mallards and Labrador retrievers, and dirty yellow curtains guarded each window. The brown carpet was dated and thick with loops, still faintly dusted, Chase had always worried, in white powder left by former tenants, a group of mountain chemists. There were two leather recliners and a flowered couch, a depressing layout overall. Chase eyed the kitchen's only decorations: carbon copies of every police citation he'd been issued in Cherokee, all taped to his refrigerator. He almost laughed, so moved by his memories of disorderly conduct, public indecency, disorderly conduct again, and public urination. He said, "One hell of a collection right there, dumbass."

A few minutes before noon, Chase finished his lunch, washed his hands, locked up the cabin, and put the note on his coffee table. He was proud of the lines, ashamed of the words. From a few feet away the message looked beautiful.

On his way out, Chase wadded the police citations in toilet paper, rushed to the bathroom nearest his bedroom, and flushed the whole ungainly ball. Someone would tell his mother about the arrests, but word would not come from his fridge. A week earlier, down the same toilet, Chase had flushed his Purple Heart.

Beside his bed he caught an accidental glimpse of the family members he could stomach, the trio he still considered loved ones, dead and alive, staring back from three cheap frames. He didn't want them seeing this. In a slow, ceremonious way, Chase lay down portraits of his grandfather, Henry, as a young soldier—baby-faced and cocksure before Korea—and a more recent Christmastime photo of his cherubic mother, Anne, her lips darkened by merlot and eyes heavily medicated. In the last frame was Jack in a Hawaiian shirt, captured mid-laugh holding an unlit cigar and blow-up raft shaped like a martini, the backdrop some azure Caribbean utopia. Chase left this frame standing and said he was sorry.

"Day like this, Jack, is perfect for a last mission," Chase said to the picture. "Just do what needs done here. Close it all down, sell it. You'll know." Chase bowed his head. "Let me go and try to accept. And please, man, keep Mom comfortable. Take her to the parks she likes and that farmers market. And don't any of you come looking for me."

Chase locked the front door but then unlocked it. He checked his pockets for the clip, the nine-millimeter, and the trail mix. He walked off the cabin grounds, stepping in his Danner combat hikers over a barbed-wire fence. He was on schedule and determined. A last backward glance, and then he clenched his teeth, leaned into the mountain, thrust one knee in front of the other, and wept.

3

Like a few other visitors who'd recently found themselves at Excellor's premier residence, Maddy Durham was an intern at Jack's radio station, Sports Talk 99 FM, The Bomb. Though her interest in sports was minimal, she'd spent her late teens adoring Bachelor Jack and his on-air buffoonery. And despite his being a chubby drunken blowhard, now well into his thirties, she'd lusted for him all summer. His wit, wavy brown hair, and command of interviews with professional athletes enthralled her. Above all, though, she adored Jack's intelligence, how he could weave social commentary and dead-on celebrity impressions into sports radio blather about quarterback completion percentages and the ERAs of Braves relievers. He could make her laugh at statistics. She was acutely aware of the danger in becoming a morsel in Bachelor Jack's smorgasbord, but unlike the other girls, she felt she could *change* him, because she had studied him. And besides, she thought, the station had never hired an intern so lethally attractive as her.

In the moment, with sunshine illuminating Maddy, Jack felt himself growing fond of her, a wholly alien sensation— but a welcome, warm thing nonetheless. She was playful, and he sensed a kindred wildness in her, though their romance had begun only the previous afternoon. Maddy scored a day's work editing outtakes in the radio room and, during a commercial break, she breezed past Jack, enveloping him in top-shelf Chanel. His attention followed her, like a puppy to chow, and she gave a brusque nod.

"Hey," he'd said. "Do you like martinis?"

From the station they caught a cab to Whiskies, a sexed-up power bar for hedge funders, the New South's lawyer elite, and impresarios with sports-world connections. Whiskies was rollicking, and the more that smart-suited men jockeyed for Jack's attention, the more Maddy wanted to unclothe him. To a broke college girl, Jack's world was an idyllic landscape of big fruit, the antithesis of dorm dates with vodka in plastic cups. She hoped the night would be her entrée into Phipps Plaza fashion circles, to penthouse parties at the Ritz Residences thrown by quarterbacks with max contracts. She envisioned trips to Rio and to a Nicaraguan haven for injured peacocks she had read about. She wanted to lounge with Jack on lavish leather couches, to call in sick tomorrow, to sip fresh pineapple juice and nurse their hangovers together.

Around midnight, Jack and Maddy kissed in a Mafia booth near Whiskies entrance. When patrons realized what was happening—in such public fashion—they reached for smart phones and snapped photos. This signaled to Jack's cronies behind the bar it was time to call a car, the chauffeured one on standby provided by the radio station.

In the parking lot, Jack and Maddy embraced against a cool breeze. She ribbed him for being short and called him genius in the same breath, asking him to talk her up on the radio. She wanted details of their date broadcasted, her name beamed into 2.7 million vehicles each afternoon, without her having to work for it. She wanted to matter like Jack mattered or to matter by proximity to Jack. They loaded into the late-model Mercedes, and Maddy smacked his left arm, across his parrot tattoo, for no reason. He liked her meanness. He liked that she was smart and difficult. Something in his abused body ached for stability—his persona be damned—and in Maddy he thought he could see that, a sort of raft in his life's debaucherous sea.

The car whipped under Excellor's parking canopy, and Jack handed the driver a bill. At the lobby doors he told

Maddy to relax, to jibe with fate, and to excuse the silly presence of a sex swing upstairs. He asked the concierge to fetch a fine cognac, to deliver the bottle to his condo in an iced cooler with, for some reason, two tulip-shaped wineglasses. He led his date to his elevator, and in the rising cosmic capsule their hands scampered up shirts like blue crabs on midnight beaches.

Maddy stared at Jack's immense door. "Does BJ mean Big Jerk?"

"Nope," Jack said. "Bingo, Jackpot."

"Huh," said Maddy. "What a Big Joke."

"Or on Sundays," said Jack, "Bless Jesus."

Inside he left the lights off and toured her past the huge windows, the chef's kitchen with Turkish marble countertops, and the stainless-steel fireplace. On the balcony, looking out, they saw the dark pools of neighborhoods, the circuitry of streetlights, and the incandescent spires of Midtown. They embraced, two wobbly silhouettes against the urban night, a painting in a jazz bar. In these moments Jack felt a decade younger, his sense of being desirable reinforced, his relative agedness a nonfactor, his game as sharp as ever.

The concierge arrived with the bottle. He reminded Jack it was Monday, or now technically Tuesday. He was eager, he hinted, to hear Jack's in-studio interview with the Atlanta Falcons' head coach at 10 a.m., a Tuesday staple.

"You might need some rest, Mister Lumpkin, for talking to Coach."

Jacked hugged the concierge, pulled the cork, and gulped from the bottle of Chateau de Montifaud.

"It's Michael, right?" Jack said.

"That's correct."

"I appreciate your concern, Michael, but please know I have experience in these matters, and this beautiful guest in my home tonight will keep me awake no more than one hour ..."

And then it was dawn.

Squinting, huffing, and sweating miserably, Jack turned away from the sunrise, glanced at his alarm clock, and was stricken with the realization that work would begin in two hours. He'd have to forfeit this game with Maddy. "Let's just rest," he said, his thrusts now lazy lunges. "I need water, and sleep. A big day tomorrow or—ha!—today."

Maddy rolled over and pulled on his face. "What've you done to me, Bachelor Jack? Four *freaking* hours!"

"Yeah, right," he said. "Congrats to us. Work is going to *suck*."

"Not to inflate your fat head even more," she continued, "but you've exceeded expectations. Blown them away!"

Jack gave Maddy his billboard smile. "Nothing," he said, "beats a lover with low expectations."

She closed her blue-tinged eyelids and said the room was spinning. For Jack the room whirled, too. He thought he could will the seafaring sensation away. When it didn't pass, he rolled from bed, stood naked at the window, put his hands against the glass, and felt magnificent, momentarily, about his station in life. As Maddy called for Jack to join her, to fill the divot left by his body, she pulled a framed picture off the nightstand. She studied the photo: an army soldier in desert fatigues, his eyes sharp and stern, his chin an anvil like Jack's but without the fleshy jowls. "Tell me this isn't you," Maddy said. "This *can't* be you."

Jack crawled back into bed. "You sayin' I'm not man enough to fight for my country?"

"No."

"You saying I'm too chubby to kill?"

"I'm saying you'd never conform like this, would you?"

He kissed the picture and tossed it on the bamboo floor, where it spun and slid and clacked against the window. "My kid brother right there," Jack said. "He's triple the man I am. With a Purple Heart to prove it."

"That's cute," she said. "You two sound close."

"We used to be. We've grown apart, with him so far away, living up in bumblefuck, near the Carolina line."

"Yeah?"

"Long story, but we're about to reconnect," Jack said. "In person, finally. He reached out to me last week, and we're going fishing. Trout fishing in the mountains. That's his big plan, at least. He sends these rambling handwritten letters."

"He's been to war?"

Jack fetched the picture and returned it to his nightstand. "You might say he's still there."

Though he could smell her sour sweat, and his own, Jack latched onto Maddy and bid her goodnight—and good morning. He felt he was hugging a precious, metaphorical anchor; Maddy saw a bloated gateway to the big time. But both said nothing and assumed the other was filled with unadulterated happiness right then. They laughed about the hour, cocooned themselves in blankets, and fell asleep in seconds.

***

Chase had charted an eight-hour hike up and over Singleton's Ridge, so that he might die in the evening, as the sun fell over lower Appalachia. In his mind the sun would burst orange, just above the horizon, in that crystalline coda unique to early autumn. The season had always been Chase's favorite, more pleasant than floral Southern springs. The rot of autumn smelled to him like Georgia Bulldogs football and the first optimistic weeks of school. He unbuttoned his jacket and cut right, around a hazardous outcropping of rocks. The day was nearing its peak temperature, probably 75 degrees, but he was not thirsty. Not yet. His boots crunched broad leaves and twigs. He was making good time, but then he erred by looking down. The earth-tone foliage was such terribly good camouflage.

Snakes had always horrified Chase—to the point that, as a boy, he had to close his eyes at the Grant Park Zoo Reptile Cave. Ravenous spiders, coyotes, even the black bears that occasionally sauntered into Atlanta's suburbs—nothing to fear. But he could not reconcile the wickedness of snakes.

In these woods, Chase knew, he was governed by snake law, which had precluded his hiking before today, except in deep winter. He could think of nothing else now. He did not want to die by snake. Nothing in his plan called for swollen feet and boiling blood. Tromping in the leaves, over gray piles of limbs, he looked for two things: the watercolor stripes of copperheads and the thick-bodied coil of timber rattlers. He'd brought extra ammunition in case he kicked up snakes. It was high season for such encounters. The tavern regulars had filled his mind with envenomation nightmares—how the rattlers would strike fast as boxers' fists, how baby copperheads would crawl into a sleeping man's mouth. The stories echoed now, and as Chase hoofed upward, he drew the gun, holding it at his right hip, pointed down.

Growing up, Jack had constantly ribbed Chase about his fear of snakes. And his lack of girlfriends. And his propensity for getting in trouble in school, even grade school, like the time Chase beat a boy named Ramon bloody on the basketball courts. When Jack was summoned to pick Chase up and drive him home to begin a suspension, Jack overheard the teachers saying "schizophrenia," "autistic tendencies," and "oppositional defiant disorder" in reference to his little brother, which made him so angry he walked Chase to his Mustang in uncharacteristic silence. That night, over spaghetti, the Lumpkin boys' father, Charles the Lawyer, as they called him, was more incensed about Chase's ruined shirt than his weeklong suspension. In his pointing Charles brushed his seersucker sleeve through the marinara. His broad face purpled with anger, his comb-over so blond and sculpted it looked like icing.

"We need to get you playing football, Chase, away from the video games and goddamn war movies," Charles had said, twirling noodles into tight cocoons. "You never used to have this temper."

"I am who I am," said Chase.

"That's right," said his father. "And your brother's who he is, too. He's nothing like you. He can function in the world. So it's not a matter of a flawed home environment, or your natural self, as you seem to be implying."

"I want to go live with Mom."

Charles dropped his fork. "Your mother can't provide what you have right now. Not your schooling, not these top-shelf fucking noodles. So you can take your disrespectful attitude, and your nasty little mouth—"

"*Gentlemen*," Jack interjected, sounding baffled but amused. "No more bloodshed today, please. And with all due respect, Dad, this is a kid you're talking to."

After dinner that night, Chase raced into the back-yard with lighter fluid, his body tense with rage he didn't understand. Behind the shed, where he and Jack had always shared contraband Coca-Cola, he doused the soiled shirt, lit it, and watched this gift from his father disintegrate in coiling flames. When fire licked his finger Chase panicked and tossed the shirt next to the shed, where it contacted over-sprayed lighter fluid, ignited dry leaves, and climbed to the structure's wooden base. Chase stepped slowly back, unable to react, and was startled to see a white flash to his left—a fast, tumbling cloud—and then in front of him, extinguishing the fire and sparing the shed.

"You *do* need counseling, shitface." Jack's tone suggested he was smirking. "Does fire turn you on?"

"You scared me."

Jack punched Chase in his shoulder, saying nothing. Falling away, Chase grimaced. Though he wanted to hug his brother, he hadn't in years, so he called him an asshead. "How'd you know I was out here?"

"You had a stupid plan written all over your face at dinner," Jack said. "I didn't expect *this* stupid, but stupid."

"I'll paint over the damage," Chase said. "It's done, in the morning."

"Bet your ass it is."

Behind the shed they talked for a while in the dark. Chase admired much about his brother beyond his skill for scoring dates. He liked Jack's honesty and envied his wit, but even as a boy, Chase felt his brother was misguided, more than Jack, his parents, or anyone else knew. "Down in Destin," Chase said, "when Grandpa would take us on his boat for mackerel, past those lagoons, what was it he called the guide things that showed you the way?"

"Buoys?" said Jack.

"No. Bigger."

"Beacons?"

"Yeah, exactly," said Chase. "Is that the way you think of Dad, like a beacon?"

"Look at you, using metaphors," Jack laughed. "Chase Lumpkin, the philosophical fifth grader!"

"I'm serious," said Chase. "And I'm asking because I don't think it's right to be like him. This probably doesn't make sense to you, but sometimes I feel like another trophy on his wall. I think that when you're grown up you should stand for something. I think Dad just stands for himself."

Jack rolled his head. "Look," he said, "you're more of a mama's boy, and that's okay. Nothing wrong with being sensitive or whatever. But one day you'll realize you're in goddamn America, and that you're blessed, and that you have no reason to complain. Dad is what they call ambitious, and there's nothing wrong with trying to take life for all it's worth. I'm sorry, but Mom's a pushover. I mean, she has trouble just leaving the house sometimes. The sweetest person in the world, but she's spent her life on the edges. Dad goes after it, and she just waits for everything to come. You can go that way, if that's your beacon, and I'll go mine."

A blister swelled on Chase's index finger, which he licked to cool. "I just wish we could be happy," he said.

"I am," said Jack.

"And together."

"We are."

"You know what I mean," said Chase. "Smartass."

In the yard, they made a pact that night to never divulge the damaged shed, the charred shirt, or any other harmful secret, for life. As they walked back inside, Jack shook his head, dropped his hands, and said, "There's something about you that scares the hell out of me."

***

A call from Jack's producer roused the sleeping pair, and they burst from bed, knocking into furniture like people fleeing aerial bombs. Jack pushed a cellular device into his ear and wetted his face, chest, and arms with potent bespoke cologne. He gargled mouthwash and tossed Maddy her blouse as she snapped her bra.

"Sorry for the rush. I'll have a car for you at the lobby," Jack said. "God, I feel like a big old bucket of shit."

Maddy donned last night's wrinkled garb, a turquoise business dress. She helped him button his Oxford shirt, and then she clutched his hand. She tried to kiss his minty mouth.

"Stop," he said.

She recoiled. "Don't do this to me."

"Just please don't cling," said Jack. "Okay?"

"Who are you calling? Just *go*," she said. "You're so late, Jack."

He zipped his jeans. "On hold for Anita, the hard-ass morning producer," he said. "I need to give her an excuse for being here, not there, right now."

Maddy turned away. "Can we see each other this weekend?"

"Can we slow down?"

"Is that no, Jack?"

"I'm taking a long weekend, heading up to the mountains, like I said."

"You're a shitty liar."

Line was busy. Jack gave up on the phone call, tucked the earpiece into his pocket. He envisioned chaos at his office down the street. "I'm serious," he said. "Four days of fishing in the mountains. I'm going up to see my brother, so it's a family thing. Call me an asshole, a chauvinist, or whatever, but I've never been a liar."

Maddy combed her hair into a bouquet of reddish curls. She followed Jack to the front door, where he grabbed two icy waters from a mini fridge. They loaded into the elevator. Jack changed the music selection to smooth jazz while circling his fingertips on his temples, pressing hard. Maddy brushed her fingers across the back of Jack's arm. "Can I come meet your brother?"

"Please, really, slow down."

"I was joking," said Maddy.

"No you weren't."

"Yes I was."

"Look, I think you're great. I honestly do," said Jack, as the elevator began its descent. "You're clearly ambitious, and smart, and what I'm feeling right now isn't the sad suck I get from other friends I've made at work. But let's take it easy. Let's be organic. And let's not talk about visits with my family. There's drama going on with my brother that's kind of personal; he's been struggling. It's a trip better made alone."

"One more question," she said, "before you run off."

"Fire away."

"Why was there a pile of baby clothes in your hamper?"

"A better question," Jack shot back. "Why were you snooping around?"

"It was obvious," she said. "Don't falsely accuse me. There were tiny pink socks in the bathroom, too."

"Ah, right," said Jack.

"Well?"

"Well, would you believe I have a daughter now?"

"No."

"Then you wouldn't believe she's three months old and lives in the suburbs, and that her mom doesn't trust me enough to grant unsupervised visits."

Maddy touched his forehead, a consoling gesture. "You're serious."

"Yes," he said, "it's serious."

"Do you get to see this baby at all?"

"Not really. Not enough."

"I can't believe I'm hearing this," said Maddy, her eyes doting. "It's not like you to withhold things on air."

"Her mom worked at the station last year," said Jack. "I don't think I can legally say anything on air. She's a real pit viper in court. And she's hungry for more money—like, *insatiably* hungry. I've done well the last couple years, but I've been reckless with earnings, too, and that's disconcerting for the baby's mom. As long as I have this lifestyle, the judge doesn't deem me trustworthy enough to watch an infant alone. So, yeah. Welcome to my conundrum."

"What's your daughter's name?"

"That's enough."

"I won't say anything about this."

"I thought that was understood."

Maddy grinned. "I mean I won't say anything—*if* you let me come to the mountains with you."

"For saying *that*," Jack said, stepping away, "your internship has been terminated, and we're not going to talk again."

"Are you serious?"

"It's a real bad morning for blackmail."

"You *are* serious," Maddy said.

"I was lying about the daughter thing."

"No you weren't. I can tell."

"Oh, I was."

"No you weren't, Jack, and you're only pushing me away, like an asshole, because you're afraid."

"You're right," he said. "I'm afraid you're psychotic."

The doors opened. Jack handed her $20 and pointed to the valet stand. "Sorry if this sounds harsh," he said, "but if you spill the beans about the baby, you'll never work in radio in this city. I was honest with you, because I really thought we might've had something at the time, back forty seconds ago."

He patted her back, bowed his head, and fled the opposite way, toward the street. Maddy yelled through the lobby, "I hope they fire your drunk ass today!"

4

With the sun overhead, on terrain so steep it felt like climbing a ladder, Chase's pouring sweat began to blind him, and he dried his eye sockets with dirty palms. He sipped from his canteen and continued up the mountain but suddenly stopped. Somewhere to his left, beyond dense lines of hardwoods, he could hear snorting, intermittent and angry. Next came the thud of fur-buffered bones slamming against each other, and then grunting, and the hiss of stomped leaves and crackle of crushed branches. Next, an explanation: the click-clack of clashing antlers. Two large bucks were fighting on the mountain, and though his destination summit was to the right and still miles away, he was lured to the sound, to see this final awesome show of brutality.

Chase aimed his handgun straight ahead and stepped gingerly into the brush and trees. But the clash sounded farther away the deeper he went, even as he hustled down a gulley, up the other side, over a mossy pile of boulders, and a quarter mile directly up the mountain in the wrong direction.

As he hiked his mind wandered, and the stench of unwashed fatigues, unmoving heat, and soil recalled for Chase the stifling noonday sun and foreboding mountain ranges in southern Kandahar, early June, 115 degrees. There, after three weeks in-country, Chase's platoon had teamed with the Afghan National Army for two recon missions. They called one ANA motorcyclist The Ninja, who on missions would wrap his face in cloth so you'd see only his eyes. He always carried a clunky Remington 700 with a scope, even in close-range fighting, and he led a nomadic crew of informants who helped the Afghan army for pay, at the risk of being executed. Near the entrance of the forward operating base, Chase ran into The Ninja one day on tower guard, shook his hand, and offered half the Florida orange he was peeling. The Ninja declined.

Chase toed the dirt. "How many children do you have?" He flattened his palm toward the ground, to indicate short-ness, and he bounced his head to mimic the frolic of children. "How many bambinos? Little kids? Babies?" He humped the air to mimic sex. The Ninja, confused, made sounds like a goat. They laughed at their useless interaction. "Yeah, sure, I fuck goats," Chase said, as orders came in from an Afghan subordinate, and The Ninja sped off. Chase turned around to resume his post, guarding the base's west entrance, but a high whine from the motorcycle's engine made him peek back over the wall. The Ninja had grown frustrated with a lumbering explosive-ordinance-disposal vehicle, and in his haste he passed the big truck. He revved his engine again and took off, passing an army escort vehicle a few yards in front of the truck, straying from the road itself, an abso-lute sin. Then Chase felt thunder in his ribs and saw a black geyser of dust and rocks and falling parts. He heard things rain to earth in periodic smacks, the sound of belly flops in swimming pools. The dirt dissipated, an eerie morass settled in, and the convoy stood still. Chase squeezed his AR15 and screamed, "Fucking shit!" as the EOD truck raced back to the base. He called for a Medevac, and through his gun site he watched the carnage and attempted rescue. The Ninja, still breathing, had lost both legs below the hip, and his shredded skin and muscles lay at the end of a gurney. Someone yelled about morphine. The rest of the convoy parked at the bomb site, and a major leapt from the passenger seat of a truck to snap photos of a long deep hole where the explosive had been hidden. He laid a cone to mark the location of potential human remains, and tossed glow sticks near loose dirt where other bombs may have been. In minutes a bomb tech arrived to investigate, as other soldiers logged the remains, and the cold efficiency of the process saddened Chase. As the convoy crept down the highway, continuing the mission, he could hear the crunch of muffler parts and spokes, and for the first time in his life he felt wholly compelled not just to fight, but to kill somebody.

After the Ninja died, Chase became both desensitized to, and strangely lured toward, death—a condition that now fueled his pursuit of violent mountain animals. He hoped to find one deer dominating the other, pulverizing the weaker opponent, he thought, so that he might have company in suffering on his last day. Finally, a half-mile from his planned route, Chase saw what he wanted: the white flashes of tails and the gorgeous, twisting protrusions of their heads, clashing.

Chase marveled from across a silent shaded bank, and in a moment the antlers thwacked again. He yearned to be closer. But his next step was snagged by something not of the forest, like a thicker metallic version of fishing line, strung eight inches above the leaves. This set off a series of red flashing lights a hundred yards downslope, each glaring but silent, and it sent the bucks into frenzied uphill retreat.

"A fucking tripwire?" Chase said. "Here?"

***

Jack jogged three blocks to the 3400 Peachtree Tower, arriving in a sweaty, pathetic state of dishevelment. Susan, the receptionist, rolled her eyes. On her desk a tiny clock radio aired the station's current program, Morning Madness with Bachelor Jack—sans Bachelor Jack. In twelve minutes the show would switch to a national broadcast. With or without its star—its "voice of unreason"—the taped program would simulcast to 195 radio stations, from Fort Lauderdale to Olympia, from San Diego to Rochester. Whatever was being taped upstairs would soon be heard everywhere.

"Coach here?" Jack said.

"Upstairs."

"What time's he scheduled?"

"I just can't *comprehend you* sometimes," Susan said. "I'm sorry, Jack, but you look like hell—"

"The coach, how long?"

"Your cohosts are filling in, interviewing him now," she said. "They're stuttering all over themselves up there."

Jack hustled to the elevators, calling back: "This one isn't my fault. We need to hire more responsible summer help!"

The office tower's elevators were antiquated, faux-gold boxes with clanging lifts and mysterious rattling sounds. They convinced Jack on mornings like this that he had vertigo, and before the doors sealed shut he knew this ride would be the worst in months. He felt so disoriented, so severely confined, he swore the elevator was twirling—a cube, in the wind, on a string. He lay back in a corner and covered his face, praying to Jesus that no one else would board. At the fortieth floor his nightmare was realized when a hot purge of bile leapt from his throat, into his mouth; the taste forced Jack to fully puke, bent over with hands on the elevator railings, damning the concierge who'd made him drink. He nosed up to the elevator doors, and when they opened, he shot into the long hallway that housed The Bomb and three sister stations. To reach the restroom, Jack would have to pass the radio-room window, where his colleagues, Ernie and Bravo, would point him out and berate him in front of the city's most esteemed professional coach. Crawling was an option but not a prudent one. Jack swept back his hair and tried to muster a genuine smile. He packed his mouth with mints. He opened the station door, and saw his producer: Anita Jones, a tall, unsmiling, broad-shouldered presence who'd once been an Atlanta track phenom and Olympic hopeful, until her knee shattered across a hurdle in college. Around that bad knee, Anita's skin still bore a web of scars, which Jack peeked at now, paranoid she might kung fu thrust it into his stomach. On days like this he constantly feared a whupping by Anita, a fitting punishment he'd be helpless to thwart. Instead, she latched a big hand on Jack's shoulder and said, "Get in there and rescue this, you idiot!"

Jack slipped into the booth, nodding to Ernie, Bravo, and Coach Riddick, a gladiatorial ex-linebacker. On air, Coach Riddick was explaining the team's recent decision to cut an unproductive defensive lineman. Callers from across the metro queued to ask questions and spew opinions.

Bravo, the color man who ran point after commercials, was a baseball fanatic; he hardly knew the difference between NFL defensive packages and basic zones, so he was useless in a conversation about gridiron minutiae. Ernie, meanwhile, a hotheaded Baltimore transplant, was the lowbrow comic relief, the buffoonish clown to Jack's more polished, knowledgeable standup comic. As Jack arrived Bravo held up his arms, incredulous and irate.

"Morning," Jack grumbled, reaching for a microphone.

The coach prodded: "Late night, Lumpkin?"

Jack nodded, smirked, and sat down, deflating into his tattered, high-back leather chair. This big pompous seat, which made Jack look like a boyish magnate, had been a present from his mother when he landed his first radio gig in Miami. Though he never told his mother, or another living soul, he suspected the chair was magic, in that it made him feel authentic—and coddled—in a high-pressure world of temporary idols and harsh opinion. He pulled the chair to the table and the microphone to his face, inflating himself into Bachelor Jack as best he could. "Okay, gents," said Jack. "Let's get serious."

"While he's inexcusably late," Bravo said into his mic, "Jack's fallen short of the record he set after last year's Super Bowl. Or whatever year it was you rented out that brewery and refereed Jell-O wrestling. What was that, Jack? Two hours late? Three?"

An intern brought two bottles of water. Jack swigged twice and tried to crack a joke: "Like my grandfather told me, God rest his soul, 'Nothing's inexcusable when you're irreplaceable.'"

The coach shook his head and tapped his Omega watch. Bravo leaned into his mic: "Before this petulant man-child wandered in, we were discussing defense."

Jack rubbed his face, sniffing cognac fumes. "Not to make this a 'me show,' but I don't understand why Bravo rips me for living the persona."

"It's not a persona when it's *who you are*," said Bravo. "You need to grow the hell up."

"Coach," said Jack, "you were thirty-five once, right? I mean, I'm a single guy. I'm blessed with this career, with a chance to chew the fat for a living. It's more than I probably deserve. What I do is normal, Bravo. It's *commendable*. Instead of living vicariously, you vilify the BJ. And we all know vilification is the sincerest form of total ignorance. Now, let's take some calls ..."

"You work *three hours a day!*" Bravo said. "And you can't make it on time."

"Guys," the coach said, "proceed."

"Forgive me, Coach, but I'm steaming," Jack said. "Can you two boys go skip around the hallway or something? Then Coach and I can get to the bottom of his three-four defensive philosophy, and how it'll face problems this year with the Saints' meaner, more diversified slate of running backs. They've got those speedsters, the bruiser, and the slippery pass-catching threat."

"Yes," the coach said, "let's move on."

"Without you pansies," Jack continued, "we'll hash out the coach's arsenal of blitzes—without divulging too much, right? Exactly. And for our national listeners, we'll go broad and talk general NFL trends. Hell, we'll talk baseball. I'm here to play tough. I'm not throwing softballs. The coach's a big boy. He can answer for his own ass. So we can do that, or I can take a nap and let you clowns ask about cheerleaders."

Ernie leapt up and tossed a dart at a hanging board in the corner. "I'm about to hurt somebody."

Bravo pushed his coffee mug against his computer, stood up, and rounded the oval table toward Jack. "I can *smell* you, man," he said.

The coach slapped his hands on the desk and said into the microphone, "Folks, I apologize ..."

Jack grabbed his mic and interrupted the coach—a broadcasting sin. "We'll be right back after these words from Bravo's man diapers," he said. "Anita, please, just cut to a break."

The coach wasn't finished. "Hats off to the station for hosting these discussions, but I won't be back," he said. "This is a disgrace. Get 'hold of yourselves, boys."

Banging on the producer's window, Jack hollered, "Commercial!" but behind the glass Anita kept rolling. Jack tossed his headphones on his chair and saluted the coach as he stepped back from the table. "I apologize for this, top to bottom," Jack said. "On your way out, be careful, Coach. Someone ralphed in the elevator."

Jack stomped down the hallway but stopped before the restroom, halted by the realization he'd never walked out on an interview. Despite his wild spending and the new expense of child support, he had enough cash in his checking account to take a significant break from this soul-sucking act. After so many on-location shows at Florida beaches, New Orleans casinos, and Carolina golf courses, Jack hadn't felt the need to take a bona fide vacation in years. His vacation time had accrued to more than a month's worth, and it was time to take off for a while, even though idleness, he knew, would leave him at the mercy of his appetites.

To announce his sabbatical, Jack stormed back into the station and poked his head in the producer's room. Anita snatched his arm and shut the door. They watched the coach berate Ernie and Bravo during commercials, and Jack winced as his cohosts offered bumbling apologies. The coach huffed to the elevator—where, shocked, he erupted again—before slamming shut the door to the long flight of stairs.

"I wasn't shitting about the upchuck," Jack said.

"Yes," said Anita, "about that ..."

Anita asked an intern to switch to national programing and exit the room. Jack suspected this was the end of his morning gig at The Bomb, his termination coming during a seismic hangover—the day he'd always feared. But Anita's long, suddenly affable face suggested more amusement than consternation. She stroked hot-pink fingernails across her tweed business dress, her bare shoulders defined like topographical maps of the Andes.

"Look, Jack," she said. "Remember the beach party we held at Lake Lanier that one year? Remember how nobody from the station went to sleep, and how we all felt awful once the sun came up? Right, yes. Well, I want you to remember that feeling, on that morning—"

"Is this your termination metaphor?" Jack said.

"Settle down."

"Is this your idea of kid gloves?"

"What I'm saying is that the best parties come to an end, okay," Anita said. "And no, to cut to the chase, you're not fired."

"Then I might have to quit."

"You don't have to quit."

"I've got to get out of here, out of this town, out of these confining buildings."

"This town is your blood, Jack. And you were born for this job."

"I feel like I'm walking the plank, like I'm at the edge and getting vertigo, like I'm really cooked this time," Jack said, clutching his face. "Something has to change. I'm like a lunatic now, a monster, and you know it. I have a goddamn sex swing!"

Anita flinched so hard her head jerked back, as if she'd nibbled rancid cheese. "That's repulsive—and a mental image that's unfortunately going to last," she said. "But it's forgivable." She squeezed Jack's right shoulder. "What's really eating at you, honey? The pressure of being national?"

"No," said Jack. "Well, maybe. That and other things. Life stuff. Family stuff."

"Problems with your maladjusted kid brother again?"

"That's an interesting way to put it," said Jack. "But yeah, partly."

Anita sighed and struck a contemplative pose, an elbow in one palm. "Why don't you extend that trip to see Chase, take a few more days? Get up there in them woods, breathe some good air, fish trout from the Chattooga or whatever. Forget about this place—this *life*—for a while, and just air out. Because, damn it, you're the most talented radio personality I've ever seen, and I don't want Bachelor Jack to kill the good guy that's somewhere down in him. You hear me? You know what I'm sayin'? We're not twenty-four anymore. You hit limits. You pump the brakes, or you crash. You can't keep pushing like you do."

"I appreciate the concern," said Jack. "The thing is, though, I can't act the part. I have to *be* the part. Nobody wants 'Born Again Jack' Lumpkin."

"Nobody wants you *dead*, neither."

Jack stood up, aggressively shook his producer's hand, and said, "Stay tuned."

He walked into the hallway, to the stairs, down through the building and out, headed straight home to pack, sleep as much as possible, and escape to the North Georgia Mountains.

***

Leading with his handgun, Chase eased down the mountain toward the flashing lights, and from fifty yards he recognized the limp shapes of military camo netting. He whistled to announce his presence and tossed a stick atop the netting, which he could see concealed a makeshift little cavern built of stacked logs and brown tarp. He bent down and crept around this setup; now he could see a primitive kitchen with a two-burner stove, aluminum table, and stacked pots. He backed away and could smell that he was near the designated restroom, shrouded from the cabin by more netting. He reached up and, with the twist of one knob, turned off the emergency red lights.

Elsewhere he saw rows of gasoline cans, a generator, extension cords, piles of bungee cords, and, beneath more netting, two large water cisterns, connected via brown-painted piping to a babbling creek. Rows of tomatoes, carrots, and something labeled "pepino" sprung up in small sunlit patches.

Beyond the vegetables, girded by young flimsy pines, hundreds of bucket-sized holes pockmarked the earth, interspersed with a few dozen marijuana plants, ranging from knee to shoulder height. The shape of the leaves reminded Chase of high school, and the few times in college he'd toked from pipes at parties, after which he'd become an awkward social hermit and retreat home to watch cartoons. He was surprised to know an Illicit farm like this had operated up the mountain from his cabin the whole time, and something in the subversion of it made him grin.

Convinced he was alone, and that no one had inhabited the place that day, Chase holstered his gun and pulled a pile of vegetables from the ground, washed them in the creek, and sat down beneath the tarp to take a short break before proceeding back east, toward the obscure plateau he'd been aiming for. He finished eating but still was famished. He sifted through capped plastic containers in the kitchen, finding an unexpired six-pack of Coca-Cola and a pile of chocolate cookies, each wrapped in plastic and remarkably moist.

Chase couldn't see or smell anything abnormal about the cookies. So he took a timid nibble, enjoyed it, and then finished a full cookie, followed by a second with walnuts. He cracked the can of Coca-Cola and felt sufficiently nourished for more hiking, lifted a little by caffeine. For a while he luxuriated in so much fizzy sugar on his tongue, the pleasurable carbonated sting in his throat. He watched the shriveled carcasses of leaves tumble down and pile up. With his boots he made a seat of leaves and decided to sit down a while.

Before long, Chase's thoughts wafted incoherently, obeying no discernible patterns, seeming at once profound and goofy, his brain a snow globe of vital nonsense. He grew keenly, horrifyingly aware of his heartbeat. His thirst was severe.

Occasional wind gusts brought down more big leaves, spiraling flocks of them, and Chase imagined the great mountain was breathing beneath him, heaving taller, its centuries of erosion reversing. The creek's nearby babble took on fascinating, almost linguistic dimensions, and the leaves of the secret crop shimmered. But then his stomach rumbled, filling with cold acidic tempests, a chemical overload, if not overdose, so he lay beneath the sky, dug his boots into the pine straw, and clutched the earth for an hour, so as not to fall off.

As evening fell across the mountains, the horizon bled orange, opening deep purple corridors. Some clouds were lithe and faint, others bold and pronounced, and in them Chase saw camels, a chucked Indian spear, and the outstretched arms of church revivalists. He sat up and felt better, his nausea gone and limbs responsive. Above the farthest mountains, more distinct than other mirages, he saw a quintet of mermaids, elbow to elbow, their tails tucked under buxom torsos. He concentrated and closed his eyes and heard their falsettos. He imagined them falling gracefully through the trees, filling Appalachia with song, encircling the makeshift cabin, and ushering a stoned soldier to some blissful place. If this was hallucinating, he didn't want lucidity.

All pleasantness ceased when Chase heard footfalls in the leaves. Instinctively, he lay flat and scooped a mound of pine straw beside him for cover. To his right, stomping up from the creek, kicking through rhododendron, he saw a bearded man with a hulking backpack, covered from bandana to boots in camouflage. The man seemed lost in his thoughts and therefore a lone traveler, someone silently conversing with himself in lieu of a companion. With his heart electrified and eyes bulging, Chase drew his handgun, aimed it at the man, and began to slowly, silently stand up. The man came to the vegetable garden, noticed the fresh subtraction of carrots, and halted. "Oh God," he said.

"Get the fuck on the ground!" screamed Chase, though being authoritative felt awkward. "Under the tarp—get under there, on your stomach, right now."

"Okay, okay," said the man in a raspy, mellow voice. His jacket was concealing a dirty-blond ponytail. "You got me. You found my racket. I surrender."

As the man crept low and lay down, Chase frisked him and found an antiquated revolver strapped to his right thigh.

He was a large man, a head taller than Chase, with oaks for legs. "Any other weapons here?"

"That's it, man."

"Why were you sneaking up on me with this gun?"

"I wasn't."

"Don't fucking lie," said Chase, so flushed with adrenaline he was struggling to breathe.

"I'm just coming back to close up for the season. If I'd have known you were here, man, believe me, I wouldn't be."

"You've seen me," said Chase.

"No, I haven't. Not really."

"You've seen me up here, and now everything changes."

"Sorry, officer, but what in the hell are you talkin' 'bout?"

"Shut up! Don't talk. Clasp your ankles together, and the same with your wrists, behind your back." The man complied, and Chase hastily unfurled the pile of bungee cords in the tent, wrapped the wrists and ankles tight and then hogtied the bundles together. An acrid, bathless odor lifted off the man.

"Whatever you do," the man pleaded, "for the love of God, don't just leave me out here like this. I'll plead to anything you want."

"For the last time," said Chase, holding the handgun at arm's length, "not another word."

In the dark they stayed in these positions for a while, possibly an hour, Chase hovering and silent, his mind blitzed with a hundred awful scenarios. When the man began to snore, in a way that seemed genuine, Chase slowly walked backward and leaned against a hardwood, refusing to blink in fear he'd doze off and lose his advantage.

As the moon rose, he watched the ebb and flow that was his hostage breathing. Somewhere in the branches two courting owls talked. Chase decided to sit, momentarily, to rest his legs, back, and dopey head. Within the hour he inadvertently fell asleep.

5

Morning sun permeated his bedroom, and Jack lay cocooned, like a diseased patient, until he couldn't snooze a minute more. Despite an alarming sixteen hours of sleep, he was still strangely nauseous and post-flu weak, with the jitters in his fingers and wrists. He fished his cell phone out of the sheets. After five calls to Chase, he quit trying.

Jack kicked Chase's framed army photo onto the bedroom floor, and he feigned stomping the stern soldier face, an assault so exaggerated it was cartoonish. "Invite me up there early, dork ass!" he shouted at the floor. It wasn't like Chase to duck his brother's calls, and Jack knew the kid rarely ventured outside in the morning. The more he thought about it the more his irritation became concern. Chase always remembered appointments, and especially something like a trout-fishing weekend. Jack called for a sixth time and left a message: "Hey, brother," he said. "I hope you're at the outrigger, preparing to catch us some river whales." He switched his tone from condescending to businesslike. "I'm coming up right now, a couple days early, because the boss wants me to air my head out, and because everything's kind of going to hell, here in the city. When I tell you what happened with Coach Riddick yesterday, it's going to blow your mind. It was hilarious. And pathetic." Jack took a long uneasy breath, and while exhaling, his lips jumped like mudflaps. "So, anyway, get extra beer if you're going in town because that'll solve everything. Let me know if you can't. I'll grab supplies. Just let me know something, man, one way or the other."

Dropping the phone, but not ending the call, Jack lifted Chase's picture off the floor and returned it to a smiley family gathering on his bedside table. "Looking forward to finally catching up," he said. "Just do us both a favor and remember the beer and bait. See you in a little while, Chase."

Jack packed a leather duffle, locked his home, and took the elevator down, wondering if he'd been too hard on Maddy—she was so young, after all—or if maybe the mountains were overflowing with ambitious women like her, minus the ulterior motives. He whistled into the parking garage to mask his lingering anguish; he was flushed with hot-flash hangover anxiety, an ailment now triggered by fear of conversations with strangers. He hustled past the private storage garage that housed his new truck—a massive Toyota so outlandishly tricked out it looked robotic—plus a dusty Harley Sportster he hadn't ridden since spring and a vintage Vespa he had no recollection of buying online. Fearing he'd see one of the many devout Bomb listeners who lived at Excellor (people who'd probably heard yesterday's fiasco, he now realized), he walked comically quick, soldier-like and stiff, as if in fast-forward. Among the seven-series BMWs and crouched-panther Ferraris sat Jack's vintage Corvette, a 1975 Stingray convertible, orange as Florida sunsets. His daily driver. It had four manual speeds, a modified four hundred horsepower, and a customized driver's helmet meant more for disguise than protection. Parking at Chase's backwoods home would make this svelte beast filthy, Jack knew, but on days like these he needed foolish speeds and a face full of wind.

He ripped from the garage onto Peachtree Road and shot north, toward Georgia Highway 400, the car's long snout pointed to the mountains, his scenic destination less than two hours north. Something felt off, though, like he'd forgotten vital luggage or a gift for his host. He thought about the PTSD book, a would-be Christmas present he'd never bought for Chase. Could he find it in a store right now? Would it be an awkward gesture? Would it kick the badger in Chase? He decided that, in lieu of the book, he'd host long, healthy, brotherly talks this week, preferably semi-sober, beginning with some humorous topics from their youth, as one online essay about mental illness had suggested. He'd always viewed Chase as a captivating, lovable sort of enigma, a fixable puzzle, simultaneously the family's physical stallion and emotional runt. His kid brother, in Jack's eyes, had been flawed from an early age, and now his recent struggles had been gnawing at Jack as proof he hadn't tried hard enough, in more formative times, to help. Behind the wheel, Jack decided he would come clean about these feelings, however soft that might be, insisting that all of Chase's failures were equally his own. In doing so, Jack thought, they might close the gaps between them, let out the steam, and help mend each other's ruptured lives. At the very least, they'd get slap-happy blitzed together, like old times, in a beautiful place.

The Corvette eased into a low gargle, and Jack's pocket buzzed. Though he hated doing it, he ignored the call—it was his mother—and twisted the radio dial from heavy metal to easy-listening fluff, a breezy ballad about palm trees in the South Pacific or something. The warm wind helped alleviate his queasiness. He passed a family in a maxi-van, a cloud of leather-clad bikers, and outdoorsy dudes in a Jeep lugging mountain bikes and kayaks. Jack put on his Ray-Bans and was relieved to see, in his rearview, Atlanta's suburban high-rises shrink to distant nubs. The detachment was real, the stress dissipating, and he felt more virtuous already. Ahead lay the lumps of lower Appalachia, a ruffled brown blanket that stretched the whole horizon.

Squeezing the wheel, Jack winced at the thought of returning his mother's call, but because she'd left a message, it was unavoidable. He had to sound chipper for a sorghum-sweet but psychologically unstable woman who didn't understand him, who rarely listened to Jack's broadcasts anymore because they made her feel guilty of lackluster parenting. In Jack's rants she heard echoes of his father, and she constantly reminded him of that—and the danger in becoming such a man. Jack didn't want to hear Anne's scolding, not on a fine day so full of independence, productivity, and unabated October sunshine. But he couldn't outrun a voicemail, so he steered with his knees and dialed.

Anne picked up on the fourth ring and cleared her throat. She'd been born a rural peach to an executive in the energy industry who moonlighted as a pastor, and she still spoke in gentle, earnest waves of Southern dialect, her vowels elongated into song. But now she was livid and unconcerned with manners of any sort. "What's gotten into *yawh damn head*, son?"

Jack winced, as if shocked by cattle prods, and he considered lying, but he knew his mother was too savvy. She was a master gardener, a cookbook author, a whiz with crossword puzzles, and above all an admirably obsessive mom, a woman who considered it her chief purpose to be molding good citizens of her sons. Despite her cunning, it had taken Anne twenty years to discover her ex-husband's infidelity, which she dubbed the "waitress safari." She was too kind to confront wickedness until it latched onto her throat. And it was this sweetness, as young Jack had seen it, that rendered Anne weak for all her life, the opposite of his confident and accomplished father, the pole to which Jack naturally gravitated. When Anne could muster a certain authoritative meanness, her stern talks with Jack had always seemed empty, however, because her inexplicable struggles with social anxiety often kept her indoors for days at a time; his dad's braggadocio, meanwhile, came across as trade secrets. Through the years, on an emotional level, Jack kept his mother at a distance, and at times during his rebellious teenage phase, she felt to him like little more than a nagging guidance counselor. To atone for all of that, and to help boost her spirits without pharmaceuticals, Jack had recently bought his mother a Buckhead Hills residence in the Dutch Colonial style. It was a birthday gift she'd never asked for and seemed embarrassed to accept, and a splurge her son could hardly afford.

"Can barely hear you, Ma," Jack shouted. "I'm en route to Chase's place. In the 'vette, top down."

"Seven or eight people called the house yesterday and this morning. It's horrible. Everyone's afraid you'll lose your job."

"Huh?"

"Everyone thinks you're out of control."

"Come on," said Jack.

"I think you need to talk to someone."

"I am."

"Who?" she said.

"My brother," he said. "Like always."

"I'm not joking."

Jack said, "Speak up," and immediately regretted that.

"Not that it's my business," she said, clutching a dainty fist and waving it around, history's emptiest physical threat, "but what were you doing before that radio show? How late were you out?"

"I had a date and slept in," he said. "A nice girl, you'd like her. Full of integrity and plans."

"How many nights are you drinking now?"

"What?"

"Answer me, son."

"Can you define *drinking*?"

"Don't do this, Jackie."

He hated that nickname. It was still a verbal whipping.

"Ma," he said, "I'm a grown man. I'll do what I do. And I know what I'm doing."

"How many days?"

"A couple," he said.

"Four? Five?"

"They say it's good for you, in the moderation I practice. Everything in my life is under control."

"I'm worried," she said.

"No need."

"I'm worried about my boys."

Boys. Eternally they were boys. Growing boys. Flawed boys. Little boys. The way she'd said it reminded Jack of a spring day in Chastain Park and a bustling farmers market near the playground, sometime in the early '90s. It had been Anne's weekend to have her boys, and she'd been acting over-caffeinated if not slightly paranoid all day. As young Chase and Jack helped their mother select cucumbers and fresh cilantro, she bumped into a former church associate and one of her ex-husband's law partners in the same queue, bookended by conversations she hadn't anticipated. Forced to speak with both acquaintances, Anne instead hunched her shoulders and stared at the dirt—until, without warning, she grabbed her sons' wrists and ushered them away from the crowds to the outfield of an unused baseball diamond. She could barely breathe, clutching at her neck and falling to her knees, a frazzled look on her face like imminent death. Chase hugged her and began to cry while Jack hollered for help, until Anne stopped him and eked out something about a simple panic attack. "But why are you *doing* this, Ma?" Jack had said. "For God's sake, you live in Buckhead, with alimony out your ears." For the first time, there in the grass, as Chase caressed his mother's trembling head, it occurred to Jack she may have passed some corrupting, emotional cancer to her youngest son, a genetic infliction her eldest knew he was blessed to have ducked.

Jack kicked the gas pedal and threaded between a Lexus sedan and peach delivery truck, then eased into the middle of three northbound lanes. "Anyhow, how's the house?" he said into the phone. "Did the roofers come by and fix those fancy shingles? They're supposedly highfalutin European roofers, with expertise in that sort of thing."

"It's all fixed," Anne said, her tone dour now. She felt a bit uncomfortable with the focus turning to her, in any situation, which is why the mirrors in her home were all relegated to bathrooms. "I don't know, Jackie," she said. "This place is gorgeous, it really is, but it's only me and my books and all these rooms—"

"It's a *two-bedroom*, Mom," he said. "Not exorbitant."

She whimpered a little, in agreement, trying to maintain the disappointment in Jack she'd felt moments before. "I know, but beyond the house, and all this quiet space, it's the actual *place*—the street. On my little bend, I'm the only household without children, and I can't help but well up with old memories just watching them, hearing them. You wouldn't understand yet. There's a certain kind of music in all kids' voices that's exactly the same. I hear my boys out there all the time, crashing their bikes and laughing, roughhousing in the grass. I hear boys that aren't ever coming back."

Jack released the steering wheel, smacked his forehead with both palms, and threw up his arms in exasperation. "Speaking of," he said, rapidly detouring from her pity, "have you talked to Chase lately? He's still taking his medications, and doing that therapy regimen, right?"

When Chase became the subject, Anne liked to take her time, parsing her words so she didn't sound frantic. She'd done all she could to keep her fragile son from the military's clutches, forcing Chase, with her ex-husband's help, to try college before enlisting. They'd seen Jack succeed as an undergraduate a few years earlier, when an admiring English professor at the University of Georgia suggested Jack's personality and media studies were a predestined marriage. If his wild brother could hunker down and ace broadcast journalism classes, they argued, surely Chase would find his calling, too.

So, for three years, Chase slumped in the back of history classes at Clayton Community College. But following his twenty-first birthday, he confessed to Anne that he'd quit college to work construction until the paperwork cleared and the military could take him. He said he was a man. She said that's true, and men are good at making bad choices.

Jack thought he'd lost the connection until Anne said, quietly, that Chase had gone off the grid, that he hadn't called her back in two weeks and hadn't written a letter in a month. She hadn't been this concerned, in fact, since the day Chase had come home—July 29, 2011—when she'd planned an elaborate celebration at Hartsfield-Jackson Atlanta International Airport with seven women from her running club. That day, her round face was pink and happy, her blond-gray hair twirled into a practical bun. Her fingernails, typically chipped from gardening, gleamed a perfect mauve. She beamed at having raised her sons into successful men—the sports expert and the hero—in spite of their father's influence. Back in Miami, Jack's first sports-talk radio show had been a smash, tripling ratings in his first year; his Atlanta-based company lured him home with a lucrative contract and promises of national syndication, eventually, which was a move his mother welcomed. Seeing Chase come home, Anne hoped, would complete her life like never before, an accomplished mother hen awaiting inevitable grandbabies.

As Chase approached on an airport escalator that day, Anne was so jovial she squealed, a rarity without uppers; her friends raised ridiculous, glittery, celebratory signs— "Congratulations!" and "God Bless You, Soldier" and worst, "Chase Lumpkin: Hero." Chase hugged them and glad-handed and smiled but, once outside, his good leg nearly buckled when he saw the prearranged cavalcade. Cordoned off by airport security, with lights flashing, Fulton County deputies

waited in tan Impalas and on bulky Harley-Davidsons. Their
duty was to escort Chase home, and at the first sight of him
the deputies saluted. Soon his mother's party flanked Chase,
hoisted the signs, and nodded for a welcome to commence.
The cops clapped and whistled. Bystanders in taxi queues
and mothers with strollers paused and applauded the injured
soldier. Chase felt weak and exposed. So what—he'd fucked
up and gotten shot, ostensibly by the bad guys? And now he
was being *saluted?* For the benefit of the crowd, though, he
tried to maintain a cordial grin, a happy wave, but his hands
went to his knees, and his vision speckled white. The air
sickness he'd grappled with all the way home from Germany
returned. Before Chase could stop himself, before he could
hobble to a trash can, he dry heaved toward the concrete,
followed by violent coughing. The deputies bowed their
heads and turned away. One of the women with Chase's
mother knelt to her knee in prayer. The children snickered.
Chase turned to his mother, who held her head with both
hands, and his voice became a tortured wheeze. All he said
was, "Help," and Anne, crushed, kissed the back of his neck
and drove him home herself.

"Ma, you still there?" Jack pictured his mother's face
constricting, her mascara melting into the rouge. "What a
little jerk, leaving you in the dark, too," he said. "I swear to
God, Mom, I'm going to sneak up on Chase, in his sleep, slap
him, and run, just for you!"

Anne shouted, "Don't be a lout, Jackie."

"He shouldn't do this."

"This isn't his fault," she said. "You aren't really your
fault, either. You boys need to reel in your lives and come
home for a while."

"Ma," Jack said, manually rolling up his window, blocking
wind. "I'll take care of this. I'll report back to you. Go for a
jog with the ladies. Get outside. Your boys will be okay. You
can trust me. I'll come through."

Anne's crying trailed off. She felt buttressed in a way by Jack's confidence, but her tone became grave. "Call it mother's intuition," she said, "but something's off. I need you to call me back tonight. No messing around, Jackie. No later than tonight."

***

"Sir ... sir ... sir?"

The quiet, desperate inquiry woke Chase, and realizing where he was, he leapt up and pointed the gun. For a second, he was disoriented and confused, numb with post-dope stupor, but the gravity of the situation snapped his mind right. His clothing was moist with dew, his neck sore from sleeping with a drooped head. The sun warmed the gulley and the secret camp, and Chase knew he'd had a dangerously long sleep.

"Sir?"

"What?" said Chase.

"I have to piss. Awfully bad. I'm on fire, really. Can you free me for second?"

"No," said Chase. "Hold it." He rubbed the sleep from his face and walked closer for a better look at the hostage. "Are you alone up here?"

"Yes, sir."

"I don't believe you."

The man took a moment to formulate a response. "Sir, it's the end of the growing season. At this altitude, in the Chattahoochee National Forest, all the cover is falling to the ground. Everything is exposed. I'd just come back to touch up and get gone."

"Touch up?"

"Well ..." said the man, though it came out as "whale." He gritted his teeth and seemed to ache from his prolonged contortion on the ground. "I mean to finish the harvest, and then bury and hide what's here. And that's a one-man job, so I'm alone. Forgive me, but if you're gonna book me, can we get on with it? I really have to piss."

"I'm not law enforcement."

The man stopped straining and put his face in the leaves. "Then I'm not a grower. I'm just a hippie hiker, shootin' the high-country breeze."

"Not a cop," said Chase. "I'm a soldier. Or I was, I guess."

"Obviously," said the man.

"What do you mean?"

The man chuckled, *hehehehaha*. "I mean, it makes sense, because this is some military-grade torture. Some George W. shit you've got going on right here, with my ankles and hands."

"Oh," said an uncompassionate Chase. "Maybe I overdid it."

"Trust me," said the captive, "I squirm less than the Taliban, I bet."

Chase nodded. "But you talk so much more." He was beginning to feel sympathetic and soft, which alarmed him. "What's your name?"

"You want my real one, or what I go by?"

"Answer the question."

"Well, they call me Prophet."

Cocking his head, Chase said, "And why's that?"

"Because I deliver the truth, man."

"I see," said Chase, eyeing the makeshift kitchen. "I think I learned the truth yesterday, on accident, with whatever you're storing in those plastic containers."

Prophet forcibly giggled now, his back vibrating with the wicked, unclever sound. "Those moon cookies are magic! It's a perfect strain, soldier. And they're so damn good when you float 'em in chocolate milk!"

"Anyhow," said Chase, "if I untie you, how can I trust you?"

The laughing petered out. "Look, man, I just want to finish up and truck my ass to Asheville for the winter. That's it. I'll be gone, and I won't say nothing."

"How many more are there? In general?"

"The hell're you talkin' about?"

"How many other growers are up here, running around these mountains?"

"Oh hail," Prophet said. "Not many left now, but in summer, we're everywhere. The cartels pay really good these days. They come to us to restock what border patrol intercepts. Plus, dee-mand is still high in a corner of the country like this, one that's all throbbin' red. We're the new moonshiners, really."

"What about higher up in the mountains?" said Chase. "I mean, on the peaks, or right up near them, in this general area? The places where everyday hikers don't go?"

"Naw, we're not up there, not really," Prophet said. "It's a little too obvious where the trees thin out, where the GBI birds can see right to you."

Chase put his boot on the man's back. "We have a problem," he said. "I can't be seen up here. And you've seen me. So now what?"

"I didn't see shit."

"Yes you did."

"Let's hold on a second here," said Prophet. "Can I ask *you* something?"

"Quickly."

"I thank you," Prophet said. "So, look, not to get uncomfortably personal or whatnot, but you been in combat, man?"

Chase looked away, down the mountain. "I asked a question."

"I see that weight on you. That soldier weight. You got those harried eyes."

"Shut up."

"There's no virtue in violence," said Prophet. "You won't find God in no gun. And you know all about that, way deep down in your center, don't you?"

"I think so."

"Then stop pointing all that death at me, man, and let's take those shackles off your mind. Let's have a pow-wow and get to the bottom of it all."

"Enough with the hippie-dippie shit."

"Suit yourself," said Prophet, "but it works."

"What do you mean, exactly? Beyond the getting high part?"

Prophet pulled his head from the leaves, a few straggling on his ratty beard. "I mean the doctors probably pumped you full of their cash chemicals, right?"

"Maybe."

"To fix physical things and head things, right?"

"Maybe."

"Then untie me, man, and I'll reverse all of that—organically. This ain't snake oil. It's medically proven, dating back to Cherokee rituals, to the dawn of man. You talk the poison out, over this fine smoke and shrooms, and you feel a-okay. Real simple, really."

Chase crouched, suddenly but silently, and whispered above his captive's head, "First, tell me: You believe in destiny?"

Prophet's eyes widened, his cheeks and forehead folding, and he laughed. "No, brother," he said. "I believe in coincidence. I think coincidence is more potent than God. But I do believe we were destined to meet each other, in a way, if that's what you're asking."

"I see," said Chase. "Then it must be a coincidence there's someone walking this way, a hundred yards across that creek, dressed exactly like you."

Prophet said nothing. He didn't breathe.

"Don't move. Don't speak. And I won't shoot both of you right now."

6

On the outskirts of Gainesville, Jack exited the highway and followed signs with cartoon pigs to a kitschy roadside shack proclaiming itself a world-famous barbecue outpost. Wafts of sweet hickory smoke permeated the air, and Jack felt better knowing his appetite was restored. Hordes of day-tripping city dwellers, heading north for early fall foliage, crowded the gravel parking lot. Jack parked in the road to spare his car from clingy white dust and hustled inside the shack, finding a low-ceilinged space bedecked with license plates from Alaska to Maine to Austria. He lifted his sunglasses and cleared his eyes with the sleeve of his T-shirt, exposing his biceps tattoo: a singing parrot, roaring drunk on rum. The ink drew the attention of the only person ahead of Jack in line, a happy-eyed man who looked like a grizzled, portly logger, his lip fat with chaw.

"You know that's a desecration of your body," the old man said, nodding to Jack's arm.

A quick glance, from toes to kind face, and Jack felt confident he could pummel the man with four punches, or at the very least outrun him. "You're a desecration of my morning," Jack said, half-joking, sucking in his belly and bowing his upper chest. "Bring it."

The man set his hand on Jack's left shoulder, but Jack smacked it away, and in doing so, they squared face-to-face in the ordering line. Beneath the man's flannel shirt Jack noticed a priest's collar, and he immediately backed away, wrapped his hands around banisters, and dropped his head. A clerk at the counter, clearly appalled at what Jack had done, braced and hunched his body, as though he might leap to the pastor's aid.

"Calm down, y'all," the pastor said. "This man's just having a shitty day." And then, to the clerk, "Bobby, can you cut him a discount?"

"Sir," said Jack, "I'm sorry a million times over. My mouth has a mind of its own sometimes. But I don't need a discount. Let me pay for your meal, too."

"No need, son," said the pastor.

"Kid," said Jack, nodding. "His lunch is on me."

The pastor acquiesced and invited Jack to sit with him outside, so that neither would eat alone, and they found a cool place beneath a spindly oak. They shook hands over brisket sandwiches, jalapeno mac and cheese, bourbon baked beans, and fresh sweet bread. They slugged tea from little Styrofoam buckets.

"I know who you are," the pastor said.

"*Wonderful*," Jack said, sarcastically. "You get the station all the way up here?"

"I have a massive antenna on the truck, and except when it's raining, I catch your programs fine. I hear you talk about that car all the time."

In this context Jack felt ashamed. He put down his plastic fork. "So you probably know why I'm going to Cherokee, to hang with my insane little brother?"

"Is that the right word to use?"

"It's not," Jack said. "Forgive me, pastor. That was stupid. I've been the kid's biggest advocate for about twenty-five years and should know better."

"I think it's noble that you care so much," the pastor said. "You're a nobler man than you know, when you're not being a pig."

Jack cocked his head, feigning confusion. "That's not the real me, I don't think. I'm paid to be like that."

The pastor finished his plate and neatly arranged his napkin atop his fork and spoon. He lofted a quick, post-meal prayer. "A proper greeting—I'm James Rutgers, of Tabernacle International, the most liberal church in North Georgia." He handed over a business card.

Puzzled, Jack accepted the card, impressed by its restrained design and classy font. He read it twice. "Since when do men of God say 'shit'?"

The pastor smiled, the corners of his lips maroon with barbecue sauce. "All I can say is that we, as a congregation, don't abide by established norms," he said. "But our mission is earnest. Our mission is to help."

"A liberal mountain church?" Jack said. "That's like calling yourself a cosmopolitan bean farmer." The pastor laughed, and Jack was encouraged: "Or a jet-setting exterminator!"

"Okay, okay," the pastor said, drawing a napkin across his mouth. "It might sound contradictory, but we stand for the good, honest truth."

When he'd finished, Jack collected their plates and tossed them in a bear-proof garbage can. He stepped toward his car, hinting at his desire to get back on the road. "What brings you here?" Jack said, turning around. "Are you the barbecue apostle?"

"I'm down here on a purchasing trip, for supplies," the pastor said, leading Jack to his car. "I live north of Cherokee. I've actually heard of your brother. I've heard from friends how he is. Drop me a line sometime. Or call me, before y'all take one of those fishing excursions. I'll show you boys how to fish trout. And we can have a good talk."

"I'm too old for conversion," Jack said. "Just so you know."

The pastor chuckled. "Shit, I don't work miracles."

They shook hands, and Jack walked to the car, where he rolled down the window and shouted back that he'd be in touch. He thought he might have meant it. The pastor rubbed his bulbous belly and said he owed Jack lunch. "I'll pray you keep those wheels on the road," he said. "And that you find your brother in a state of peace."

The pastor tilted his head and raised his hand, as if to make one last point, but Jack tore away, bound for mountains so close he could see their veiny yellow ridges, furry conifer wisps, and deep legions of shadows.

***

Chase crept behind the tent and waited, crouching, for Prophet's counterpart to arrive. The footfalls crunched big leaves, slowly closer and closer. When the sounds were within ten feet, they stopped; so Chase flanked around the tent and burst upon this camouflaged figure from behind, shoving the face into the ground, hopping to his feet, and aiming the nine-millimeter straight down.

A frantic, young, dreadlocked blond woman rolled over, saw the gun, and screamed. She lifted her arms and legs and fluttered them like a roach.

"Shit!" Chase shouted, lowering the weapon. "I'm sorry, miss. I wouldn't shoot you. Just calm down—calm down."

Beneath the unkempt hair, Chase noticed, she had vivid green eyes and a prominent, pointed chin that quivered as she stared up, cowering in his shadow. Smeared sweat shone on her forehead, and to Chase her face seemed pure, uncreased by time or worry. He studied her without meaning to. And he gawked. She looked equal parts college cheerleader, subversive Atlanta street kid, and Special Forces hard-ass.

"Just lay down, baby," Prophet hollered, the loudest that Chase had heard him. "He's a nice guy—a real American hero."

"Shut *up*," said Chase. "You lied to me. You're dead to me."

The girl flopped on her stomach, next to her comrade, and said, "I'm sorry. We're sorry. We were just hiking and stumbled into this place. I can't go to prison."

"You're both liars," Chase said, gauging this weird new predicament, this time-killing diversion. "I don't wanna have to keep covering you with this gun, miss, so I'm going to tie you up with these bungees, too. Okay. Okay? I've never done this with a woman, and I don't want to hurt you, so relax and don't fight it. Just lay on your stomach. There you go, thanks. I promise not to leave you like this long. What's your name?"

The girl pouted into the leaves. "You'll have to finger-print me to find out."

"Look, I'm not the police. I'm not the parks service. And I'm not here to take your shit," said Chase. "But I don't trust you, and I need to think." He roped her wrists and ankles together and stretched the last cord between the two bundles, leaving her in the demeaning position of a hogtied captive, which, to his surprise, pleasantly accentuated the shape of her muscular lower half. She was so petite he could've lifted the cords and carried her out of the woods, like a package. As he stood up, he snuck a shy glimpse at her gymnast physique, then looked again while standing straight. Prophet shuffled around, seeming antsy, almost panicked.

"Please just tell me your name."

"It's Yonah," she said.

"Okay, wow," said Chase. "That's different. But nice, I mean. I don't think I've heard that before."

Prophet laughed hoarsely. "Soldier, it's the Cherokee word for bear."

Chase rolled a heavy boot across Prophet's vertebrae and contemplated sending a stronger message with a heel to the ribs. Instead, he sat down on a log and said nothing. He felt despicable for ogling another man's woman, but it had been a long drought for Chase, since before basic training, as his blurred dalliance with the Cherokee bartender, Carrie, didn't count for anything, the way he saw it. This Yonah was such a magnetic blend of prettiness and spunk his eyes were acting independently of his brain, until he reached up his hand to rub them, intentionally blocking his vision and ending his despicable voyeurism.

"Listen, man," Prophet said. "Give me the benefit of the doubt here. I didn't know what you were going to do to me. I couldn't tell you that my girlfriend was trailing me back to the site. What if you skinned me alive? I couldn't set that trap for her, too. Okay? Wait—why are you doing that?"

Chase's hands trembled severely. He clasped them together over the gun and forced them into stillness by pressing downward in his lap. "Happens when I get stressed, and you've got me stressed," said Chase. "But go on ..."

"Any-hoo," said Prophet, "that's the only reason I lied. That's my logic. That's my motive. I'm a truthful man otherwise."

"He really is," said Yonah.

"We're honest, good people," Prophet continued. "You should cut these ropes, and we'll talk it out, like I said. We can help set you straight, especially with two of us here now. We're not running narcotics, man. We ain't poisoning kids. We do good in the world. Like you did."

Chase rolled his head and stood up. "You've made your case," he said. "I hear you. And I see you've pissed your pants, so you'll be good to lie down there a while." With his boot Chase budged a pile of crunchy leaves over the expanding wetness. "I just need to sort out some things in my head."

**

Ten calls now to Chase, and Jack knew nothing. After a fourth ring on the cabin's landline, he canceled his call. Two miles later he decided to call once more, and into the answering machine he threatened, in a boyish whine, "Why are you leaving me in the dark here, man? This was your idea. You can't ignore me and think it's okay to back out. I'm here, in the mountains now, and I'm coming straight to your house. I swear to God I'm not getting a hotel, and I'm not sleeping on your porch—I'm *kicking in your door* if you're not there." Jack bashed his palm into the steering wheel and tossed the phone onto the passenger seat. He considered turning around and sleeping at home for the rest of the afternoon, but the wind and sun and liberation of travel felt wonderful.

Banking into a curve, Jack tried to recall the last time he'd actually heard Chase's voice, instead of reading it in the occasional, weirdly fanciful letters dispatched from the mountain. These last few weeks had seen the first sustained silence between them, as even while Chase was overseas they constantly volleyed emails to each other. Wartime correspondences between the brothers had initially been weird and formal, but soon the awkwardness gave way to perversion. As Jack's first sports radio show began to find an audience in Miami, he would email photos to Chase of his conquests, grainy cell phone images he'd taken of women posing beside him in bed, each provocative but none pornographic. Chase felt contemptible for looking and called Jack a Neanderthal, but in truth he found the photos intoxicating, if not a little artful. They were redheads, brunettes, and a raven-haired Latino baseball correspondent from the radio station whose navel was ringed with black tattoos. Their bodies under silk sheets were sleek as sand dunes. Any accompanying messages from Jack would be tantamount to the language of snickering boys—"he he he he," and "woaaaaah." He was living an extended adolescence, while Chase risked his life beside Afghan National Army soldiers whose names he couldn't pronounce. After a quick glimpse, Chase would delete the photos, which felt to him like setting women free.

Jack drove faster as the elevation climbed, eager to reach Chase's place, unpack, and knock back cold ones beneath a swirling, smogless sunset. The pines momentarily receded, unveiling a landscape of dramatic, bucolic beauty that to Jack seemed otherworldly. Boulders girded the road; some were ancient, half-buried, and moss-covered, others freshly fallen, lodged like axe heads in the culvert. The highway dipped into a valley and opened into a long scenic straightaway. Black cattle dotted far green hills. Next came roadside farmers markets, decrepit filling stations split by tree growth, and abandoned horse barns reclaimed by kudzu. The highway climbed a rocky mountainside, revealing with each gap in the white pines and sweet gums a more spectacular vista beyond. Jack thought he should be savoring the moment, not burning through. He pulled into a little roadside parking lot for sightseeing, exited the car, and found himself alone and inspired. The serenity was strange but invigorating. The spires of Pentecostal churches poked up from the valley like distant pencils. Beyond them, a creek carved faint snakes of leaflessness through amber foliage. Jack wondered for a moment if he could cut ties with the city and settle down in the high country. He breathed musky earth and pine, which got him thinking about gin, so he loaded back into the car and roared off to town.

Shadows slinked across the streets of Cherokee as Jack arrived. To him the town seemed an apt setting for a Jimmy Stewart movie, a really hokey one, with its gaudy street clocks, proudly antiquated storefronts, and rickety wooden homesteads. The inhabitants all seemed to walk around in complacent states of obliviousness. Drivers at stop signs waved and smiled at Jack to proceed before they did, as if their appointments were secondary to his. This struck Jack as eerie and insincere. "Why are you all so *satisfied?*" he said, under his breath. "Are you even real?"

Downtown the people stepped gingerly, almost theatrically, from store to store, house to house, street to street, gourd stand to pumpkin stack. It was high season for tourism, and the townspeople were clearly upholding their reputations as warm, welcoming, entrepreneurial hill folk.

The quaintness amused Jack, and if the dates—1831, 1832, and 1923—weren't etched into the facades of most buildings, he'd have thought they were fabrications. The Molly Theater's resuscitated marquee flashed on one corner, while next door the ice cream parlor teemed with people, the happiest of which were kids attacking drippy waffle cones. On the square stood the Georgian-style inn, with its glorified archways, a wine shop, an Irish pub, and the fanciful toy museum. Jack knew this town had been fossilized by design; its insularity was famous. The men, especially, beamed as they walked downtown, as if to gracefully warn national retailers and Yankee profiteers away. On air, Jack had laughed at news of Cherokee's no-outsiders controversies, the rumors of its closet Klansmen and cults, but he'd always wondered if this place wasn't onto something.

At a stop sign Jack let at least ten tourists pass. He nodded to a sheriff's deputy in khaki uniform. The deputy eyed the Corvette, front bumper to back, pursed her lips, as if moderately impressed, and turned up her thumb. Then she hooked both thumbs on suspenders that looked tactical and serious, as if designed to hold grenades. Her hairless forearms were like machinery, bronzed by a long summer and defined by swollen cables of muscle. The fingers, Jack noticed, were cut and scabbed in tiny slashes, as if clawed by rodents fighting for their lives. Her jaw was thick and athletic, too, though not so disproportionate and fan-like to make her fair face overtly masculine. There was a pretty blond shine about her. Nonetheless, she terrified Jack.

"Good-looking ragtop," the deputy said. "Nice to see one that old being babied. Cherokee's mayor had a 'vette, about the same model, when we were growing up. The star of every parade."

"Much appreciated, officer," Jack said, in his best John Wayne.

"It's deputy," she said.

"Apologies, deputy," Jack said, still cowboy. "But yes, ma'am, I reckon she's a great fit for these hairy old mountain roads."

In his rearview Jack saw two cars queued, but he figured no Cherokee driver would dare interrupt a law enforcer's conversation.

"You enjoy your drive."

"Which way to Highway 27?" Jack asked, though he knew.

"A right there," the deputy pointed to the next stop sign, opposite side of the square, exposing her hands, "and you'll T-bone right into 'er."

"Much appreciated."

"You bet."

"Not to be nosy," said Jack, "but what happened to your hands, ma'am?"

"Oh," she said, balling her fists. "A little taxidermy hobby. That's all. I'm a novice, just learning, still clumsy. I'm good with any Glock, but those damn sculpting tools are something else."

She couldn't have been much taller than Jack, he noticed, which would qualify her as practically dainty, but something in the proud, stiff-shouldered, excessively trained way she held herself made her gigantic. She was maybe thirty-two, or maybe an ultra-fit forty-two, or hell maybe twenty-five, he couldn't tell. "Let me guess," said Jack. "You've been sewing up the black bears and cougars you hunt for fun?"

"Get movin', sir," she said. "Drivers are lined up behind you."

"I beg yer pardon, miss."

"Just be careful up there," the deputy said. "Sounds like thunderstorms. With all that power and those bald tires, you're bound to slip. You're not on Peachtree Street anymore."

"You know, that just did dawn on me."

"Have a good one now," said the deputy, flashing beige pearls of teeth, which matched the nondescript studs in each ear. The smile seemed genuine, and the jewelry feminine enough, but nothing, strategically, a fighting crook could loop his fingers around for leverage, pulling her head to places she didn't want it. "Don't smash that car in the rain, hotshot."

"Hell," Jack smiled, patting his door. "She needs a shower."

The deputy winked and walked behind the car. While scratching the blond hair at her temples, slicked back and shiny in a tight braid, she studied the license plate. Jack pretended to look away, and he slowly turned right, all the while watching his observer in the side-view mirror. The deputy slipped a folded paper and pencil from her chest pocket, just below the sewn nametag, and she wrote something down while walking toward a pub.

At Highway 27 Liquors, Jack grabbed two cases of lowbrow beer in gray-green cans called Chuck's Lager. To Jack it tasted like pencil shavings, but his brother had mentioned in letters how he liked—and could afford—it. Jack emptied his shopping cart at the register and asked how the brook trout were biting.

"Don't fish," said the teenage clerk.

"*Pshaw!*" Jack acted crestfallen.

"Fishing sucks," the kid said, rolling his eyes. He beeped a case over the barcode scanner. "You're going fishing in an antique Corvette?"

"Such an observant boy," Jack said.

The clerk sighed and asked for twenty-two dollars and five cents.

"Here's thirty, and the change is yours, on one condition ..."

"Can't wait to hear this."

"Tell me the last time you saw a taller, strapping sort of dude in here," Jack said. "Former army soldier, lives up the road, drives a four-door Honda. I know he's been here. Probably recently."

"He's in here all the time, buying this same horse piss." The clerk was amused by his beer description, his hand atop Jack's purchase. "I saw him maybe a week ago. Maybe less."

"Not more recently?"

"I don't think so," the kid said. "He's a pretty, I don't know, *uneasy* guy. I've seen him sort of arguing with himself in the parking lot before. Like he's debating whether to come in or not. One time, last summer, he came in hammered and started saluting me. All the customers, too. It was so weird, sir. Is that enough for the tip?"

"So you'd call him a heavy drinker?"

"*Oh*," said the kid, "he's good for business."

Feeling alarmed, and a little disheartened, Jack loaded his cache into a shopping cart and walked out. To calm down he cracked a warm Chuck's in the car, sipping it surreptitiously, his head slinked down with one eye over the dashboard, weaving up the mountain. Chase's cabin seemed smaller than Jack remembered it from pictures, almost solemn under peach skies of late afternoon. Chase's battered Honda sat in the driveway, beneath a netless basketball goal. Seeing the car encouraged Jack, as Chase couldn't have wandered far without it, he thought. He raised the ragtop and called his brother's name into the woods. He rapped on the dusted windows of the garage door, peeking in to see defunct table saws and the gutted carcass of a four-wheeler. At the front door Jack gazed off to the mountains and cracked a second beer. To his surprise the door was unlocked.

Inside, the house was dead, not a fan buzzing or appliance humming. It felt so abandoned and smelled so stale Jack feared he might find what he did not want to see—a crime scene, a human lump of decay, or worse, lumps. Scanning the room he saw the note on the coffee table and felt relief, expecting to read a pacifying explanation for his brother's absence: an overnight stay with a barroom girlfriend, maybe, or a surprise obligation of his probation. Jack flipped on the television and walked to the kitchen. He retrieved his bags and beer, loading the forty-eight cans into a barren refrigerator with rusted metal grids for shelves. He packed four cans in the freezer, returned to the living room, and sat down on the sofa. He let out a loud, happy exhale.

As he read the brief, beautiful note, Jack stretched the paper tight, squeezing with both hands. Then he tossed his full beer can against the wall. Suds burst across the paneling and a plastic mounted eagle. Jack leapt up and felt the need to pray but had no words. Instead, he clutched his face, gritted his teeth, and kicked the coffee table. He ran downstairs screaming, *"Fuck you!"* To his mind the note could've been a morbid joke. He yelled and slapped the basement walls to thwart his brother's sick prank. Satisfied the basement was empty, he ran to the main level, then through the upstairs bedrooms, kicking beds, scything his arm through closets, until he came breathless to the stairs, and slowly walked back down.

Jack stood over the note and felt eviscerated. He was alone in this house, in this town, and he didn't know where to begin. Chase had slipped off into the wilderness to die, and Jack had never felt so unqualified, so small. For a long time Jack stood still, breathing heavy with clenched fists at his hips, watching beer trickle down paneling cracks. Every word of the note was like red flags waving, the manifestation of the warning signs Jack had known about since high school, since his brother's suspension for playground fighting. That incident had spurred Jack and his mother to visit the Buckhead Central Library and research the terms Chase's teachers had used, specifically "autistic tendencies" and "oppositional defiant disorder." In their quest to understand Chase, Jack formed a sort of team with his mother, and he'd never felt closer to her, before or since. Together, over the course of one summer, they dug through stacks of medical journals and self-help books in crinkling library plastic, eventually diagnosing Chase as a sufferer of divorce-induced depression and uncontrollable, crippling defiance. As a possible solution, they devised a plan to organize a family dinner, during which they'd present their findings and ask Charles to fund therapy sessions. Standing in Chase's living room now, Jack almost smiled in recalling how proud Anne had been of their thoroughly researched plan, how they high-fived each other by the library card cabinets and those big primitive computers.

As afternoon gave way to evening, and the windows began to purple, Jack called his mother. She sounded startled and hoarse, as though she'd just dozed off during Jeopardy.

"He's fine," Jack said. "Found him sleeping on the basement ottoman, down in the dark. Had a rough night. But it's nothing greasy food and lightweight meds won't cure."

"Oh Lord," Anne said. "Good."

"A lady friend of his, maybe a real girlfriend, was here with him."

Anne cleared her throat. She was so excited she could have leapt from bed and spun across the hardwoods, a sexagenarian breakdancer. "Put that boy on the phone!"

"Can't," said Jack. "He's in the shower. Has been for an hour. I'll tell him to call you, maybe tomorrow, and to stop ignoring your messages. In fact, I'll yank his ears—like Grandpa used to—for doing that to you."

"Jackie!"

"Okay, I won't," he said. "We good, Ma?"

Anne was silent for a moment, scouring her mind for pressing questions that Jack might know the answers to, possibly supplying details to tide her over until morning. When no specific inquires came she merely smiled in silence, luxuriating in this notion of her sons being reunited in a quieter, calmer environment—and Chase having finally found himself a lady.

Meanwhile, Jack's shoulders clenched in fear of an oncoming interrogation. His thoughts danced with fantastical lies he didn't want to deploy.

"Now, quickly, about earlier," Anne finally said. "I want you to know that I love my house, and I love that you did this for me. Okay? If I was complaining, it's just me thinking out loud, being unreasonably nervous, because there's so much to adapt to. When you get old, these situations are harder to mitigate. But I really cherish your thoughtfulness, all of this stuff, and the craftsmanship of this old home."

"I know you do, Ma."

"And I'm proud that you were *able* to do this," she said. "Don't get me wrong. I didn't want you thinking—"

"I don't think anything, Ma," he said.

"You checking on Chase like this gives me hope, too, that your life isn't fully corrupted," she said. "Warms my heart."

"This was *his* idea, this stupid fishing adventure," Jack said, sounding angrier than he'd meant to. "We'll get through this. Everything is good. Let's just appreciate things while they last, while we have them, right?"

"Sure," said Anne. "Now talk to your brother about making me some grandbabies with this love interest of his. I don't have eternity."

"You have more than you know."

"Excuse me?"

"Nothing," said Jack. "I said I have to go unpack."

Anne thanked her son again and sighed. Jack could tell she wanted to stay on, to keep this lifeline open. Instead, he said goodnight, hung up, and peeked out the back windows, up the steep mountain, into the jagged blackness of pine, the wild everything, the endless nothing.

Part II

Part II

7

In the cooling, blackening forest Chase nudged the captives with his boot, awakening them from naps. Immediately they moaned and complained of aching joints and difficulty breathing. Through a mouthful of carrots Chase said he had decided to set them free.

"You're a damn good soul," said Prophet. "A noble man, yessir."

"Not really," said Chase, swallowing. "I just don't trust you to stay tied down, with you working in tandem, if I fall asleep. Now, please, can one of you build a fire?" He bent down and unlatched the cords binding Prophet and Yonah, alarmed to see deep, red, snakelike indentions all over her arms and legs. "God, I'm sorry," said Chase. "I guess these were tighter than I thought. Either that, or you've really been fighting to get free over here?"

Ignoring the question, Yonah thanked Chase and sat upright in a yogic position, flexing her arms and hands. Prophet gingerly stood up and began gathering pine straw, twigs, and branches.

"These dark woods mess with my head," said Chase. "I can't shake the feeling they're hiding something horrible, just beyond what I can see."

Yonah said nothing. To Chase she appeared to be stewing, planning. He worried that captivity had physically hurt her more than she was copping to.

"How common are bears up here?" Chase asked her. "Are they less active, more hidden now that winter's coming? Or is this peak season for them to be roving around?"

"Guns make me nervous as hell," she said, nodding to his weapon. "But you'll probably want to keep that handy."

Chase stole a glance at the shivering woodline, where Prophet was mutilating trees while biting through a carrot. Chase liked the buffer of another man, especially an upright ox like Prophet, between him and deep woods. "Here," said Chase, to the girl, "I cleaned some vegetables. You must be famished, and I'm sorry. But I needed time to formulate a plan."

"Who *are* you?" she said.

Chase took a big bite of carrot. "That's not important," he said.

"Are you running from something?"

"You could say that."

"What do you want from us?"

"I want you to forget you saw me," he said. "Like I didn't exist here, and that we never met. How do we accomplish that?"

"Poof!" she said. "It's done. You're gone. You never happened."

"No, really, I can't have witnesses."

"Jesus," she said. "You're strange."

Chase dropped a handful of vegetables in her lap and felt a pleasant sizzling—a burst of guttural electricity—with his hand in that region. "Let's sit beside this fire," he said, "and I want you to put my mind at ease that I was never here, that you won't say anything to anyone. And then we can go off to where we have to go. I'm not leaving until I'm convinced."

She bit into a fat carrot with her molars, tore away the root and chomped like some starving jungle omnivore while shaking her head. "I don't *get* you," she said. "You give off a really morose, wounded sort of energy. But you seem like one of us. Like one of God's misfits, too, you know?"

"No," said Chase. "I don't know."

"Like you're meant to be wandering, I mean. Like your only real home is the world at large. I don't know why you can't relax, put down this wall you're building, and just join us."

Prophet returned and doused his findings in gasoline. Around a heaving, throat-high inferno they ate deer jerky and vegetables and drank cold creek water. Chase watched their faces dance in firelight. "Do you have jobs?" he asked. "I mean real jobs with legit income? In the offseason or whatever you call it?"

Yonah licked the jerky salt off her fingertips and gulped water. "That's a difficult thing to have in this country, with felonies in your past." She spat a wet, mischievous giggle. "Second chances are for wealthy people and politicians. Otherwise, the world turns its back. At least for people not willing to compromise, you know?"

"No," Chase said again. "I don't know."

"There's no way in hell I'm serving fries out a shitty little window or mopping the YMCA at night," said Yonah. "I'd rather rot in jail."

Chase nodded. He was convinced he was empathizing, that he understood, and that he might be infatuated with this scrappy blond vagabond.

"In short," Prophet said, "we choose to be on our own wavelength, living by our own standards, our own decree. We're not so stupid to think we've figured out a way to be above the law, but we're sort of beyond it out here. Most of the time, at least. It's a helluva fun life, really. Trying to stay one step ahead of the man and societal norms and all that shit. It beats the commute and cubicle."

Yonah was nodding, acting either excited or increasingly nervous. "There's a whole new life underground, an untethered life, if you have the *cojones* to live it," she said. "You might see a little hippie chick sitting here, but I came up through orphanages and juvenile detention, and I've got heart like you wouldn't fucking believe."

Prophet bounced and wheezed with laughter. "A fire-cracker, boy, ain't she?"

Chase's wrist ached, so he switched the gun to his left hand, letting it be seen in the firelight. He felt that Yonah was ready to pounce, which he didn't necessarily dislike. "Is there some sort of commune you retreat to, in the winter?" Chase said. "Some place that supports you, or that you belong to, or whatnot?"

Now Yonah laughed, a high-pitched, stuttered shout. "Listen to all these questions! Sounds to me like you wanna grow out your hair and run free with us," she said. "The latent wild child in you wants born. I can see it!"

"Oh," Chase deflected, "I didn't say all that."

"Don't you have military family or something?" she said. "People to fall back on?"

"I don't need anyone else—"

"I think I *get* it," Prophet interrupted. "I see it now. He's just a lost Boy Scout, looking for his metaphysical bivouac. Am I right?"

All three laughed. Chase felt his neck muscles relax.

"Truth is," said Chase, "I don't really belong to anything, not anymore. I'm never going home. I've raised too much hell. I've hurt too many good people."

Prophet grumbled and stroked his face. "Isn't that what soldiers do?" he said. "I mean, technically, that's the gig, right?"

"Not what I meant."

"Come on," Prophet continued. "Enlighten us to war, in the spirit of a good campfire like this."

"I don't talk about it," said Chase.

"Ah, man," Prophet whined. "Just give us a little something from the front line. Something real and visceral. Something awful."

Whether they verbally asked or not everyone wanted to know what killing someone meant to you, once you'd done it, once you'd lived with the aftermath. Prophet's tone reminded Chase of the nagging emails his brother had sent him overseas, missives that begged for the dirt on killing. Jack had been rabid for such details during the war. Ten months into his deployment, Chase finally acquiesced, but he made Jack swear to Jesus he wouldn't mention a word of it on air. In response, Jack emailed a photo of his hand atop their grandfather's Bible, and Chase subsequently agreed to describe in writing his first insurgent kill, convinced it would force him to take the healthy step of documenting his feelings. One night, he slinked to the food tent, home to the nearest internet connection, careful to ensure he was alone. He brushed aside a *Sports Illustrated*, toed up to the base's antiquated public computer, but then strangely, physically seized up. He couldn't counter the beauty in the photos Jack had sent of his posing girlfriends with plaintive talk of death. And he couldn't admit—even to himself—what he'd done, not in writing, despite the fact the first dead fuck had been trying to kill him. Without typing anything Chase cut the lights, hustled outside under pulsing summer stars, and walked the base, feeling agitated if not somehow violated. Three weeks later he was shot, critically wounded, and then headed home for good, where he'd heal his wounds, settle into his mother's home, and forge his poisonous cone of silence.

Despite Chase's reluctance to talk, Prophet pressed on, and in a moment the prying began to grate on Chase. "Just shut the fuck up, man," he said. "It's hard to talk about."

"You know what I think?" Prophet said. "I think you're bluffin'."

"If you weren't there," said Chase, "I can't 'enlighten' you to jack shit."

"Oh, hail, come on. What's it like to cut a little man down?" Prophet said. "I mean, it's a mismatch, right? I see these primitive resistance fighters on the news taking on tanks. The way things are—modern-day warfare, I mean—it must be relatively easy, right? Goliath for them, a push of a button for you. Just tell me that."

Prophet's curiosity sounded reasonable enough to Chase, and something in him was eager to prove he wasn't lying, that he'd bled overseas for a cause that once seemed justified. "Fine," Chase said, "but just in general terms. That's all you get."

"Right on," said Prophet. "Whatever."

"So, look," Chase said, tensing up again. "Some of the guys who got the best scores in basic, once they got overseas, they ended up running away from firefights. Why? They can't kill a person. It's a lot different when your crosshairs are on a target; you can hit it all day long. Put a body on the other end of that, and a lot of tough motherfuckers shrink. But it's different when they're shooting at you. Or if somebody has a radio. It's not a weapon, but we considered ICOM deadlier than guns, because they bring the ambushes. And when they start hurting or killing guys that you've known for a while, you stop caring. They become less than human because they took somebody away. But I mean you still had to watch who you kill—"

"I'm not buying this," Yonah interrupted.

Chase cocked his head, pissed. "Buying what?"

"This soldier yarn," she said. "I think you're undercover, trying to infiltrate us."

"Please," said Chase.

Prophet cackled again. "Play nice, girl," he said. "Or you might break this fragile G.I. Joe."

Chase didn't laugh. From ribs to back to neck his body tightened, coiling, his hands jumping. Seeing this, Prophet reverted to the serious, reverent tone he'd had in captivity.

"If you're really not a cop," Yonah said, pointing. "You'll smoke with us right now."

Unnerved by the proposition—or by the forceful way it'd been delivered—Chase leaned away, like a wary child offered the stove that'd seared him. "No way in hell," he said, waving off the idea. "I found the truth last night, in those damn cookies."

"So you're *experienced*," she said, lifting her dainty arms, as if in epiphany. "The first time's intense. The second's euphoric."

Chase engaged the safety button on his weapon. "I can't believe I'm saying this, but maybe one puff," he said. "Could help me sleep tonight. Wherever I end up."

"Now *that's* the truth," said Yonah. "And, really, it'll help you know where you're going. On a permanent basis, I mean."

"Whatever," Chase said.

Prophet finished eating and stoked the fire to fill the camp with light. He counted footsteps away from the tent and tapped his boots on some hollow place. He bent down, brushed away leaves, and lifted a wooden door, unveiling a burrow. He reached in blindly and opened a padlocked tin box and returned to the fire with a tightly rolled joint, so plump he called it pregnant with twins. "Who wants the honors?"

"Hand it over now, man," said Yonah. "It's been two days."

With a burning branch she lit the joint, inhaled big, and made fish lips of the exhalation, slipping into a demeanor of deep, dazed satisfaction. She repeated and handed the spliff to Chase, who said, clumsily, "Cheers!"

He took a tiny pull and hacked wildly, coughing so hard he felt the strain in his earlobes and chest. Barely able to breathe, he balled his fist and repeatedly dropped it on his knee like a hammer. He felt like a fool.

"The cookies, by the way, are child's play," Prophet said. "This here's the big leagues. It's a strain from another galaxy, man. I've been working on this since the '90s."

After another wheezy moment Chase composed himself. "I'm done," he said. "I'm there."

The others finished smoking and in a few moments built up the fire again, shooing the deep-forest chill. They stood on the opposite side of the flames, facing each other.

With narrowed eyes and a dumbfounded smile Chase asked, "What are you two whispering about? You've been standing there for something like eight minutes."

"Who's whispering?" said Yonah.

"I just heard it. I heard, uh, sibilance over there. Didn't I?"

"You're tripping, soldier," said Prophet.

"Whatever, man," said Chase.

"We've got no secrets," said Prophet. "But we do have a proposition."

"A proposition?" Chase smiled. "What're you talking about?"

Behind the fire Yonah grinned. "I think it's best to show, not tell."

"Yes, of course," said Chase. "What in the fuck does that mean?"

"Sit tight, soldier," she said.

"Man," said Chase, "I don't know about you guys."

The fire dimmed to a squat, thick-flamed dance. The stars pulsed hard and gorgeous through the trees. Without warning, Yonah walked around the fire, gently lifted Chase's chin upward, and filled his mouth with a sensual kiss.

"*Wait,*" said Chase, pulling back. "What the hell?"

She clutched his cheeks and moved in again. "It's okay. Just relax now. I know you feel this."

Chase shook free and looked at Prophet, who was observing beyond the flames, his face stoic in the flickering light. "Is this trespassing?" Chase said. "Whatever this is?"

"You're going to fit right in, soldier," he said. "I'm going to lay down over there, and I'll leave this blanket on the ground here. Let the night go where it wants."

Chase raised his hands and cupped the back of Yonah's thighs. She shed her jacket, ripped off a sweatshirt, and her breasts shone pale in the moonlight. She clasped Chase's hand and walked backward to the blanket, stopping intermittently to kiss his lips and lick his chin. She lay down on the blanket, lit warmly by flames, and pulled down her pants and panties, nodding for Chase to help untie and remove her boots, which he quickly did. He slinked down atop her, buried his face in her chest, and he could hear her heartbeat drumming in his gleeful head. With both hands she pushed his face lower, to the dirty blond silk and spice, and just as Chase opened his mouth, projecting his tongue, Yonah latched her legs around his neck and hooked her ankles behind his head, leaving only the top of Chase's head exposed. She shouted, "Now!"

Prophet tore away the camouflage netting and rushed in, wielding a metal water pipe, which he swung and bashed with loud, hollow precision atop Chase's captured skull.

Chase heaved up once but fell back between the legs, silent and twitching. Yonah dug her heels into the blanket and scurried away from the fire. She screamed, "Shoot him— shoot him in the fuckin' head!"

In a clumsy, panting rush, Prophet unfurled a burlap sack and produced another old revolver. He stood over Chase for a long contemplative minute, the unconscious head between his feet, until finally he dropped his shoulders and spat on the ground. "Just wouldn't be right," he said. "Cop or not, I ain't no killer."

***

In a daze Jack walked from his brother's living room to the porch. He did his best to calm his breathing, but it didn't feel right to be at ease, either. He tried to gauge the night, to predict how long he had until total mountain darkness. But he knew nothing about that. He knew nothing about anything, and his usual crutches—his agent, his boss, a concierge—could not swoop in and make this right.

If he ran into the woods now, he might catch Chase and reason with him, maybe coax him back home to drink Chuck's Lagers and talk about brown trout and football. But if Jack wandered too far and became lost in the forest, his mother could lose both sons tonight. The police? Could he call them and report a suicide threat? Would they expend resources for that? Jack's hands quaked. He grunted in frustration and stomped back into the house, to the refrigerator, swallowed a beer in six dumb gulps, and used the wall phone to call 911. The operator chewed gum and sounded so bored she must have been fighting sleep. In the background a television hissed game-show applause.

"Yes, hello," Jack shouted. "I have a note, a cryptic note. And I have reason to believe my brother is lost in the woods."

"Calm down, sir," the operator said. "How old is he, your brother?"

"Twenty-eight, I think. Yeah, that's about right."

"And why would he be lost."

"Maybe lost isn't accurate."

"Is he injured, sir?"

"I'm not sure."

"In distress? You'll have to be more specific, please."

"Look," Jack said, "I don't want this going public, in case it's a false alarm or whatnot, but my brother, Chase, he's seen a lot of shit, in the army, in the Middle East, you know. And he's struggled with his mind, shell shock and all that. I came up here from Atlanta, for a weekend of fishing on the river, and he's not here in his cabin, but there's this note. I think it's real."

"Real?" the operator said.

"He says he's going to 'end it, in a painless manner,' whatever that means. In the letter he's talking to my mom and me, because we're all he has. Look, this might sound strange, but I have some clout in the city, and I don't want this getting out. I don't want it hurting my family—"

"Emergency calls are public record, eventually," she said. "But let's not concern ourselves with that. When was the letter written?"

"I don't know, but it just *feels* like he's been here recently," Jack said. "Can you dispatch a search team, or a plane, or something, before it gets completely dark? I need help in the worst way."

"I'll send a deputy to your address."

"No, sorry, to hell with that," Jack said. "I can see what any deputy can. We need to get something in the air. Or some dogs in the woods. Or something else, I don't know."

"What makes you think your brother has gone to a remote place?"

"Ma'am, it's spelled out in front of me, that he's gone into the woods, that his flesh won't burden us, and all this other rambling shit."

"I'll have a deputy there in just a few minutes."

"*Jesus!*" Jack said. "We need more than that. We don't have time!"

"Sir, just sit tight for me." The operator sounded distracted, her attention waning. "Everything's going to be okay. I'm sure your brother is fine."

Jack bashed the phone against the receiver and went for a beer. Soon a dial tone squawked from the dangling phone, so he kicked it and watched it swing like a tetherball, still squawking. He opened the beer and slipped outside to wait for the authorities.

In twenty minutes the same deputy who'd spoken with Jack on Cherokee's town square responded to the cabin, her cruiser chewing gravel up the driveway. The rain she had predicted started to fall, tamping dust.

"Ah, hello," said the serious blond woman, even more cop-like than Jack remembered, donning a ranger hat that matched her khaki uniform. On her belt was a large pistol and a larger leather pocket of handcuffs. She noticed that Jack was panting and seemed agitated, a contrast to the lackadaisical tourist she'd met that afternoon. "If it isn't mister sunglasses and his orange Corvette."

"Yeah," said Jack. "Small town." He waved the deputy inside and held the door open behind her. Then he fetched the note, saying, "What's going on is laid out right here, but it's not exactly a road map to where Chase is. This is a legitimate missing person we're talking about."

Instead of reading the note, or asking to see it, the deputy did a lap around the living room, so peppy and optimistic she almost bounced when walking. She set her hat on a kitchen island and sat down on a barstool, hoisting up her rugged, clay-flecked hiking boots. She fiercely chewed gum, which made pulsing, rippled plums of jaw muscles beside her ears. Jack could sense she was the type to religiously track salt intake and body-fat percentages.

"I'm sorry, miss, but bar's closed," said Jack. "You're acting like this is happy hour and not a life-or-death emergency. I'll run out that door right now, if you swear to follow with more deputies and dogs—or whatever protocol is."

"How do you know the kid who lives here?" the deputy said, scratching shiny manicured nails against her palms. From Jack, she was getting the vibe of an unhinged bourbon magnate, or a failed yachtsman, set adrift in midlife grief.

Jack dropped his arms, deflating. "Brother."

The deputy brought a palm across her wide, pink, rain-flecked face. "Never seen you," she said. "You get up here much?"

"With all due respect," Jack said, "I made an emergency call, and you're sitting on the barstool interrogating me. A rainstorm's sweeping in, and my brother—"

"I feel like I *live* here," the deputy interrupted. "Been dragged here so much it feels like home. Petty stuff, usually, but this shack is familiar to our entire force." She gauged Jack's reaction; he was stunned, not breathing. "In fact," she said, "Sheriff Gaylord ordered me up here on a gun sweep a few weeks back, for some reason. We pulled out an arsenal of really crappy pistols." She nodded to Jack's hand. "Looks like you have the same taste in beer as your brother. Hope you don't share his fondness for pissing in the street."

Jack tossed the note onto the living room floor, fetched a fresh beer, and stomped to the back door. He put his nose to the window and saw dense thickets of pine, blackened now with heavy cloud cover. "I know he's a handful, but deep down he really is a good kid, and he holds a Purple Heart," said Jack. "He's always had this thing about pushing back. Revolting. Rebelling. You're the latest in a long line of authority he's clashed with. Please don't take it personal. And don't use it as a reason to ignore what's happening."

The deputy got up, slowly walked to the center of the room, retrieved the note, and relaxed on the couch. "Your brother likes to push our buttons. No doubt about that."

"What's your name?" said Jack.

"McLaren," said the deputy, nodding. "Apologies, friend. Deputy Rhonda McLaren."

"You realize that's not just a suicide note," Jack said. "Read the thing, please, and you'll hear a call for help from a guy who really wants to live but is confused." Jack pointed to the paper, repeatedly jabbing his finger. "You have a tax-paying, depressed citizen lost in these woods, and you're choosing to ignore that."

"No, Jack, I hear every word you're saying."

Jack scoffed. "However you know me, I see your badge number—I won't forget it—and I've got friends at the state level, at the Georgia Bureau of Investigation. I don't know your rules, but I can tell that you're violating something, just sitting here—"

"Your tag," McLaren said, forcing an oversized smile, an attempt to calm her erratic subject down. "Your name is on the back of your car."

"Oh, right, damn," said Jack. "Sorry."

The deputy read the note, went to the back door, dropped her shoulders, examined the rain, and sighed. "There are procedures ..." Her voice, firm but with that floral North Georgia dialect, reflected off the glass. "Don't accuse me of subjectivity. Okay? Not me. Been doing this around here twenty years, and I know when resources are about to be wasted in the woods and when they're not."

"Forgive me," Jack said, "but this talk of *resources* is just bullshit."

McLaren rapped her knuckles on the window, the meager wedding ring rhythmically pecking glass. She turned, walked to the barstool, and as a docile means of venting, pulled her hat down so tight her bundled hair loosened and burst out like hay. She stared into Jack's tight face and saw a desperation she couldn't help but admire. Several years earlier she'd led an expedition to rescue four lost Florida hikers, and upon finding them all alive, their eyes held silent pleas for food in the way Jack's wanted guidance now. "If your anger wasn't coming from a good place," McLaren said, "I'd take you to jail for the night." Her thumb sat atop the asp baton in her belt, and she cocked her head. "You hear me?"

Jack gave an exaggerated smile, an exuberant thumbs-up.

"Call the station if anything changes. If nothing does, you can file a missing persons report in ninety hours from your initial 911 call."

"*Ninety* hours," Jack said, lifting his beer to point the deputy to the door. He followed her out, pouting, and stood on the porch.

McLaren turned around, hands tucked in jacket pockets, fighting a twinge of regret about the county's longstanding protocol. "Ninety hours is typical, across Georgia," she said. "And the rain would've thrown the dogs off anyway tonight." She pounded down the stairs in her heavy boots and swept twigs off her windshield. She started the cruiser and backed away, lowering the driver's side window and staring at Jack, who refused to make eye contact. "These last two years," McLaren said, "your brother was full of threats. I don't know what you know, but he was. This is probably one big empty threat."

"Go write a parking ticket." Jack pointed in the general direction of town.

McLaren smiled. "Don't drink too much—and don't go doing anything drastic. Like I told you, man, you're a long ways from Peachtree Street."

"I'm a long ways from law enforcement with morals, that's for sure."

"No," she said, "you're not."

"Be safe, Rhonda," Jack said, turning toward the cabin.

"Eastern chipmunks!" she shouted. "Gray squirrels, mice, possums, and every so often an Appalachian cottontail rabbit, but they're pretty rare. You asked about my taxidermy. That's what I do. Or that's what I'm trying to learn. I find the ones that are roadkill, or that've been mauled by whatever, and I try to make them respectable again."

Jack's mouth popped open. He couldn't respond, this information was so unprompted and foreign.

"I'm trying to tell you I stick up for the little guys," she said. "Just be patient, Jack. And in the meantime, don't accuse me, or anyone else around here, of lacking morals. From what I hear, you're the last person to talk."

The deputy drove away, and Jack felt enraged, offended, motivated. He grabbed his brother's raincoat in the garage, loaded some apples and white bread into a plastic grocery sack, and hustled out the back door, hoofing past the shed and into the woods. Wet pine straw clung to his boots and jeans. Bands of freshly fallen leaves were slick, ubiquitous obstacles. He changed course after a few dozen yards, then again, zigzagging up the mountain; it was an energy-sucking fool's route, he realized. Despite the chill, he could feel sweat seeping into his hair, so he unbuttoned the raincoat, which smelled like rotting trout, and tied the arms around his waist. He pumped his knees, one before the other, until the aimlessness of his trek overwhelmed him. Five minutes into the search, Jack's legs burned so badly he thought they might convulse; he regretted the beers and his deplorable physical condition. Daunted, he walked the mountain laterally for a while, until his breathing calmed and a cluster of white oaks supplanted the pines. Above, the clouds broke, stars shone, and the jet stream blazed a blurry red, like a vast astral carcass, split long and laid open upon the world.

In a clearing Jack screamed for his brother: "Chase ... hey ... Chase ... come out, come out ... jackass!" He saw a burst of little birds about a hundred yards away. He heard more rustling elsewhere—somewhere—and was encouraged. For a fleeting second, it all felt like the hide-and-seek contests the brothers had routinely played around their grandfather's big Tudor house. Being years older, Jack would feign cluelessness as to young Chase's hiding places—obvious choices like the alley-facing shed and the lower branches of a front-yard loblolly pine—to make the kid feel clever. Later he would train Chase on ways to better hide himself by burrowing into autumn leaves or clinging to the underside of trucks; Jack had called that useful knowledge, should the cops ever be on Chase's heels, and he now regretted every bit of that subversive wisdom. "Come on!" He rushed back into the woods and screamed so loud a third time the words were unintelligible. The canopy was too thick for echoes.

The forest and its shadows horrified Jack. He lunged ahead, scanned the mountain above, and set a goal: to reach a crop of rocks, piled around a bulge of granite, in five minutes. He wanted to be atop the rocks before the sky became ink.

Soon the trees dissipated around him, and Jack hoofed up craggy boulders and sat down. He wiped his sleeve across his face and scaled the granite lump, an off-white anomaly in so much timber and leaf. With a few more lunges Jack summited the rock, and now he peered across the tallest downslope hardwoods, into a valley that shifted with wind-swept mist. The immensity of the wilderness lay before Jack now, and he had never felt weaker. "Mountains," he said, tossing his arms. "The fuck am I supposed to do with mountains?"

He paced the boulder several times but saw nothing. Above and behind him stood steeper slopes he could not climb alone. He faced east, away from the cabin, and tossed the bread and apples as far into the woods as he could, to separate himself from the scent of food. And then Jack lifted his dirty trembling hands, at first in front of his face, then higher, over his head, and balled them into fists, screaming, "Goddamn it!" He tripped around the rock, from end to end, throwing his voice in every direction, and then collapsed into a tired pile. He struggled for breath. Sweat dripped off his face and dotted tan stone. After a moment Jack rolled onto his back, and his first real glimpse of shimmering stars alarmed him. He leapt up, scrambled across the rock, and ran screaming his brother's name down the mountain, aiming for the sickly amber glow of cabin windows.

**

The fire had dwindled to a breathing orange heap, not two feet from Chase's face. He revived slowly, belly on the ground, soothed by the warmth of embers and the smoky scent of happy camping times.

When he fully awoke, a cold bolt of pain shot from the crown of his skull to his back teeth. The left side of his tongue was lacerated and swollen where he must have bitten it. His brain seemed to pulse, his cheeks shivered, and his vision blurred and fuzzed like screens of broken televisions. He hurt so bad he felt feverishly ill.

The evening's odd events came back in nonsensical flashes, and he wondered for a second if he'd fallen off Yonah and struck his head on the stove, a log, or some stone he hadn't seen. When he tried to stand up, however, it was clear the captives were now captors. Worse, they'd mimicked his hog-tying proficiency, and escaping, he worried, would be impossible, as would quick death. Starving, right here on his stomach, would accomplish his objective of dying, ultimately, but he couldn't imagine the nightmarish suffering between this and there. He jerked and pulled against the cords until he feared his wrists would snap.

The dark woods were still and quiet. There was nothing to distract Chase from his pain. Nothing but his panicked thoughts. He wondered if being shot in the head felt like this, and he thought of all the godawful protrusions of brains he'd seen overseas. Exposed brains were the hardest things to forget. Chunky brains. Brains splattered like confetti. Brains the color of roses in Peachtree Road boutiques, the color of baby toys. Fresh brains so pink Chase had thought they were white. All brains were blatant proof a living man was but a husk, a slab of what wouldn't be again. Chase recalled the day an ANA soldier had been standing to his left as they waded through a field of low, scrubby grasses. The first enemy round was the one that hit the soldier square in the forehead, just beneath the brim of his helmet, the bullet exiting through the back with a tiny metallic burst. The soldier fell into a fighting position on the ground, his antiquated M16 pointed in the direction of the sound, and Chase thought he was still alive, still fighting. The 240-gunner wingman, flanked to the right, blanketed the perimeter with at least 200 rounds. Chase took his usual fighting position—head ducked, weapon up, spraying in the direction of the enemy, until someone shouted to ease off. Five hundred meters away, they saw turbaned heads in retreat, bounding for cover, and Chase thought of white-tailed deer. They scurried to the downed man. A medic rushed forward and flipped off the helmet, exposing a bouquet of white intestinal knots. The medic shrieked and leapt back, as if the brains might detonate, and Chase caught him as a dozen more soldiers rushed in from the grape rows. "A jack-in-the-box, ain't it?" a corporal from Kansas named Riley had said. "Fucking brains just jump out." Chase shook his head at Riley and walked around the body. He knelt to the man, his dead face half-smiling, his teeth jutted out and green eyes dull.

"Did anyone catch his name?" Chase said, standing up.

Riley cleared his throat. "I think it was, maybe, Raul, or Rafule, or something," he said. "He liked you, Lumpkin."

Something in the brain pile shifted, and Riley groaned. "This would be fucking me up right now, if it was us," he said. "We have better luck, better instincts, but it doesn't make sense, you know. They've fought over this dirt for two thousand years. Somehow they ain't learned shit." To shut Riley up, Chase bent down, latched ahold of the soldier's leg, and dragged him backward, in the direction of their forward operating base. Three others assisted, grabbing the body's wrists and ankles. The leg Chase was holding twitched, as if electrified, and for an instant Chase paused, hopeful, until Riley said, "Fucking rigor mortis." They walked together through the grass, a long morbid mile, and Chase wondered how much more intolerable the day would've been if the man had spoken English, let alone been American. That they hadn't shared a word would make it easier, Chase hoped, to forget.

As with most trauma, the forgetting never fully came, and for an hour Chase fought memories of twitching dead soldiers as he struggled against the cords, rocking on the forest floor. Each desperate thrust of his legs felt like it could slip his shoulder blades through the skin of his back. He wanted to scream and rage and pull until something gave, but he kept quiet and finally accepted that he was helpless. All but his stomach was wet with rain, and to counteract the chill, he rolled so that he faced away from the ember's heat. Soon his clothes began to dry. He struggled to extend his hands, to maybe snap the cords with the heat of embers, but instead he singed his fingertips and gave a pitiful yowl.

A strange wooziness set in, and Chase studied the unmoving woods. No glimmering barrel tips. No sinister grins in the dark. No trace of anyone. He wanted to rewind time and shoot the fighting whitetails for distracting him, for delaying his task. He wanted to slap himself for being so gullible, for ending up wallowing, wounded, captured. Yet he began to feel calm in captivity—sullen to the point of inertia—and absolutely finished with this fraudulent world.

Eventually, a breeze swept through, and the hush of windblown trees lulled him back to sleep.

***

In the bathroom mirror Jack's face was frantic and tired. Gray sacks sagged beneath his eyes. He pulled from a Chuck's Lager.

"Come on—*think*."

His cell phone buzzed in the kitchen. He ran out of the bathroom. The caller was his mother, and he stepped away. He could not speak to Anne right now, not without losing it; he'd lied to her enough for the night. She hung up and called back twice more. When the ringing finally ended Jack felt terrible, so he hustled to the couch and laid down a pencil and notepad. It was time, he decided, to formalize a plan, to put his options on paper. He devised what seemed four viable tactics, writing:

1. *Call mother, father, friends, close ATL relatives. Ask for assistance with searches. Boots on the ground, eyes in woods. Charter a plane, too. Search dogs? But $$. And where to begin?*

2. *Wait for Chase to return. In cabin, fish, booze, call Maddy from radio station. Too optimistic? Too stupid?*

3. *Go home. Wait for protocol time to elapse. Force cops to help. Or call lawyer, threaten lawsuit against town, department, deputy. Push them. Approach Cherokee newspaper.*

4. *Mount search party. Leave family alone, unalarmed. Call that cussing pastor. Find brother myself.*

For a second Jack felt okay. He was proud of his list and initiative. He reclined into the soft, worn, stinking couch.

With his pencil he circled the last option, over and over, until the lead was thick and flaky. "Tomorrow!" he said, lifting a toast to nobody. "Number four it is!"

Tonight, he was tired, buzzed, and useless, so he would drive to town in the morning and mount the search team. And maybe, he thought, he'd find Chase in Cherokee, shacked up with a barfly after all, laughing at his own elaborate, sadistic prank. Jack leaned back, lifting his muddy jeans onto the couch, and on his phone he thumbed through photos of his twelve-pound girl—his blurred but earnest attempts to capture her first reactionary smile. She had his wild eyes, his mad laughter, his mess of hair. She was constantly reaching, upward and outward, grasping for great big things, presumably ambitious. Jack wasn't scheduled to see her again until after Halloween, but thoughts of her in elaborate costumes— a pumpkin, kitten, or jug of lemonade, with a flat silver hat for a lid—ushered him grinning to sleep.

**

In the middle of the moon-bright night Chase awoke shivering, tremoring in captivity beside the faintest hints of hot coals. He'd had these same shakes upon coming home from war, when he was gaunt and tired with skin pale as a chemo patient's, when his old neighborhood looked foreign and suspiciously happy. For nine months Chase lived in his mother's basement and did very little but drink cheap beer, race exotic cars in video games, and sit on the rocking-chair porch, which had a blue coffered ceiling and fans with drooping blades. His mother's retired friends would occasionally drop by in their Lexus SUVs and fluorescent sneakers.

"Hi, Chase."

"Hello, ma'am."

"My name's Denise. I jog with Anne. She's the sweetest. We've never officially met."

"Good to meet you, ma'am."

"Looks like you're healing up."

"Thanks."

"Hang in there."

"I'll try."

"You know, it's really great, what you did."

"Thanks."

"I can't imagine being in that place, enduring that hell. But you did it!"

"I did," said Chase.

"Uh-huh."

"Maybe," he said, "hell's here, too."

"Excuse me?"

"Nothing, ma'am."

She leaned forward and studied his solemn face. Chase felt a mix of shame and irritation.

"You look more like your mom than your dad," she said. "And that's a good thing."

"Thank you, ma'am."

"Seriously, Chase, hang in there."

"Oh, I'll try."

Soon Chase felt caged at his mother's place. Or in the company of anyone who wasn't military. For his last year in Atlanta, he holed up in a shabby one-bedroom apartment, whiling away the months and disability checks. He'd bought a small flat screen in a Buford Highway pawnshop and incessantly watched it, frequently seeing Jack in late-night commercials. Jack had parlayed his growing radio popularity into ridiculous TV spots for a European motors dealership, in which he used a pirate sword to chop paper numbers in half—"We're slashing the MSRP, folks!"—while wearing designer suits and sniffing incredible stacks of cash.

"Jesus Christ, Jack," Chase would say to the television. "You're the second coming of Charles the Lawyer. You're better than this!" As Jack's media star rose and Chase plummeted further into struggles to achieve basic normalcy, the more a strange gulf between siblings widened and the more the younger Lumpkin felt irretrievably cast aside.

In his apartment, Chase's insomnia intensified, to the point he yearned to prowl the streets at night and execute the criminals who made the news. Against his army training, he knew, common street thugs wouldn't last two seconds. And he couldn't shake his urge to patrol. One evening, a news team's investigation enraged Chase. Westside heroin peddlers were selling to young girls in three blighted apartment complexes. The poppy fields all over again. "Pap, pap,

pap!" Chase screamed at his television, jutting his elbow and aiming a loaded AR15, feigning kickback. "Those are kids, you fucks—*pap!*"

After that he had to quit the evening news. He'd turn off his radio, too, silencing his brother's voice and watching the street from the apartment's bay window, a means to keep himself occupied and sober. He watched the street at all hours, learning the bedtimes of his neighbors, the barking habits of dogs. But when even that began to make him nervous, he found a functioning vehicle for $1,000 and landed a job delivering pizzas. The routine was good— brief nightly missions with no fear of ambush—if a little confining and trite. Being around civilians began to feel right again. When he wasn't working, Chase walked the quaint and funky streets of Cabbagetown, his neighborhood, still slightly limping. His quaky hands were always plunged into the pockets of his shorts, popping the safety on and off his nine-millimeter. In a way, he wanted guys to jump out from the shadows, buck up, and try to take his money. Other times he just wanted a woman's bare belly pressed against his in bed, a soft primal contact that seemed an impossible luxury.

Before any of that could happen, Chase saw the taped- up advertisements in Realtors' windows, pictures of cabins that included what would become his. He thought of those pictures now, on the damp forest floor, as signs pointing the wrong way, errant guideposts toward a mistake even graver than his decision to join the military. He whispered the word "stupid" until sleep pulled his squirming brain away.

8

The morning sun made dingy ghosts of tulip-patterned curtains in the living room. Jack sat up, yawned, and remembered his objective. Sullen thoughts would anchor him to the couch if he didn't get moving. He had a goal: drive to Cherokee, cut a few checks, and mount the best private search party in North Georgia history. He showered, choked down toast, milk, a cup of strong instant coffee, and said a silly but honest prayer: "Lord, please, I need your clues. I need your light." He leapt into his car and sped to town.

At a stop sign he clutched his hairless chin, worrying another bitter hangover was beginning, when he spotted the Ash County Jail, a squat, two-story relic from Cherokee's gold-mining heyday. Jack parked and hustled inside, where deputies congregated in the lobby. The tallest of the bunch was telling a joke about divorce. In the back, through a door, Jack could see the tiny jail, three cells with steel bars. Closer, he saw the cubicle-divided office, where every few seconds a head would emerge and vanish, like prairie dogs on the plains. Private offices flanked the cubicles. The largest room on the left bore a painted gold star on the wall. In there, Jack guessed, was the asshole sheriff of Ash County. Up front sat a card table that functioned as the receptionist's desk, without any discernible security measures.

The receptionist smiled. "Step up here, son, away from these loud men." She winked to the deputies.

Jack recognized her voice as that of the indifferent dispatcher. "I want to ask about your inmate population," he said. "I'm looking for somebody."

"Oh," the receptionist said, "you again."

"Look, I apologize for last night, for mouthing off on the phone," he said. "I'm just a passionate guy, and this is my kid brother we're talking about."

The receptionist swiveled her chair and faced the back of the office. "Hey, Gerald," she called out. "We got anybody in the suites back there?"

From the cubicles a man's voice said, "Nope."

The receptionist turned back around and propped her elbows on the desk. "Records show he ain't here."

Jack nodded. "Thank you. Like I said, I didn't expect him to be."

"Deputy McLaren, one of our best, was dispatched to assist you," she said.

"And what a help *she* was," Jack said, careful not to let the deputies hear him. "Is there a chance I could speak with the sheriff himself? I have just a few quick questions."

The receptionist nervously stroked her fingernails across her palm. "Sheriff will be back at one o' clock, after his lunch at the diner, if you want to request a meeting."

Jack pressed his fingers into his temples, thinking, calculating hours left in the crucial day. "I'll grab lunch, and I'll be back at one," he said. "And I'll keep the meeting as civil as possible, okay?"

"Sir ..."

"Thanks again," said Jack, backing away. "See you in an hour."

He hustled to the sidewalk, gritted his teeth, and struck a bargain in his mind: It was time for a drink, but only one, to be followed by a sandwich with onions, and then peppermints to mask his breath. The meeting with the sheriff, he decided, would be better if he was relaxed, his angry edge a little dulled.

Ahead, in a brick corner building with a rocking-chair front porch, Jack saw what seemed a suitable lunch destination: the Lonesome Cub Tavern.

Inside, Jack felt better, almost coddled by a dingy place with low standards. The room was long and deep and dark, its exposed brick dotted with ragged continents of plaster. The bar itself was so ornate with carved wood—mermaids, anchors, and detailed, mountainous landscapes—it seemed gothic. On each side of the hulking bar glowed two neon signs: "LONESOME" and "CUB." Elsewhere hung a congregation of dusty animal heads: gazelles, big-horned rams, three snarling black bears.

Four customers sat at the bar in such relaxed poses Jack knew they had to be regulars. Each man smoked a cigarette and watched college football highlights on boxy old televisions. A smiling, bearded bartender pushed through swivel kitchen doors, spotted Jack, and waved. "Welcome, friend," he said. "Hop up to the bar, if you don't mind. I like my ducks in a row this early."

Jack took a stool, keeping three empty ones between him and the nearest local. "I've got business with the deputies down the street, so I probably shouldn't imbibe, but as long as I'm not slammed, I'll—"

"Got it," the bartender said, pulling back a tall tap. "That's you in the Corvette, right? I won't let you crash an American treasure like that. Relax, man."

Jack gave the menu a glimpse and ordered the burger, extra onions. He slurped his beer and blurted, to no one in particular: "Gentlemen, I need to mount a search party. I want the best trackers in town. I have money, and I'll spend it."

Each head at the bar turned toward Jack.

"You're a little early," said one rough guy in a Braves hat. "Gun season for deer and bear don't start until Wednesday, unless you're good with a bow. Somehow, I don't see you being good with no bow."

Everyone chuckled, and Jack joined too, deploying his best knee-slapping hillbilly impression, sounding obnoxious.

"I'm talking about tracking *somebody*—a hiker way up in the crest line or whatever, higher than I'm willing to go by myself," Jack said, his smile fading. "Honestly, I don't know what I'm doing up there. I don't know exactly where he is."

Another man, the one closest to Jack, scratched his young, pocked face. "Is that the business you have with the sheriff's department?" he said. "Because that sounds like a police matter right there."

Jack slugged his beer, smacked his lips. "No offense, but your local cops have shit for brains."

No one responded. All momentum died. The silence, the embarrassment, warmed Jack like a wool suit. He felt sweat trickle down his back. He wanted to make a joke about accidental sacrilege but doubted anyone would be sympathetic, so the heavy silence hung. Jack stared at a single cracked peanut on the bar like it might suddenly leap up and dance.

A few seconds later, the bartender emerged from the kitchen again, and Jack welcomed his lunch with a ravenous growl. "Your deputies have a grudge against my brother, I mean, because he's been raising hell up here, and I need a third party to help," said Jack, shouting over a loud TV commercial. "Simple as that, y'all. It's a shame, because the kid's honestly, literally an American hero."

The bartender relaxed against the oak cabinetry—and then sprung back to the bar. "Hold on, you two *look* alike," he said. "I thought you looked familiar, walking in here. Your brother owes this place a lot of money, to be honest with you, so maybe we can start by settling that."

Jack dropped his burger on the plate. "Good God," he said. "What next? Was he running a puppy mill, too?" He stole a glance at his cell phone and placed it in front of him. "Just tack the damn thing to my bill, sir, if you don't mind."

"It's more the principle," the bartender said. "I've never been stiffed, not in Cherokee."

"How much?" Jack said.

"He ran a tab for $250 one night, buying shots for a table of teachers up here on sabbatical. Then the dickhead disappeared."

"I hate to hear that," said Jack. "But I can tell you for sure he's not a thief. He probably stumbled out, not realizing what he left behind, which I think we can all relate to—"

"It don't make him less of an ass," said the bartender. "In fact, can you go ahead and pay for that burger now, up front?"

Leaning back on the stool, Jack felt his heart kick, his lungs restrict. He pushed his lunch away and emptied the beer glass. "I *like* this town," he said, smiling. "There's no bullshit in you people. No agendas. You say what you think."

Jack slid his Visa to the bartender, ordered a vintage whiskey from the locked cabinet, neat, and said, "Eat, drink, and be merry on me, gents. I'm not stiffing anybody here—in fact, the opposite. Just give my proposal some thought, okay? Or tell me who to call for help. Because I'm at a loss. There's good money in it, though, and you could be heroes."

The whiskey came, but Jack ignored it. Instead, he pulled a business card from his jeans and punched in the numbers. The pastor didn't answer. Jack heard the kind, recorded voice, and he talked quietly, plaintively: "Hi, Pastor Rutgers, it's Bachelor Jack, from the barbecue joint yesterday. I'm in a bad way in Cherokee, mixed up with a bunch of lazy yokels. My brother, the one I was coming to visit, is missing. I'm afraid he's shot himself in the woods, and I need to find him, but I can't find any help here. Please call back immediately."

Jack hung up, pocketed the phone, and drained his whiskey. He slurped the onions from his burger like noodles, had a few big bites, gave two thumbs up, and stomped into the street.

On the sidewalk Jack packed his mouth with peppermints. The whiskey had loosened him; he could feel its toxins. As he crossed the street, a familiar physique came into focus, standing beneath the sheriff's department awning, impatiently pacing and craning her neck to either end of the block. Deputy McLaren spotted Jack and offered a nod, raising her excitable arms as if overwhelmed with happiness. Jack wanted to avoid this awkward reunion, but he saw no other entrance to the building, so he sulked for a second, plodded ahead, fashioned a smile, and saluted.

McLaren shook Jack's hand and cocked a weird grin. A radio device of some sort was clipped to her button-up shirt, in the middle of her chest, and Jack noticed that no feminine lines showed there, just a hard vest between shoulders, a little wall of authority. "The sheriff's back now," she said, "a little early, and he's willing to speak with you."

"Terrific."

"We have an open-door policy, but there's not much he'll say that I haven't."

"Point me to him, please, ma'am. I'd just like to meet the man."

"Okay," said the deputy, her eyes pinched and worried. "It's your show, hotshot."

Jack trailed McLaren through the reception area, around the cubicle maze, and into the cushy office of Sheriff Monte Gaylord. The room was long and formal, paneled in mahogany wainscoting that reminded Jack of Britain. He waved his head around, taking it all in, fascinated. A bank of dirty windows, reinforced with hexagonal wiring, framed an alleyway beside the department. The office walls were bedecked with military honors in shadowboxes; that much encouraged Jack. One medal near a window looked like a Purple Heart.

The sheriff—his full gray hair parted on the left and primped, his brown uniform sharply pressed—scribbled furiously into a checkbook. Judging by the splotchy skin of his hands and gaunt cheeks, the sheriff was older than Jack had expected. His chair, beige cowskin with barbed-wire gashes, arched over his head, caressing him like a worn baseball mitt.

Jack walked closer to the big desk. The sheriff closed his checkbook and leaned back into his chair, offering the forced, reptilian smile of a politician. Jack was impressed with the sheriff's straight white teeth and tan face; the rest of his authoritative pomp made Jack squeamish. The sheriff offered his hand, his wedding ring chunky with gold, and Jack squeezed until he felt the contours of old bones.

"Whiskey for breakfast?" the sheriff asked.

Jack backed off and sat in one of two occasional chairs. He glanced at McLaren, who stood behind the second chair, arms down, head high, ponytail cocked back, on guard. Her demeanor reminded Jack of an overeager softball pitcher he'd dated in college, the one who'd claw her cleats in the dugout like bull hooves, anxiously chewing great wads of bubblegum, starving for the thrill of competition, the clash.

"Quite a nose you have, sheriff," Jack said.

"Comes with experience."

"I bet it does," Jack said. "Maybe they should leash you up, send you out sniffing in the woods."

Jack could hear McLaren shuffle behind him, emanating cop sounds: the crackle of a polyester belt, some jangling keys.

"So, comedian, you always drink brown this early?" the sheriff said. "Or is this just how you act on vacation?"

"This is how I act, quite frankly, when someone fucks with my family."

The sheriff gave Jack a wry half-smile, entertaining thoughts of clubbing this quick-witted city scum with his asp baton. "I understand this is a troubling situation, what with your errant brother," he said. "But your mouth'll get you nowhere, and neither will drinking all day. This county used to be dry—can you imagine? Back when the Baptist contingent held full sway, when people in general had stronger morals. They changed the books to cater to Atlanta money, the folks who started building second homes up here. It's ironic that y'all come for the views and then muck them up with your tri-level, prow-fronted homes. But it's nothing new, nothing unexpected. Certainly isn't surprising. Just the way of the world and market demand, I guess. You'll have to forgive me; I'm a little protective of my county. Nothing against outsiders whatsoever, so long as you're the kind that behaves."

"Don't worry, sir," Jack said. "I'm just passing through."

The sheriff nodded. "My deputy here says you have a procedural question?"

Jack turned and nodded to McLaren. "I didn't come to town to make threats or crack jokes, but I'm getting desperate, and I noticed the newspaper's just down the street. I'm willing to bet someone there will recognize me, and they'll listen to me when I file suit against the sheriff's department—"

"*That* tone," the sheriff interjected, "sounds threating to me." He scooted away from his desk, a hand under his chin. His eyes bounced from wall to wall, taking in the moment, the competition, the interloper.

"Call it whatever, sheriff, but you've got a civilian lost in your jurisdiction, and you've done nothing to help him," Jack said, leaning forward. "I'm a fish out of water, just flopping. But I've got friends who'll find malfeasance in this, because it isn't right. And let's be honest, your protocols aren't holding you back. You have a grudge." Jack eased off a second to catch his breath. "I don't know you from Smokey Bear," he said, "but I've always had a knack for reading people, and it feels like there's something you people aren't telling me."

McLaren gasped, stomped forward, and latched ahold of Jack's shoulder, digging into the flesh. "Enough," she said.

"Not another word, Jack. Stand up, turn around, and walk out."

"No, actually," said Sheriff Gaylord, "could you give us a moment alone, deputy? Just shut the door behind you. Maybe two minutes, tops? That'll suffice."

Slowly, McLaren let go of Jack and obeyed orders, pulling the office door tight.

"Now, son," the sheriff said. "I'm guessing maybe you don't know this, but your boy and I got to know each other a bit. We got along all right, until we didn't. That's fine. Not everyone likes the law. That's between us. But I have to ask you ... do you know the extent of what he's running away from?"

"Sir," said Jack, drooping his head. "He's no saint. Never has been. Never will be—"

"He's a damn *war criminal*, Jack."

"Enough."

"It's true."

"Chase has a Purple Heart."

"For getting his ass shot," said the sheriff. "What he's not telling anybody is that he also shot one of his own. A platoon mate who'd become a liability. Your boy's a killer, Jack."

"Fuck you."

"Naw, son, fuck you."

"If you knew that, you'd arrest him."

The sheriff's face reddened as he leaned back, deep into his chair. "Look," he said, "I've struggled with this, I'll admit it. But when Chase confessed to me, I gave my word it'd be in confidence. I tend to keep my word. Besides, if it's not my jurisdiction, it's not my concern. With all the damn meth and weed up here, I've got enough on my plate." He leaned forward again, to drive his last point in deep. "I'm truly sorry for your family, but Chase is irreparable. He's gone. That degenerate doesn't need prison to repent. He'll burn himself in hell, all on his own."

Jack didn't move. He couldn't. The sheriff's half-smile was a wordless taunt.

"Sorry," said the sheriff, "but it's just the way things shook out—"

"This sounds to me," said Jack, now yelling, "like an awfully convenient excuse to not go searching."

McLaren burst back into the room, and she put a leg between Jack and the sheriff, shouting, "Out!" and pointing to the door.

"Naw, deputy, let him stay for a bit," the sheriff said. "Let's teach him how to act."

To Jack the chair felt confining. He contemplated tossing it across the desk, into the old man's chest, but days or weeks in jail would bring him no closer to Chase.

"I'll put it another way," Jack said, more calmly now. "This is probably going to sound egotistical, but sometimes we've got to beat our chests to be heard." He pushed himself out of the chair and stood at the sharp corner of the desk, and the sheriff leapt up, too. The three of them now formed a triangle, a standoff. Jack continued: "Do you know that every afternoon, three million people in cars and offices—in twenty major markets across the country—tune in to hear what's on my mind? You understand that? Can you comprehend the reach of my pulpit?"

"Son," the sheriff said, "I could give two shits who you think you are—"

"Give me ten seconds," Jack said. "I've worked hard for my position, for what I have. I fetched coffee for AM radio clowns in Miami for five years before they gave me a chance. No one's given me a damn thing I didn't earn. I might not look like it, standing here, but I'm a dogged man. At some point, I'll have to go back home, to my job in a big important building, and if I find out that something's happened to my brother, that he's up there dying while you sit on your hayseed asses—I'll never forget that. I'll air my grievances with the nation. And you, sheriff, will be my whipping boy."

The sheriff pounced forward, thrusting out his finger. "You little shitbag!" he shouted. "Don't barge in here with that. This is disorderly conduct if I've ever seen it!"

The sheriff limped around his desk, and Jack leaned toward him, chest out, two bantam cocks colliding. McLaren shot her forearm between them and struggled, momentarily, to rope Jack away. She held him in place.

Jack pulled against McLaren's grip, but he could feel an intense sort of leverage in her compact stance, something borne of specialized training, that he was helpless to counteract. "All of this is horseshit," he said, nodding to the sheriff's medals. "My brother's dying out there—and you know it. He might be a fuckup, but you can't just let him go."

McLaren planted a leg behind Jack, flipped him over her hip, and drove his trembling chest into the carpet. Jack felt a knee and shin on his spine. He didn't resist; his hands were wrenched behind him and then locked into cold metal. The sheriff squatted next to Jack, set one hand on the carpet, and peered into the pained face: "I tried to help your brother from the moment he crawled up here," the sheriff said. "He's a punk. He's unstable. I don't give a damn where he's been, who's tried to kill him, or how decorated he is. And I don't care if he rots in the high country for now. He's nothing to me until *ninety hours* have passed. That's county protocol. That's the rules. You reported this last night, so we've got time. Go sit your ass in a cell until you've got some sense."

The sheriff stood straight and pressed down the wrinkles on his uniform. McLaren lifted Jack by his elbow.

"Sir?" McLaren said, breathing heavy, but trying to disguise it. "Charges?"

"We've got disorderly conduct, and on top of that, public intox," said the sheriff. "Charge him, get a blood sample, and don't let him out before it's dark outside—compliments of the whipping boy."

"Come on—*jail?*" said Jack, wincing against the deputy's grip. "You're serious?"

"Goodbye," the sheriff said.

"How about a ticket? A fine? I can't waste time in a cage, not today."

"Please," said the sheriff, "get this piece of shit out of my face."

McLaren dragged Jack through the offices, back to the hoosegow. A lady with a bob hairdo and thick black glasses gasped at the sight of Jack. She recognized him, which deeply alarmed him. He winked to the lady and gave his best billboard smile, but her face showed only disgust and shock. McLaren dropped Jack in a cell and rolled the clinking door closed. Looking around, Jack said, "Can I get a pillow?"

"No, you can't," said McLaren. "Unhinge the toilet paper roll. Sleep on that. Goodbye."

"Don't you need a blood sample? Fingerprints?"

"You're not drunk—you're just an ass."

The deputy stomped past the jail desk, back into the office, closing a thick metal door behind her. Jack unrolled the toilet paper and wadded it into a pillow. He lay on the concrete bench and studied the walls, rough with overlapping bricks and mortar. He'd seen a few drunk tanks from the inside, but none that looked so easy to chisel out of. As the adrenaline ebbed, a deep sadness and sense of failure set in. Jack pictured his body spinning, whirling around a huge toilet, his disappointed mother standing over the bowl, her face angry, hand on the handle, flushing again and again. He'd never been so frustrated. Or felt so gutted. Compared to this disaster of a week, his life had been a long summer swim. He hated the cell already, the dead moths in its single overhead light canister, its odor of cleaning chemicals. Through slits of tall, barred windows he could see a large bird, above the town, kiting on the wind, graceful and indifferent, several hundred feet up. He wondered if Chase could see the bird, too, or if that predator had eyes on Chase.

***

Throughout the morning, Chase lay on his stomach, terrified that he'd been abandoned, left to starve. From the ground he could see that all the remaining vegetables and illicit crops had been harvested in the night. The makeshift kitchen was missing every piece but its heavy stove. A brown tarp lifted and bowed in the breeze, but otherwise nothing moved. Chase heaved his weight and rolled onto his back to see the creek. And then Yonah was standing over him, her boots next to his ears, her face cantilevered over her crotch.

"The baby-killer woke up," she shouted.

"Please," said Chase. "You can't do this. Show some mercy. You're better than this. Don't leave me here, wallowing."

"Shush."

"Just cut me loose, and I'll take off," he said. "We'll go our ways. It'll be over. I'll never be a problem again."

Prophet's graveled laugh wafted up from the creek, and Chase looked down to see him pointing both antiquated revolvers uphill. "Told you he'd come to eventually," Prophet said. "That's a tough bastard right there."

Yonah pressed her boot on Chase's forehead, rolling it across his nose and lips to leave an insulting red-clay imprint. "Look," she said. "We're done here. We're packing up and advancing. This camp is useless now that you've seen it, so don't get any big ideas about ambushing us here next season."

"For God's sake," said Chase, "I am *not* the police—"

"Shut up," said Prophet. "Enough out of you, soldier. That pounding headache you have, I'm sure, was our only option. Not my first choice, necessarily, but I'd say it worked out. Nobody died. And you're right, it's over. No bad blood. No more violence. Goodbye, and thank you for your service."

"*What?*" said Chase, sounding desperate, even childish. "Please, you can't leave yet. You're reasonable people and leaving me stranded will haunt you. You can't just let me starve."

"I'm gonna roll you over, go all God Bless America, and give you freedom," said Prophet. "And then you're gonna bound off into them woods, to the east. If you so much as look back—I open fire. And I won't stop until your camos are soaked red, until these guns gut you like a buck."

Yonah stomped the ground in protest. "I'm telling you, I don't like it."

"Please, yes," said Chase. "My family—my mother—will be indebted, for the rest of our lives."

"Don't make me regret this, solider," said Prophet, slowly approaching. "But I can't have starving you to death on my conscience. I meant it, to a degree, when I said we're good people." He bent down, cuffed Chase's shoulder, latched onto the cords and flipped him back over on his stomach. "Undo him, baby, while I keep these aimed at his head."

Pouty, cautious, and mean, Yonah unlatched the primary cord and freed the ankles, standing on them to thwart upward kicks and inflict pain in achy joints. While unfurling the wrists, she gasped, with a smile. "Damn, pig, you're bleeding like Christ."

Chase lay flat on the leaves and groaned until the trembling left his extremities. Prophet shouted for him to get going, to quit bitching, to head east forever.

"Just give the blood a minute to get flowing," said Chase. "Afraid I can't even walk straight right now. I think I'm still a bit dizzy, a bit concussed."

Prophet cocked both barrels and hovered the weapons— almost touching, as if to form one mighty cannon—not two feet from Chase's face. Yonah screamed to pull, just pull, because this cop wasn't cooperating, was slowing them down, was dangerous with those crazy eyes.

"She's right," Chase said. "Listen to Yonah."

Above the barrels, Prophet cocked his head. "Huh?"

"Do it, man"

"Calm down, soldier."

"*Do* it!"

"I'm telling you," Prophet croaked, "don't tense up like that. Breathe easy. Lay there, and we'll just walk away. Don't think of bucking up, or I'll leave you here crippled."

"No, right in the fucking head—*do* it!" Chase yelled. "Get it over with. Save me the embarrassment. Save me the trouble."

Prophet stood, stepped back, and nodded for Yonah to do the same. "Stop this batshit talk," he said.

"You really want to know about my war, to be 'enlightened'?" said Chase. "That's what you want? An inkling? Well, I've got an inkling for you ..."

"Go easy," Prophet said. "Don't move. Keep flat. We're gone."

"I deserve to die," Chase shouted into the leaves, the earth. "You're looking at a worthless piece of shit. You're looking at the worst soldier in US history. You're looking at a killer who should be put down, like a dog. If anyone deserves an execution, it's me."

"Stop this shit!" Yonah screamed at Prophet. "End him like he wants."

Prophet shuddered, sighed, and leaned back over Chase, eyeing him curiously. "Soldier, what the fuck are you talkin' about?"

Chase's mind went back to the fighting in southern Kandahar, to the nonsensical chatter of Afghan allies, to air impossibly hot but not Georgia July thick; to blooming poppy fields and leafy grape rows, to the gun in his hand; to the kid from Ohio standing downhill, not twenty feet away, the crybaby kid, the kid who could get them all killed in action, the liability. The kid whose eyes twitched with confusion once the bullet went through him, whose mouth fell open as if sucking Himalayan air, whose lips stretched white; the kid whose mother was known for corned beef and Rotary speeches and Buckeye pride, whose son was dying around the world, beside the canal, in the shadow of Chase Lumpkin, a war-tormented fellow countryman who'd aimed with precise, insane purpose.

"I shot a member of my platoon in Afghanistan," Chase suddenly said. "This kid from Ohio, who'd stopped fighting and kept giving our position away. He was falling apart on us." He paused to breathe, pushing back the urge to weep. "It's hard to explain, but we all wanted him gone so bad. It became my duty to do it—or at least I thought that. And no, it wasn't some friendly fire accident. It was on purpose. I guess you could say it was murder. Technically I think that's what it was ..."

Shocked, Prophet shook his head, the ponytail dancing. "That's a serious demon right there."

"For the love of God," Chase begged, "just shoot me *right now!*"

Prophet leaned away. "Sounds like you qualify, but you'll have to make a better case. Tell us the whole story. How'd you do this shit, exactly?"

"Jesus, you morbid fuck," Chase said, deflating in the leaves. "That's the most I've ever said, and it's enough. Let me take the details with me."

"Nope," said Prophet, taunting. "I'm still not buyin' this."

Chase tremored with frustration, clutched his damaged head, and emitted a long, low growl, fighting his memories but eventually giving in. "His name was Mason. We teased him so much you might call it hazing. We would call it fun, a distraction, boys being boys. But there was value in it, too, because his skin was thickening. At least that's what we thought." Chase continued by recalling Mason's face—his big honking nose, like a red drinker's nose, and how he was going bald at age twenty; not from the top but up from the temples. How he looked like Midwestern Dracula. And how he was so scared, right off the plane, at the first sight of the dusty, ancient chaos in southern Afghanistan. How Mason never saw war like they did, and how the more he just stood there during firefights, the more the platoon worried he'd get them all sent home in pieces. On Mason's third night in-country, Chase took him behind the shed where they kept the personal computers, saying he'd scored whiskey in the mail and was dying to share it. Instead, Chase did his best to put the fear of Jesus in the chickenshit, pinning him against the shed, by the neck, and telling him he'd never last.

"This is why you wanna die in the woods?" Prophet interrupted. "For a worthless piece of shit like that?"

Chase clenched his eyelids. "The Taliban killed our brother Roddy on a Sunday; we packed him up and sent him home and went back in the field, mad as shit. The whole platoon was strung out, and this Mason cried like a bitch after every firefight. Imagine trying to sleep when your nerves are fried and you've got this asshole weeping next to you. Imagine if being tired the next day meant that you might die. That's why we started calling him Fetus. And Fetus didn't like that shit. The kid was fried and losing it more by the day; others were watching, waiting for someone to make a move."

The platoon was in the seventh straight day of fighting, Chase explained. On a mission that really wasn't a mission, just a bait thing that put them in the sizzling shit to gauge where the enemy was hiding. Chase strayed off with Mason and flanked down toward a berm. The firefight scared Mason, and he all but quit, hiding in some grass like a kid in the bushes. At that moment Chase knew he was finished—with Mason, with the filth, with almost dying and not dying.

There was no finality, just one dilemma, one atrocity after the next, and so much pressure in trying to survive for the sake of other people.

In the ditch, Chase's arms bounced and face twitched, he was so mad. When the fire got heavy again, Chase yelled for Mason to move out ahead. As Mason came up on all fours, and without really thinking about it, Chase pointed his rifle up and shot him in the sternum. The bullet must have cut Mason's throat because he started spitting foam and blood, and his eyes were huge and scared. He clutched his T-shirt into a ball, just below his chin, and fell straight back, his muddy boots pointing up, like a cartoon death. Chase had seen enough to know that what he'd done to Mason—he couldn't *undo* it. Then it all hit him, all the paranoia, and he started screaming about fucking up, mindful his superiors could trace the wound to his weapon in five minutes. With bullets whizzing, he ducked and started to move, trying to get down a hill, which is when he saw his thigh explode. With his eyes Chase traced the trajectory, and he saw that Mason had raised his rifle enough to fire one round—the last decision of his life. Chase gripped his leg, which felt like it was melting, and fell face-first into a pile of dusty stones, immobilized.

"Jesus Lord," said Prophet. "This is fucked up."

Yonah stepped away once but stopped, enthralled and sickened by the confession. Chase groaned in the leaves.

"Was there suspicion?" said Prophet. "That you were guilty, I mean?"

Chase slowly shook his head. "The guys start calling for medics, to save both of us. I'm trying to fess up about this 'accident,' but they're not hearing it. I was getting woozy, but I wanted to see how the platoon guys looked at me before I passed out. And I'll be damned if some of them weren't smiling down—like *wink wink*, motherfucker—even though they were scared for me. Last thing I remember, before blacking out, is hoping my casualty didn't survive, couldn't testify to the look in my eyes when I fired into him. God knows I've had his face in my mind since—"

"This is *fucked*," Yonah shouted. "Come on, babe, let's move. Right now!"

"Fine," said Prophet, stepping once toward the creek, with Yonah behind him. "You're free. None of this ever happened. You didn't tell us shit; you weren't here. Now go. Get the hell gone."

Disappointed, Chase shook his head. "Okay, then, I will," he said, sitting up and stretching. "I'll head that way, where I was going, as you go that one. Just give me my gun back."

At that, Prophet broke into loud, sarcastic laughter, though he kept his eyes focused downward. "Yeah, let me go ahead and call 911, get the medics on standby, and I'll hand over a loaded nine-millimeter to a batshit commando cop—because I'm sure he won't shoot me in the face and split my girlfriend's wig. Do I look like a dumbfuck, man?"

Chase whipped his head back and forth. "Where is my gun?"

"Gone."

"Fuck you it's gone. Where's my gun?"

"Buried," said Prophet. "Far, far away."

"No, your hippie ass is lying again."

"Just lay back down, man, and we're gonna slip away. Nice and slow. Super easy. You're making me antsy as shit."

"Jesus Christ," Chase said, sitting up straighter, clutching the crown of his head. "If you don't shoot me dead, or give me my gun, I'm coming after you."

"Enough!" said Yonah. "I'm done with this lunatic." She looped her arms through her overstuffed knapsack and turned toward the creek. "Do what you want with him, babe, but I'm putting some distance between me and all this."

At the instant Prophet looked her way, Chase sprung up and clasped both barrels, pulling them outward and Prophet down toward him. Chase thrust his head into the soft pit of belly, just below the ribcage, with as much leverage as his arms could muster, and he felt the left weapon discharge, and then the right. With a violent yank and backward tugs the weapons tore away, into his hands, but with the triggers unreachable. Aiming high, he swung both butts across Prophet's face, connecting with cheekbone and eyebrow; he watched him drop, and then turned toward the fleeing girl, hollering, "Fall down now!" She complied, nosediving into leaves.

Chase stood over Prophet. "Fuck with me now, do something stupid, and my confirmed kills climb to seven, okay?" he said. "Crawl over here, Yonah, next to him." Again, she obeyed.

"Now," Chase said. "Where is *my* gun? I need that specific gun—not these pieces of shit—right now."

"It's in a holster, made of ropes, around my ankle," Yonah said, lifting her pant leg.

"Put your leg in the air, way up, and your hands over your head," said Chase. He tucked the old guns into his belt and ripped his nine-millimeter free from Yonah's leg. While doing so he had a wonderfully vengeful idea. He wrenched off Yonah's boots and socks, and ordered Prophet to hand his over, too.

Chase slowly walked over and fetched Yonah's knapsack, emptied some fruit and cloth, and deposited in it the boots, socks, and both old guns, careful to keep them separate from the vegetables and remaining jerky. Deeper in the bag he saw both of their wallets, some cash, and North Carolina IDs.

"I have your real names here," said Chase. "I'm taking all of this back to the department, to my sergeant, and if you make it out of here on your bloody-ass feet, don't think of stepping back in this state again. You didn't see me, but we'll have eyes on you."

His gun outstretched in front of him, Chase crept backward for a hundred yards, back uphill, and before he turned and ran, he watched the couple embrace in horror, lifting their bare feet above them like squirmy apparitions.

9

In his cell, Jack dipped in and out of sleep, his tousled hair surrounded by a pile of unrolled toilet paper, his pillow. The guilt that made his guts feel cold was so potent it kept pulling him awake, and he felt despicable for not being in the woods right now, for becoming his own impediment and not doing more. It was a familiar feeling, one that Jack had first come to know well when he was sixteen, following the panic-attack episode in the park with his mother. One summer afternoon Jack drove to his father's downtown Atlanta office for a surprise visit and a proposition. Charles cut short a meeting with a client in the strip club industry and welcomed his son, always eager to exhibit his corner office for anyone. Behind Charles, big clean windows framed the Westin Peachtree Plaza's shimmering high-rise cylinder and a centerpiece park under construction for the Centennial Olympic Games. Jack took a seat, dropped his backpack, and immediately started making his case. "I think I've figured it out," he'd said, "and we need to get Chase into the best shrink in town."

Charles yanked at the knot of his tie and leaned back in his leather executive chair. "You've figured what out, son?"

"If she didn't tell you, Mom had an episode—a bad one, in public—a couple weeks ago," Jack said. "It really got me thinking. She wants to plan a family dinner, so we can all talk about this, but she's balking on actually doing that. So I thought I'd come down here, and show you what I've found at the library ..." Jack reached into his bag and exhumed a stack of Xeroxed pages.

"Whoa," said Charles, raising his hand, as if testifying. "I'm pressed for time here. Just give me the condensed version."

"Right," Jack said dejectedly. He dropped his prized research. "I think Chase has inherited Mom's weird gene, the social nervousness tic. But he's also, I think, Exhibit A for what they call 'oppositional defiant disorder.' It all makes sense, according to these books. Apparently, though, the only real fix is going to a good psychiatrist—"

"Hold on," Charles interrupted, sounding offended. "I appreciate your initiative, but just slow down."

"Why?" said Jack.

"Well, for starters ... who would take Chase to the clinic?"

"What?" said Jack. "I mean, I guess, you? Or us?"

"Right," Charles said. "That's the problem, Jack. My face is on every phonebook from Alpharetta to Peachtree City. You know what it could mean, in terms of client trust, if I was seen at a shrink's office?"

"Fine," said Jack. "I'll take him. Or Mom will. Or we'll send him on his bike. Sorry, but that's way beside the fucking point here—"

"Watch your mouth," said Charles.

Jack dropped his head and said, "Apologies, sir," but didn't mean it.

"And who's going to *fund* all this?" Charles said. "You?"

"Dad," said Jack, "come on. I can't believe what you're saying."

"I'm sorry, but believe it," Charles said. "Listen, I appreciate your efforts. And your research. It's valiant. You're a sharp kid, Jack. And you've got so much potential to really make some waves. But frankly, you're still a teenager, wading deep into adult matters—"

"Stop it," Jack said. "Stop talking like I'm some little dumbass."

Charles leaned forward, put his elbows on his immense oak desk, and folded his hands together. A long sigh, thick with pity that was obviously, shamelessly forced. "Have you considered that your brother might just be a weird kid?" he said. "I mean, it's not the end of the world. It's really not. In my experience, weird kids typically become the highest-achieving adults."

Jack didn't say anything. He felt underestimated, ridiculous, angry.

"Worst case scenario, it's a phase, Jack," Charles continued. "Chase will naturally come around if we give him space. And he'll come to terms with his anger about the divorce. All kids eventually do. I know I did ..."

For reasons he would never understand, Jack leapt out of his chair, tossed his piled research into the air, slammed both palms on his father's desk, and with a veiny throat howled like a deranged wolf, before storming into the hallway and out.

In his half-conscious state on the jail bench, Jack recalled the feeling of leaving that office—tail firmly between his thighs, watching a harried secretary rush to Charles's aid— and he clenched his jaws in frustration. Unable to sleep, he lay back with his eyes open until he heard the jangle of keys, of mercy.

"Up, man, *wake up*," deputy McLaren said, in her best warden. "Time's up. You can go."

Jack shot upright and rolled his stiff neck, trying to gauge the time of evening. "I wasted all afternoon. I can't believe it," he said, slapping his face. "I'm so far behind."

"Flush the toilet paper you've wasted and get out. Now."

Jack walked back through the offices as quickly as he could without drawing more attention. The woman who'd recognized him earlier perked up again, over a different cubicle. Jack held a finger to his lips and said, simply, "Please, not a word of this." She nodded to him but seemed worried.

"I'll get you season tickets to everything," Jack said. "The Falcons. The rodeo. Whatever. I promise. Just don't tell a soul I'm in here." She didn't respond.

McLaren trailed Jack through the lobby and onto the sidewalk. Sarcastically, Jack smiled at the deputy, saluted, and walked toward the tavern. She let go of the door and, with a few determined strides, stepped in Jack's way.

"I'm retired army myself, on the ground and airborne, back with the Global War on Terror campaign," McLaren said, without eye contact. "Not supposed to tell you that, or much else, but I want you to know you're doing the right thing, Jack. You're just going about it like an idiot."

His interest piqued, Jack took cover in the shadow of an awning, so as not to be seen cavorting with the opposition. "You want to do what's right, I can see that, but you're hamstrung by a bunch of political horseshit." Jack handed the deputy a business card, which, to his surprise, she accepted and tucked in a back pocket. "I'm counting down the minutes until the three days are up, until you can help me like decent people, but we both know it'll be too late then. So I'll be resorting to extremes, like emptying my checking account, trying to *pay* for help." Jack nodded ahead, toward the tavern. "We have to get started tonight, to start tracking him as best we can despite the dark. I know it might not sound like his character, but when Chase fixates on doing something, he doesn't mess around, doesn't waste time. So we really don't *have* time."

"You don't understand, Jack," said McLaren, looking high above rooftops, squinting her eyes. "It's a different kind of dark up there. With things that get hungry at night."

"Imagine this was your family, your blood," Jack said. "Picture your kid brother up there, and then complain to me about darkness—"

"Don't mention my brother, damn it," she said, darting an index finger into the dough of Jack's midsection. "Don't go there."

"Apologies, deputy," he said.

She withdrew her hand. The eyes did not relax.

"Clearly, though," Jack said, "you feel what I'm saying here."

"I'll tell you right now..." the deputy said, her tone somewhere between schoolteacher and drill instructor, but she couldn't finish her thought; the harried contortion of Jack's face distracted her, opened sympathetic reserves in her, soft spots in the cop veneer. Suddenly she wanted to put a hand on Jack's shoulder, if not two consoling hands on both shoulders, but she decided against such blatant, public compassion for a Lumpkin. "Don't get your hopes up of finding any sort of team who'll set out tonight. It probably won't happen. I'm sorry, but I've got a little girl, a good husband, a new house. It's too much to risk by breaking protocol and putting on my guide's cap to help you. I can't do that right now."

A tipsy herd of tourists walked by burping, and Jack tossed his arms up. "What do you expect me to do then?" he said. "Call it a night? Have a pizza and cavort with these drunken sightseers? I'm lost up here, ma'am. Give me a call when you find your human soul."

Jack rushed toward the tavern, but McLaren quickly caught up, and she yanked him in front of her, point-blank. "If you repeat this, I'll deny it, and no one will believe you," she said. "I don't think the sheriff wants your brother found, as bad as that sounds. He's not lying about our protocol, but I've never seen him act like this. He won't get into details, so I don't know everything, but I know the blood's real bad between him and your brother."

They stood silent. A pumpkin truck lumbered down Main.

"What'd Chase do to you?" Jack said.

"Nothing, really. Not personally. He tended to be gracious around women, in fact, even when sloshed."

"Then how about this," said Jack. "If you can't help, why not tell me what to do?"

McLaren nodded, the streetlight shadows sliding around her face. "In the tavern, by seven this evening, like every evening, you'll see a codger in dirty overalls, sitting at the bar," she said. "The man's the best guide in the county, knows the mountains like nobody else."

"Fantastic!" said Jack. "But give me a name, or something. There's got to be forty dirty codgers in there already."

"There won't be forty Black ones with white beards."

Jack gasped. "*Diversity?* Here? No!"

"He's half Indian—American-Indian," McLaren said, turning right to the jail as Jack went left. "I know that sounds a little *Lone Ranger*, but he's the best around here. And for your cause, he's invaluable."

"Your soul is hereby saved!" Jack shouted, lifting his arms.

"I don't need saved."

"Yes, sorry, of course." He reached his arms out beside him, then toward her, so swept up by new hope he wanted to hug anybody, anything. She stood still, declining him without words. "Just tell me, really quick," said Jack. "Why this? Why here? You could be anything, anywhere, and you choose to run around the woods, patrolling Cherokee with the local boys?"

She scoffed, throwing back her head, although the compliment, once it registered, made her cheeks feel warm. "Because this is my place, my home," she said stiffly, sounding more offended than she'd meant to, the blood pulsing now. "I know this region, and I love every last damn gulley—"

"Okay, okay," said Jack. "I get it. No worries. I just thought there might be something deeper, more specific. You've got this burning passion on your face, always, for what you do here."

"What's my motivation?" she said, loudly cracking neck vertebrae. "Is that what you're asking me, Jack?"

Jack put on his best begging puppy impression, still beguiled by the strange benevolence of his only high-country ally. And what he thought was a grin on McLaren's face was instead her tensing, trembling lips, struggling against a surge of obvious internal torment. For a minute she stood there saying nothing, awkward and quiet, save for the sniffling nose.

"You remember, back in the early eighties, that famous photography book they put out about hunger in the poorest parts of Appalachia?" she said. "Remember the dirty kids with swollen bellies, peeking out of shacks, the images they call iconic now?"

"I can see the kids' ribs as we speak," said Jack. "It's seared in my head."

McLaren leaned back into a street shadow, a reticent half-woman now, bold and uniformed on the right, shy in darkness at left. "Exactly," she said, her voice lowering. "Not that it's your business, or anyone's, but me and my little brother were in that book, at the house we shared with Momma, up north of town, when she was around. We were starving. We posed for that man, and two years later, I woke up on the floor mattress we always used, and my brother was nothing but a dead body, next to me in his little basketball shorts. They called it a lack of nitrogen. His body consumed itself. I knew on that morning, eleven years old, that my life would be used to help unfortunate people, and that I'd never allow myself to go hungry again. That answer your question?"

"Crushing," said Jack.

"It's past."

"I'm sorry."

"Don't pity me," she said, reestablishing the veneer. "Stay focused."

"Not to jog bad memories," Jack said, "but was your mom charged?"

McLaren shot Jack a barbed glare and stomped the opposite way, without another word.

***

A big moon lit the mountains almost gray, illuminating greater Cherokee, the high rocky outcrops of distant cliffs, and the deep burgundy of faraway, deciduous trees. Chase studied this pale world, wishing he could paint it. Across the valley, night-black pine forests stretched over rolling mountain passes, dissipating with elevation, until the mass became a single renegade tree, defiant and isolated. Below that, headlights flashed on serpentine highways. Two lakes shone like mercury.

Chase thought he'd come far enough and high enough to dispose of the growers' belongings and rid himself of the extra weight. He reached back and launched the knapsack with the boots and antique weapons over a cliff and into thick brush a hundred feet below. It all landed in a hiss of leaves and was sufficiently gone. In doing that, Chase felt he'd cut loose his last tie with the functioning world, and for a moment he regretted sending that couple unarmed and shoeless into the wilderness, until the bruised knot atop his skull pulsed sore and ended all sympathies. He was exhausted and filthy, but he hiked a mile more through the moonlit landscape, heading both upward and laterally, until he was convinced he'd reached his destination: an indistinct and rugged plateau he'd picked from yellowed guidebooks in his cabin's garage.

***

After composing himself, but still dazed by the bluntness of Deputy McLaren's story, Jack turned away from the sheriff's department and hustled to the tavern. He burst into the bar and pointed at the bartender. "Shut her down!" he cried. "The pillaging of my open tab ends *now!*"

The bartender, this time, was a brunette in blue flannel, with rolled-up sleeves and a tiny, tattooed flame jutting from the top of her sports bra. A little gold pin clipped to the bra said her name was Carrie. She unlatched a microphone from the wall, round like a CB radio, and said to the Lonesome patrons: "Party's over, y'all—dickhead's back." A dozen slumping men slapped angry hands on the bar. Others moaned from the pool tables. From some unseen corner an elderly female voice hollered, "That cheap sumbitch!"

Ignoring them, Jack feigned an arrow to the heart, and instinctively he stole a glance at the bartender's navel. "You," he said, nearing the bar, "have an extraordinary belly button."

She tilted her head, blushed, and looked condescendingly at Jack's midsection. "Yours is a damn mess."

Now Jack gripped his heart and belly, dramatically faking excruciating death. "Hey now," he said. "I've worked hard for every expanding inch."

"And you think that's desirable?" said the bartender, grinning.

"Well," said Jack, "I guess it's less intimidating, being imperfect but real."

At that she fully smiled. "Nothing's less attractive than a man who thinks he's perfect," she said. "And there's no such thing as a perfect man."

Jack laughed hard, wheezing and slapping the bar.

"You play up that flirty, cuddly thing well, don't you?" she said. "I see what you're up to."

Beside Jack, a college kid in fraternity letters toppled off his stool, stood up, and blamed the free neat whiskies. The bartender, visibly pissed, snatched a dry peanut, bounced it off the kid's face, and pointed to the exit. He left without protest, and she turned back to Jack: "Aren't you worried about the total?"

"Total looks just fine."

"I mean on the card," she said, topping a draft beer and sliding it to Jack.

"What's your name?" Jack said, just to hear her say it.

"To you, it's bartender." She pulled her hair across her shoulder to hide her golden nametag.

"Oh come on," he said. "Play nice."

"If you need to call me something," she said, "call me queen. You look like the type to whistle at bartenders. Queen, the way I see it, is the opposite of whistling."

"That's very random," Jack said, "but as you wish, Your Majesty."

"Tell you the truth, I'm three sheets to the wind myself, thanks to you," she laughed. "Wish more celebrities would get jailed up here." Her smile was tricky, scheming, almost devilish. "I speak for everyone when I say taking advantage of your ass, all day and night, has been fantastic." She paused to toss a peanut into Jack's chest, which he caught on the bounce and ate, shell and all. She almost admitted that his sloppiness—both in disheveled, post-captivity appearance and horndog tact—was somehow cute, but she caught herself. "Now, I'm going to ask you what you did to get arrested, and let's see if you can answer without being a pervert."

"Good Lord," said Jack. "It's like I've sprung from hell and met the devil herself."

"That's not a compliment," she said. "So I guess that's progress."

"The devil in angel disguise, I mean."

"*Stop*," she said, without humor. "If this is you sober, I can't imagine tipsy. Now, seriously, you got an answer?"

"Basically," said Jack, "I mouthed off to your esteemed sheriff, and he wanted to teach me a lesson, so I spent the afternoon in time-out."

She nodded and leaned in closer to Jack, whispering in a sloppy loud rasp, smelling of hops and girlie teenager perfume. "That weird old man has been stalking me for years," she said. "He's great at his job—an ace detective or whatever—and he's got a big heart for the right situations, which I know firsthand. But the secret bouquets on my porch got creepy two years ago. If I was you, I wouldn't feel too bad for stepping on his toes."

"That sounds like actual stalking, in the legal sense," Jack said. "And it's even more despicable because his office is covered in family photos."

"*Exactly*," she said, her head filling with memories of porch roses and tiny, terrible poems on cards. "To think I'm driving families apart because these local dickbrains don't know better ... that hurts a girl like me. I'm honorable, raised right. I can't say I'm totally innocent, but it's not my fault really, and never has been."

"Sorry to hear all that," Jack said, "but thanks for the dirt. Maybe I can blackmail the sheriff into helping me." She raised a fist to portend an oncoming punch, but Jack deflected by saying he was kidding and would keep quiet. He scanned the room for a white-bearded Black man, not seeing one. "Anyway," he said, "I'm up here to find my brother. Former army guy, super studly, named Chase. But I need backup. I need to recruit right now—and set out tonight."

With a wet bar rag she wiped a place free of shells and spills and invited Jack to sit. "Your brother's a bitter boy, but I don't really mind him," she said. "Cute as all get out, in that dark cowboy stranger kind of way. He looks like the 'after' version of you in a health commercial, really. Where'd he run off to?"

Jack gulped beer and looked around. "You took advantage of me. This whole place did."

The bartender smiled. "You wanna know the number you owe?"

"Ah, let me get a buzz first, then tell me," Jack said. "Hell, keep it open a little longer. It could help with community relations."

Carrie retrieved beers and scotch for two regulars who called her by name. Jack watched her work, the perky way she interacted with everyone, chortling at old men's jokes and bounding on rubberized floor mats, graceful despite her tipsiness. He could have slapped himself for flirting in a time of crisis, but he was enthralled, again. She had a purer sort of magnetism than he was used to, a slaphappy but cunning way that didn't seem corroded by materialistic city ambitions and years of self-aggrandizing on social media. She looked, in short, like a farm girl, but one wise to the undertow of boozy nightlife. And something in the way she commanded the attention of drinking men without trying—blithely transitioning from one bar-top conversation to the next, leaving desperate faces dangling in her wake—made Jack burn to be dominated by her. To his distractible mind, the challenge of a drink-slinging mountain woman, however inappropriate tonight, was magnetic. Jack's ogling was interrupted by his telephone, which buzzed in his pocket, but he didn't answer. He waved to get her attention, and she came, sweeping her hair into a long brown ponytail.

"I need to a find a guy I'm sure you know," Jack said. "An older Black guy with a white beard, some sort of voodoo Indian tracker."

"You mean Pronto?" she said. "He'll be in."

Jack choked on beer and inhaled fast, desperate to keep it from his nostrils, which teared up his eyes. All of this made the bartender—had they called her Carrie?—laugh. "Pronto?" he said. "What kind of stereotype nonsense is that?"

Up close her lips were lavender. They bent up with a smile, revealing an orthodontic masterwork in white. To Jack she seemed immensely satisfied with her life, charmed by the presence of all people, even a desperate stranger just sprung from the pokey. Or maybe, he thought, this all could be a disingenuous, seductive front, a vacuum for regrettably enormous tips. "I think his name's Presley, but on account of his heritage, they call him that," she said. "He should walk in around seven, or anytime about now, really."

Jack thanked her and pulled his phone from his pants to listen to the message. He heard a friendly singsong drawl: "Mister Lumpkin," the pastor's message said. "James Rutgers here of Tabernacle International. I got your message, and I understand you're in need of assistance in Cherokee. I'm at your disposal, sir."

"Thank fucking God," Jack said, clasping his phone and dialing the pastor, who answered halfway through the first ring. He asked Jack to summarize his plan.

"It's being formulated as we speak," Jack said. "Could you come down to the Lonesome Cub, this bar at the town square? I'm kind of pegged here at the moment, but I need to fill you in—tonight."

The pastor was silent for a moment, humming loudly and crunching what sounded like potato chip bags. "I'll be there soon," he said. "Let me finish some church matters and ready tomorrow's sermon."

"You're a kind man. Please hurry," Jack said, hanging up.

Jack eyed the entrance in want of the white beard. Instead, more locals waddled in, a few backslappers in overalls. Someone kept playing progressive rock operas on the jukebox, and as Jack was trying to determine the culprit, his phone relayed a puzzling message from his agent: a series of question marks and exclamation points. Jack responded with question marks of his own.

The agent called, and Jack answered. "What the hell were you doing *in jail* today?" the agent, Rudy Dillinger, barked. "I thought you were resting up there?"

Jack felt dizzy, sick.

"Answer me, Jack!"

"How do *you* know about jail?"

"It's a big deal," Rudy said. "It leaked. There's a preliminary incident report online already, at each outlet. You've made the Atlanta news, brother. At least three channels. You need to tell me what we're going to do about this."

"What do you know?" Jack said. "Did they mention my brother at all?"

"Something about accosting police in the mountains—that's it. They made a mugshot of that stupid billboard promo you've been using, the one with the fireballs and that tiger. It's a really bad look, man. Anyway, is Chase incarcerated, too?"

Jack heard the question but didn't respond.

"We've got to get a handle on this," the agent said. "We've got to be in front of it, with a press statement."

"Listen, Rudy," Jack said. "I've got a lot on my plate. Family issues like you wouldn't believe. I've got hiking plans for the next couple of days. Fresh air, autumn leaves, all that."

"People will think you've gone *missing*, man. I don't like the silent tactic—"

Jack hung up and drank two beers. He watched the door until a man who had to be Pronto sauntered through—tall, broad-shouldered, nervous, non-white. To Jack he looked incredible, an ethnic hodgepodge of high cheekbones and a thin nose, but with a deep mocha complexion and squashed cloud of white hair. He carried a camouflage jacket and wore overalls with, of all things, a mauve dress shirt underneath. He claimed an empty two-top at the end of the bar and waved excitedly at the bartender. Carrie poured Pronto a tall glass, and before she could deliver it, Jack wormed through the crowd and called to her.

"Whatever he likes, it's on me," Jack said, patting the man's right arm, then pointing to the ledge of bourbons.

Pronto held up a large cautionary hand. "I don't need help paying for drink."

"Relax, sir," Jack said. "I just need a minute. I have a proposition."

"That beer right there is all I'll need," Pronto said to the bartender, then to Jack, "Take your money and liquor-up some hot piece of ass."

Jack liked Pronto's bluntness, and something about the syrup in his dialect made him seem trustworthy. "I've been told you're the man who can help me," said Jack. "I'll pay you and, if all goes well, you'll come out of this a hero."

Pronto latched ahold of Jack's right shoulder. "Not interested."

Jack backed away and ordered two shots of single malt scotch. The drinks arrived, and Jack saluted. "Join me, Pronto, or I'll drink both of these and do something stupid." Jack handed over the glass, which Pronto readily took. "You're cool with me calling you that, right?"

"Buy me high-dollar whiskey like this, and you can call me Bitchtits." Pronto swallowed the shot without grimacing, savoring the aftertaste. "Now tell me this plan, man."

Jack told Pronto his name and explained the rescue mission. Pronto only clutched his beer, slouching on his bar stool.

"I need a tracker," Jack said. "I need *you*. I can pay two grand for your assistance, and five grand if we find him—in the next two days or sooner."

"I appreciate the offer, but I've got a life going."

"Double what I just said, all of it," said Jack. "But no more. That's the offer."

"Man, do you have any clue, any direction, where your boy went?"

"I know which way he started," Jack said, "and I have a note that might tell you more than I can. I'm meeting someone else here shortly—a local who's agreed to help for free—and then we can scat up to my place, have a look at this document, and get going."

"Oh, I ain't going nowhere tonight," said Pronto. "That's not how this works."

"Bullshit," said Jack. "Deal's off then. I'll take a flashlight, grab a sleeping bag, and accomplish this myself."

"So long then." Pronto turned back to his beer. "Best get your will in order first."

"What if I sweeten the final offer? Fifteen grand for leaving tonight and finding my brother by tomorrow. How's that sound?"

"It sounds like you wanna get all three of us killed," said Pronto, puffing his chest and sounding aggravated. "I ain't going nowhere in the woods tonight. Not for a million bucks and a whole fifth of old scotch."

"Fine," huffed Jack. "I should've known better. I heard you're the best and bravest and yada yada, but that was horseshit." Jack set down his drink and rolled his thick head, shaking bad ideas free. He stewed for a moment and formulated an even more haphazard plan: He'd conspire with the bartender to get Pronto so liquored up and full of confidence that charging into the wilderness to prove his valor would seem logical. "So it's two grand for your assistance tomorrow, and five grand if we find him alive."

Pronto contemplated the proposition. "I have to work at the textile factory the next two days, and I've never called in sick, but I'm thinking I will. We'll have to go early, because I want to see the dew."

"You got it."

"The lesser amount," Pronto said, "can you pay that up front?"

"You got it."

"And I've got to tell you something, to come clean a little bit," said Pronto, leaning closer.

"Go ahead," said Jack, almost whispering. "Swear on my daughter's eyes, I won't say a word."

"Don't repeat this," said Pronto, "but I'm not really a powwow Indian. Okay? My people came over from Madagascar, way back when. Everything I know about tracking I learned on the internet at the library, but I'm *damn* good, man. Been tracking for ten years now." Looking around, Pronto pulled Jack closer and softly spoke, directly into Jack's ear. "The Indian thing is good for business, and these morons don't know the difference. They started calling me by this dumbass nickname, and I just ran with it. But that's between us right here. Keep it hush-hush. If not, you'll ruin me, and that won't be good for you."

"Talent is talent," Jack said. "Makes no difference to me. My lips are sealed."

When Pronto leaned in to say something else, his eyes swelled, looking behind Jack, who instinctually flinched. A thick old hand landed on Jack's shoulder, and he swung around, leapt to his feet, and welcomed pastor Rutgers with an obnoxious hug.

The pastor unzipped his jacket, unfastened his plastic priest's collar, and leaned against a wooden beam, his belly falling over his belt. At first sight of the bartender, he sucked it all in. "Carrie, my dear," he hollered, "I'll have the amber, please."

Jack acted stunned. "A beer-drinking, high-country pastor!"

Pronto laughed and nodded to the pastor; Jack felt ashamed he hadn't made the introduction, so he asked them to shake hands, and then by force of habit, he turned to the bartender and ordered three more whiskeys.

"Been a long time, Presley," the pastor said.

"Has, sir," Pronto said.

"Sweet *Jee*-sus—they know each other," Jack said, his arms raised. "I love small towns!"

But the pastor's face was solemn. "Up here, Jack, just so you know, it's hard to find folks who want to vanish," he said. "Let's get that straight immediately. We've got a job ahead of us, but we've got the right number of men. I can leave church duties behind, but just for a day. I know these mountains—not like Presley, but I know them—and I have some ideas for where your brother might be."

Delighted, Jack clapped and yipped. "Look at us, gentlemen," he smiled, gathering the whiskeys and nodding to the barroom mirror. "We're the greatest posse Cherokee's ever seen," Jack said. "So let's talk this out. Let's game-plan to the nines, and after one more round, let's go *find my brother!*"

Pronto reached out and latched ahold of Jack's collar. "Not tonight, I said. You deaf as you are loud?"

"Oh, Jack," said the pastor, gently lifting Pronto's arm away. "I understand the issue of time sensitivity here, but you can't think of setting out in the dark. That's walking into death's jaws right there."

"Fine, I'll amend that declaration," Jack said, pouting. "Let's talk this out, let's game-plan to the nines, and at *the crack of dawn*, let's go find my brother!"

By midnight, the posse's ambitions had all but derailed. Pronto and pastor Rutgers had fallen into deep philosophical talk about Islamic fanaticism, sitting knee-to-knee on barstools. Jack, meanwhile, sat at the corner of the bar, nearest the exit, holding the bartender's hand, schmoozing into her smiling face. After a while, Jack asked her for a deceptively strong liquor that might trick men into thinking they were George Rogers Clark in the middle of the night. Carrie looked puzzled.

"I thought you had a busy morning ahead of you, playing in the forest," she said.

"We do," he said. "But we can't wait until morning. We need to climb into the woods right now, as stupid as that sounds. The unfortunate thing is, though, I can't get these two compadres of mine to budge."

Carrie's eyes brightened with an idea, and she dug around under the bar, before suddenly emerging and burning through Jack with a distrustful, squinting glare. She lifted an eyebrow and, as best Jack could tell, began analyzing each impure chasm of his corrupt soul. Then she looked away.

"I just don't know," said Carrie, careful to not relinquish power in this equation. "I really don't."

"About what?" Jack said.

"You seem dangerous to me," she said. "Like a fast city guy. Like a lothario."

Jack feigned a stabbed heart. "Honestly, sweetheart, I'm softening, and in more places than my gut. But I like this. I find your skepticism refreshing."

"Call me sweetheart again," Carrie snapped, "and I'll gut you with car keys."

Leaning away, Jack raised both arms, like a football referee, then blew a kiss to the sky with both hands. "You are *too* much," he said. "It takes talent—real oratorical talent, I mean—to make death threats sound like poems."

"Excuse me?"

"You should consider radio."

"You mean that ancient medium still exists?"

"It's more popular than ever, in fact."

"No thanks," she said, waving goodbye to an elderly woman. "My goals are more humanitarian. I'll be doing genuinely good things one day for a living. Seriously. Stop smirking." She swatted Jack's nose and tried unsuccessfully to rein in her wobbles. "My plan—and I do have a plan—is to work for the Red Cross. Either that, or I'll move to Atlanta and help the homeless, once I get back in school, graduate, and get away from here. Not that it's a bad job, or life. But it's a small population here. Slim pickings. And I'm not bragging when I say I have ten stalkers in town, beyond the sheriff. These wolves are always circling, always married. But I'm not looking for an anchor—hell no. Not yet, if ever. So you won't be seeing me at age forty in a place like this, drinking past midnight with a bad boy like you—"

"Stabbed again—ouch!" Jack said. "But you're convicting me without all the facts. I'm a good man."

"And what's your nickname again?"

"Look, my job is show business, plain and simple," he said. "I'm an actor, like we all are."

"I'm not acting," Carrie said. "This is me. Unscripted. Real."

"And who the hell are you, really?"

"I'm the town skeptic," she said. "But I'm getting less skeptical the longer I stand here. And that scares me."

"Not to pry," said Jack, "but what's the root of all this attitude?"

"You haven't seen attitude."

Jack rolled his eyes. "I mean, you know, where's this vinegar come from? Everyone up here seems to have a fascinating, fucked-up backstory, a whole trove of secrets. Has your lumberjack boyfriend been running around? Are there daddy issues you want to get off your chest?"

Carrie waved goodnight to a group of chatty VFW men and leaned over the corner of the bar, expecting to smell jail on Jack but instead catching complex cologne. "Listen, my daddy was a park ranger here, the most bighearted man you've ever seen, and the closest thing to a saint Cherokee's ever had. A decade ago, he was working overtime through the summer months, keeping track of some issues with tree parasites up in the high country, and he was shot. He'd stumbled onto a drug house at the edge of the national forest, and they sabotaged him, we think. Wrong place, wrong time, God's will, whatever, he was gone. Ripped out of our lives. No man at my graduation, no grandfather for my future kids, all of that. And they may have never found him if the murdering idiots didn't set their place on fire to destroy evidence. Long story, but three teenagers ended up convicted. Kids I knew in school, kids who were my friends. One of them was—or I guess is—a distant relative, a second cousin, though we won't correspond. Somehow my family— my brother and mom, I mean—found it in them to forgive, over time, but I'll make sure all three are caged until they're too old for anything." As her hands began to jitter, Carrie took a deep slow breath. "Yeah, I've been a pretty skeptical girl ever since, because those were awful days, the kind that harden you. There's no acting about it. It's a survival thing. It's healthy, and it won't change. Now prove to me you're a good man or shut your beer hole and run off in the woods."

Jack set his hands atop hers and told her he was sorry to hear.

"I'm serious," she said. "State your case."

"Okay," said Jack. "Wow, pressure—"

"Tell me why it's on you to save your brother's ass."

"It just always has been."

"Why?"

"I don't know," Jack said. "It's just my job."

"But why *you*, of all people?"

"It's something I've always done, since boyhood, basically," he said, slumping over the bar. "I remember Chase as a kindergartener being bullied because he was so quiet. He'd always be sitting under these ancient church windows alone, trying to figure out little puzzles or bashing plastic soldiers against each other. This one day, when I came in that classroom and saw these punks slapping Chase around—I'm a few years older, keep in mind, so I couldn't just punch these little fuckers—I knocked over this easel, covered them in orange and purple paint, and called it an accident. The whole room started crying, just wailing kids from wall to wall, but Chase wasn't so terrified after that. He told me he felt protected, like he could count on somebody—somebody with no reason to judge him. We're so damn different, and I've never had his struggles. Maybe that's part of it, if you really want to know—that I feel guilty. And in this savior role, maybe I'm trying to atone for being the one who isn't cursed."

"That's deep," she said. "I'm impressed."

"And as for proof that I'm a big softie, and a decent human being ... well, for one thing ..." Jack paused and looked over both shoulders. "I have a big secret myself."

"About?"

"About something that could turn you off, being as young as you are."

"Best keep that secret then."

"Or," Jack perked, "you might really love it—"

"Hey, Cupid," the pastor hollered. "If we're going to accomplish our mission, or even start it, we'd better get moving." Jack ignored him, so the pastor shouted. "Jack, have you made *any* arrangements? Have you stockpiled supplies? We'll need an adequate compass, and food high in protein. Almonds, damn it, we need almonds!"

"Amen!" Jack said. "You're right. Let's do it!"

He started to stand up, but Carrie curled her finger, and Jack leaned back in. She whispered, and he nodded. She crouched under the bar and emerged with four shot glasses that brimmed with a neon-green substance. Jack clutched two shots to assist her and gave a troublemaker grin to his new comrades. He walked around the bar without spilling, and she did the same.

"Preacher man," Jack said. "When's the last time you had absinthe?"

The pastor and Pronto slipped the glasses out of Jack's hand, and they all held them to the pendant lights above, apprehensive but curious. "Don't tell anybody," Jack said, "but our bartender smuggled this bottle through customs— back when she was in college—straight from the Czech Republic. It'll make us all very, very brave."

Without a word, Pronto tossed the shot into his mouth, winced, and said, "Another, please." Jack set his glass beside the pastor's and danced a wobbly jig. Carrie refilled Pronto's glass, the pastor retrieved his, and together they toasted the night.

"Godspeed to idiots!" Jack said.

"What?" said the pastor.

"It's something Chase and I used to say, growing up, before we'd do something big," said Jack. "I don't think it means anything, but I've always loved the sound of it."

"Then Godspeed to idiots!" shouted Pronto, and they hoisted absinthe into their throats.

Once they'd finished, Carrie looked around the Lonesome, dimmed the lights, declared last call, and set the remaining absinthe atop the bar, like a dare. Jack went for the door, but Pronto caught his elbow and pointed to the bottle. "Best finish what you started," said Pronto. "I won't accept no quitters in my posse."

**

Chase stood at the base of a sheer rock wall, near the summit of a nameless mountain. Overall, it was a bland, rounded mass, not even a knob, poorly illustrated on hiking maps, as if the cartographer was insufferably bored. And it was just as dull as Chase had hoped. There was no terrific vantage point, no flat grassy expanses for picnicking, nothing that couldn't be found an hour closer to town or to greater effect on higher ridges. The hike was too difficult for rock climbers weighed down with pulleys, ascenders, and bags of carabiners, he thought. No untrained searcher would climb this far for Chase; if trained ones did, they would have done this before, and on those treks they'd surely seen worse than one decomposing man. He could see no paths trod by deer or wild hogs, no bait for hunters, though he knew almost nothing about such things.

In his pocket he found a carrot from the camp, but he was too nervous for eating. Instead, he touched the gun, ran his fingertips along the barrel, and beheld it in the moonlight like a dark harbinger. "Chase Lumpkin," he said, "a real American quitter."

Truth was, Chase liked the idea of the mystery as much as knowing the burden of him would be lifted off his family. There was melancholy romanticism in being the guy who vanished, he thought, as selfish as it sounded.

Maybe his story would become yore, the Ghost Soldier of Lower Appalachia. Maybe conspiracy theorists would think Ash County's sheriff had finally disposed of the town scofflaw—put his bones in a lake, fed him to black bears, buried him deeper than staurolite crystals. More than likely, Chase knew, the town of Cherokee would forget him by Christmas. His Atlanta roots—like the obscure doings of his Scotch-Irish ancestors, the people who'd carved a modern civilization from wilderness here (once the original human occupants were mercilessly driven out), and whose tragedies and dreams and triumphs were nothing now—would wither and vanish. He'd be the troubled young man who was there and then simply was not. And like his battle buddies who didn't come back, the ones he'd ranted about on the help hotline, his name would depreciate and wane, a pretty good guy but touchy subject, another son lost to a tired cause.

10

pon its founding, Cherokee was supposed to have stood for something greater than gold nuggets, faux pioneer cabins, and whiskey-swilling profiteers. The town's forefathers had prided themselves on establishing a mountain outpost that would double as a paean to patriotism. The grand main entry of the historic courthouse was built to face Washington, DC, and for a century and a half, no less than 10 percent of Cherokee's maintenance budget had been earmarked for upkeep of the Civil War cemetery. Municipal leaders across Georgia looked to Cherokee's Memorial Day, Fourth of July, and Veterans Day parades as benchmarks for patriotic small-town revelry. For all these reasons, three consecutive storefronts on Main Street were perpetually festooned with every sort of American paraphernalia: trinkets, Stars and Stripes blue jeans, flag-bedecked plates with matching silverware, dog collars, cat booties, baby hats, and red-white-and-blue boxes of ammunition.

Awash in dazzling moonlight, these storefronts summoned Jack after so much exotic drink. He stepped into the street and breathed the smoky autumn air. He was dying to sing.

At the Lonesome's entrance, Carrie fumbled and dropped her keys. She laughed and slapped Pronto, who was mocking her, on his back. The slap sent Pronto into the street, where he tripped headfirst into pebbly asphalt. The pastor keeled over with maniacal laughter.

"*Enough!*" Jack said. "We need a ceremony. We need to cross the street. We need to get a grip."

"You look like kids," Carrie cried. "It's so *cute!*"

Jack darted across Main, leapfrogged a bollard, and raised his arms. Before him stretched these three American shrines, a grand wall of phosphorescent kitsch. Jack called the others over to marvel with him. "Pastor, I'm feeling inspired," he said. "Could you lead us in some sort of worship, some good-luck sacrament for our journey tonight?"

The pastor tipped back his white-haired head, lost in boozy thought. "For the last time, Jack," he said. "We'll go at first light—*not* tonight."

"Prayers, please!" said Jack. "Or a song!"

"I can't believe what I've done," the pastor said. "I can't believe what you've done *to me*, Bachelor Jack."

"Bachelor *what?*" Pronto said. "Man, who *are* you? You've got me twisted in the mind, knocked out on green drink. I mean, what *was* that shit? I'm not brave right now—I'm confused."

"Please, troops, hush," Jack said, entranced by the store-fronts. "All of these stores are a beautiful omen. *Look* at this. It's no coincidence. *This* is the truth. We're doing the right thing. Now, pastor, I thought you were going to make some prayers?"

Pastor Rutgers waddled over, in front of the others, his back to the middle storefront, and like some crazed and portly maestro he commanded them to group tightly together, shoulder to shoulder, and they obliged, but the pastor was at a loss. He had no sermon for lunatics; they'd done exactly what they shouldn't have done in a time of such high stakes, and his empty thoughts felt like penance. "Jack," he said, "I hate to piss on this parade, but I think your vices have gotten the best of us, and I'm afraid we've jeopardized our morning hunt."

"Preach!" Jack yelled. "Let me worry about logistics."

"Any requests?" the pastor said.

"Preach about unity," Jack said. "And courage! And hiking!"

Everyone fell quiet when the pastor eked out the first verse of "My country, 'tis of thee" in a reckless vibrato. Then all three joined the pastor until their off-key chorus filled the streets of Cherokee, lifting into chilly night. *"Land of the pilgrims' pride ... From every mountainside ... Let freedom ring!"* None of them knew another verse, so they repeated the first a half-dozen times, with Jack emphasizing "mountainside" more with each rendition. The pastor, beaming, waved his hands wildly, until their proximity to the sheriff's department dawned on him, and he called an abrupt stop to the singing.

"The cops are coming—I know it," the pastor whispered. "I'll lose my job, my church, if they lock me up, y'all. We have to go. *Where* do we go?"

Jack tossed his arm over Carrie's shoulder and said, "To the cabin! To *headquarters!*" They hustled to the Corvette, and as Jack let down the convertible top, the trio stacked themselves in the passenger seat, the pastor on bottom and Carrie on top. As they drove, her hair blazed darkly in silver wind. They roared through Cherokee and onto the highway, breaking the speed limit, but no one complained, so caught in the thrill of Jack's machine.

"Shit!" Jack screamed over the wind, a mile from home. "I forgot to close my tab!"

***

Chase dropped his hands and studied the ground. The last task was to find the right bed of rocks to sit and die upon. The plateau was a garden of massive angular boulders, maybe fifty yards wide and equally long, like a place where something great had stood, fractured, and crumbled. It was the right place, he thought.

Naturally, as his heart began to kick, he procrastinated. He squinted to see the streetlight grids of Cherokee and tiny white shimmers of towns in other states. He looked for any indication—any godly sign—that his actions were not the right path, that he was imprudent despite all his planning and introspection. Deep within himself he knew he didn't want to be down there, or anywhere else, but here. He trolled the rock piles and ran his hands along the cliff wall, which bulged overhead with teetering boulders. He thought of his platoon mate from Ohio, his American victim, and how the blood had seeped from the kid's chest and undershirt like the first dab of watercolor paint on paper. Chase violently shook his head to expel such thoughts, running his fingernails along the mountain stone. It was ironic, he realized, that his fixation on violence had ruined his life, led him to this miserable juncture, yet presented just one viable cure: more violence.

For Chase there was a distinct point—a frigid, suburban night—when fighting and the infliction of pain had almost become sport, and he thought of that despicable crossroads now. By his sophomore year in high school, Chase's tragicomic stunts at beer parties had earned him respect among the more popular students. At one winter house party, in the jurisdiction of a rival prep school, Chase acted on a dare and fired a BB gun that knocked a Swisher Sweet cigar from the quarterback's lips. Teammates took umbrage, naturally, and there was a brawl. With an uppercut Chase knocked an older kid out; he ducked and dived to avoid a flurry of other fists. When the cops came he filched a fifth of Johnny Walker and ran to a pay phone, where he called Jack for a ride. Later, in his father's basement, the brothers gulped the burning drink in victory, together. Jack, drunk, kept saying, "You've done me proud, you ignorant bastard." The fight had given Chase confidence in a way that socializing could not. He was finally good at something, he felt, and in the adrenalized brutality of fighting he found a sort of artistry and a platform. Deep into the bottle, swaying in his favorite recliner, he tried to describe that night as being a chunk of Tennessee River Rock, upon which he would build a distinguished career. To a mind so eager for sacrifice, toughness seemed a natural segue to heroism or, at the very least, genuine purpose.

"God, *idiot*," Chase said on the mountain, squeezing his skull with his left hand and knocking the gun against it with the other. "One stupid idea after the next. Year after year. *Why?*"

As deep night set in, Chase said what he thought to be a sinner's prayer, calling the Lord into his heart and asking for a chance at repentance in death. This path, his plight, the war before it, and all before that, he said, was his choosing. But, he said, he did not choose what those things had done to him. He prayed he would not be found, stumbled upon, or otherwise identified—only eulogized, in vague terms, when time killed hope for his return.

A crop of smaller, suitable rocks glowed white. He sat between two jagged stones, a tongue between teeth, away from the base of the cliff, so that he might fall back and face the stars. He filled his magazine. The bullets were fresh, the better for reliable velocity. He had studied how to die, watching horrific online footage and pulling morose forensic data from the bowels of the Cherokee Public Library. The studies warned against chest shots, even for trained marksmen; nervousness could make the shooter miss the thumping heart. Same with a chin shot, which would cause flinching and possibly nonfatal damage to the brain or spinal column. No shot was guaranteed to work, as best he could research, but a cold barrel buried in a warm mouth, pointed upward, seemed the tactic with the best completion rate. The gun itself was older than Chase was comfortable with, but it was all he had left. He'd considered bringing something with more bite, but a shotgun was out of the question for several reasons: He could not afford to buy—and couldn't possibly shoplift—such a big piece, nor could he stomach the idea of total mutilation. He preferred a clean, quick departure. He looked straight up and blew a long nervous sigh.

In the stars Chase could see the winged horse and beyond it an incandescent galaxy. Silently he prayed for his brother and mother and for his grandfather's soul, now reprieved from pancreatic cancer. The terrible power of a weapon in his hand had never seemed so real, so cold. This moment had played in his mind several thousand times, but despite the mental practice he felt paralyzed. He lifted the gun and thought of a river, a fluid progression of intent. "Don't hesitate, Lumpkin," he said. "Just go. Pull. Don't flinch." He leaned over and bit the metal, cocked the barrel slightly upward, closed his eyes, squeezed for one slow second, pulled harder, flinched, and it was done.

Smoke and phlegm and hot blood shot from the edges of his mouth, now closed, and at the back of his skull he felt pressure and instant coldness, a snap of bone, and the fleshy burst of the bullet's exit. Rivulets of blood snaked down the back of his neck and into his shirt. Around the bleeding he could feel the molten, sizzling specks of bullet fragments amid loose tissue. Chase's head snapped back, his eyeballs tugged deep into their sockets, and his tongue burned. But then, confusion: Somehow he still had consciousness, a working mind. He heard the *tink-tink-tink* of the gun as it flipped from his hand onto rocks near his boots. The stars pulsed with fuzzy pink halos. He tasted coppery blood and metallic soot. The force had thrust his head back so hard his shoulder caromed off a stone beside him, and he now lunged forward, and back again, his torso teetering for a moment, before he finally toppled backward. His skull thudded at the cliff's base, popping open his mouth, and hot blood trickled from both sides, down his cheeks, slowly pooling in his earlobes and spilling into his hair. In a moment the bleeding seemed to stem, at least momentarily, as his ears emptied of liquid, and his hearing returned. Besides a swish of wind the night was silent.

Chase knew he was not dead, that he'd failed to execute a simple mission, a total death. He'd lost with methods by which 90 percent of people, he'd read, had succeeded. His chest lifted and fell with frantic breathing, but his arms and legs would not cooperate. He had no tactile capabilities. His training kicked in, despite the circumstances; he rolled the back of his head and neck in dirt and dust to pack the wound, a primitive means to stop from bleeding out. His vision went black, then returned, and black again, then back. He wanted to panic but physically he could not. His throat slowly filled with blood, and he reflexively swallowed, before letting it fill his bulging cheeks. It seemed impossible to drown this way, but he thought that he would try.

A tremendous pounding pain filled his head, and Chase couldn't help but scream, a weak sound that bubbled up and went nowhere, a wet whisper. He wondered if he'd missed the brain entirely, instead catching spine with his errant shot, ironic for a sharpshooter. If he was injured enough to die, he feared death would take many hours or maybe days; he'd heard stories of the Taliban leaving soldiers in states like this for a week before they perished. He watched the leaves and feared the forest was just coming to life, the moonglow of old night a nocturnal cue. As he quit his panicked gargling, he peered into the trees and daunting blackness, wondering what the echo of his gun might have rustled up.

***

The Corvette heaved up the driveway, and the solemnity of the rescue mission draped over Jack and his newfound compadres. The ridgelines above the cabin were sharp against the stars, and Jack wondered what hideous, blood-lusting creatures were roaming those woods now. He parked, and

Carrie slipped onto the streamlined backside of the car, as Pronto stepped into the grass. In the sacred mountain quietude their minds drifted off.

"Here now," said Jack, standing in the yard, uphill from the others, taking a general's posture and fighting wobbles. "We've made headquarters. We survived. We're energized, and comradery is high. Now let's *go!*"

Pronto turned away and stared into the trees. Carrie and Pastor Rutgers said nothing.

"I'm serious," Jack said. "It'll be light in a few hours. We can get a jump on that, can't we?"

The pastor groaned. "Go sleep it off, Jack," he said. "God's in your heart right now, but Lucifer's in your liver—"

"Look, I have to be honest," Pronto said, sounding ashamed. "I'm trying to make sense of what this hill is sayin', but I couldn't find your brother in a parking lot right now."

Jack stomped around the yard for a moment and faked like he was running into the forest before finally conceding that a few hours' rest was in order. "But just a nap," he said. "I'll be back with the nightcap."

To lift the mood Jack raced into the cabin and fetched a grocery sack packed with cold Chuck's Lager. He came back to find the pastor groaning in the yard, on hands and knees. Pronto had lain next to Carrie on the car's trunk and fallen asleep. Jack tossed a beer to the pastor, set one beside Pronto, and mumbled an attempt at romanticism in Carrie's ear. She flashed an approving smile, and Jack led her by the fingertips to his brother's disheveled bedroom.

They embraced near the bed, and Carrie relented to a full kiss. Together they staggered across the room, silently ricocheting off the dresser, waltzing along the wall, and stopping against curtains made bright white by the moon. Jack pinched her jacket at the waist and attempted to snake his other hand upward, but she shivered and latched ahold of his forearm.

"I can't," she said, smiling, although in truth she wanted to. She replaced the smile with an all-business glower. "Seriously, I can't."

"Oh, but why?" pleaded Jack.

"Because I never have."

Jack stepped back, his mouth dropping open, as if beholding royalty. "You're kidding me, right?"

"Do I look like a bullshitter?"

"How old are you?"

"That doesn't matter," she said. "And it's not a church thing either. I'm not all that churchy."

Jack tried to touch her cheek, but she tugged her head aside. She enjoyed seeing him want and not get. Her pit bull, which she'd named Antichrist to spite her mother and religious friends, had used the same expression as a pup when begging for squeak toys. She almost laughed now at the thought of her tall slim figure being one big, succulent squeak toy dangling before this dirtiest of dogs.

"You think I'm going to lose interest by the morning— is that it?" Jack pleaded. "I swear to God I think you're amazing."

"Honestly, no," she said. "I'm just very picky."

Clearly she was serious, and now Jack clutched his face. "Well," he said, "I want to thank you for lowering your standards thus far." He snatched her right hand and kissed the back of it. "And it wouldn't be right for such a lowdown, city-slicker scumbag to deflower you."

Carrie giggled and shook her head, her hair drifting in translucent sheets. Then her smile faded again. "Before we take this any further, I have to tell you something," she said.

Jack gasped.

"Settle down," she said. "I just think you should know that I've been here before, with your brother, a couple years ago. But I guess you could say it was more for charity than anything."

Dropping his head, Jack stepped back. "What do you mean?"

"I came up here because I thought it would help him, really. He seemed like he was dying to talk to someone. We barely kissed."

Jack stepped forward into the moonlight, and his face slackened in astonishment. "I can't tell you how much I respect that."

She held her hand to his chest, stopping the advance. "Now," she said, "what were you going to tell me earlier?"

Leaning back, Jack grinned and hunched his shoulders. "Would you believe that I'm a daddy?"

Now Carrie bent over with laughter, wheezing downward into shaggy carpet. But when Jack said nothing she stood back up, composed. "That's your big bad secret?"

"It is."

"Boy or girl?"

"She's a chubby little girl, a butterball already," he said. "Full brown hair at three months."

"This is interesting," Carrie said. "A total surprise."

"It is."

"What'd you name her?"

Jack flinched, turned away, and ripped off his jacket at the foot of the bed, flopping backward in T-shirt and jeans. "It's late," he said. "We can talk for a minute when the sun comes up, before the rescue."

"Fine," she said. "You stay down there, wild man. And I'll be up here on the pillows."

Jack promised to behave, and he curled at her feet like an obedient bed dog. Without another word they lay still and fell asleep.

***

Chase guessed it was two in the morning, or thereabouts. In the moonlight he could see his watchstrap, but his wrist lay open to the stars, covering the watch face, concealing the answer. The dirty wound at the back of his head no longer felt warm.

He bit his tongue so hard his teeth nearly connected, deeply dimpling the flesh, and that pain was real. He was alive, his vision crisp again, his consciousness unwavering, and his mouth tasted like gun residue smelled. His tongue, warm with new blood, explored the shredded roof of his mouth. The wound swayed and shut like underwater foliage, but the terror of it had subsided, and Chase's mind wandered. The stars shone like pinpricks in a battle helmet. The town lay below in distant white patches.

The thought of living past midnight bothered Chase for another reason: The locals had said that high-elevation temperatures could be arctic this time of year, a climate on par with Connecticut December, but usually only in the dead of night. He wondered if the air was already bitter cold. His hands and feet sent no clues. He did not shiver—or maybe he did.

Chase had another, more upbeat thought: hypothermia. Dying by cold could be a quicker alternative to blood loss, starvation, infection, or assistance from the woods. "You," he whispered to the wind, to the jet stream beyond, "grow some balls, freeze me out."

The constellations shone in odd geometric groupings, cosmic Chinese puzzles. They were slow to reveal the basic patterns Chase strained to recall, Orion and so forth. In his wooziness the stars intermittently seemed eons away and so close he could kiss them. This false nearness excited Chase; he confused the sensation with that of being lifted, with rapture. He turned his face side to side to fully see the cosmic panorama, and the rocks against his skull confirmed that he was grounded like never before.

A searing pain dragged across his face, down his neck, and into the marrow of his chest bones. He let loose a gargling, tormented scream. In a moment the hurt was tolerable, which he thought could be the onset of shock. His eyes began to close against his will.

A rustling in the forest awoke Chase—cracking twigs and shuffling leaves. He screamed, hoarsely, "Stop!"

He strained to lift his head and check the perimeter. He yelled again, a primal sound without words, reflecting his harried voice against the sheer rock face behind him. He paused to breathe. He winced in expectation of a howl, roar, hiss—some desperate animal plea—but all he heard was weight shifting on leaves. He gave his most guttural scream, pushing until his lungs quit.

The woods began to rise, drop, and shake around Chase's base of rocks. He shifted his head and loosed a stone that tumbled down. The footfalls retreated—a slow, downhill parade of weak thumps and breaking branches.

Blood surged in Chase's temples, and he felt the muscles around his ruptured vertebrae throb. He regained his breath and screamed again, not for protection, but in frustration. Though he lay in open wilderness, he felt the onset of claustrophobia, imprisonment within himself.

By the time Chase settled down his teeth were chattering. He convinced himself the visitor was very small, as evidenced by the gingerly patter of its retreat. *A gray squirrel,* he thought. *At worst a fox or two.* He would not sleep again, he knew, until sunlight burned the cold from the woods. He whipped his face from side to side until he broke down, moaning in clouds of breath, "Oh God, oh God, oh *God.*"

11

A deep thud woke Jack. He thought it was the concierge knocking. He kept sleeping, until the thud came again, and he opened his eyes to an atomic headache and mouthful of alkaline. Carrie lay beside him, abundantly clothed. The sight of her made Jack feel better, until he saw the alarm clock beside her and screamed, "*Nine twenty!*"

The outburst roused the slumbering household. Jack darted into the living room, where the pastor shivered on the floor, half-covered with a quilt. "Rutgers—up, *now!*"

The pastor flipped over, revealing that the back of his shirt and pants were wet. He groaned. "I keep falling off the couch."

"Good God, sir," Jack said, hovering. "Did you piss yourself?"

The pastor quickly sat up. "No, Jack, I woke up in the yard, face to the sun," he said. "Presley's still sprawled on your car; I couldn't budge him. This isn't good. This is not an early start."

Jack rubbed his temples. "Can you splash water in Pronto's face while I fire up coffee?" he said. "We need to eat something as fast as possible and go, go, *go*. We're wrecks, man."

In a minute the pastor returned with Pronto, and they both took seats on the couch, slumping over their knees. The pastor guffawed at the sight of Jack drinking a hair-of-the-dog beer, but Pronto extended his hand longingly for a cold can. "Oh, *hell* no," Jack said. "I'm not paying for a tracker with dulled radar." Carrie sauntered in, and Jack begged her to make eggs and toast from stale bread as he darted away to shower. Pronto called him "city bitch" and warned against wearing cologne. Jack could hear that Pronto was still very drunk.

Jack returned quickly, his hair inexplicably loaded with mousse, and he bore thick black dashes under his eyes. The others looked confounded. "It's eye black, like football players use, to deflect sun," Jack said. "I had some in my travel bag, from Falcons training camp. Clearly now, I mean business." Somehow he was in the mood to taunt, which he thought, in turn, would motivate. "I thought you lumberjacks could handle your liquor," he said. "Look at me. I'm ready."

"Why?" the pastor begged, face in his hands. "I mean—*why?*"

Jack winked to Carrie and came into the living room, where he tugged both men up to their feet. "Let's be positive here," Jack said. "We're a few hours behind, but I think we achieved something last night—real unity. I think it will aid us today."

"No," said the pastor, plopping back into the couch. "Last thing I'll be doing today is humping supplies into the hills. I need to rest."

That angered Jack. He turned to Carrie and asked if she was working the evening shift. She said no. "Then you two stay here, in case Chase comes back," said Jack. "You tell him we'll be back soon, but don't move too fast, because he doesn't know you. Make yourselves at home, but leave a little food, because we'll be hungry as bears."

Jack thanked Carrie for cooking and readied two plates with eggs and toast and handed one to Pronto. They ate quickly and gulped several glasses of tap water. Pronto ducked his head under the kitchen faucet, rubbed his wet face, and said he was ready; he laced his boots tight and led Jack into the backyard to gather his bearings. From the pocket of his overalls Pronto produced a long retractable knife and checked its sharpness against his palm. In another pocket he found a compass the size of a gumball.

"I don't rely on this," Pronto said, proudly. "Just use it to verify my intuition."

"The internet gave you intuition?" said Jack.

"No," said Pronto, "practice did."

Jack reached over and cuffed Pronto's shoulder. "Do you think we'll even find my brother?" he said. "Be honest with me. It's all so big up here, and that scares me."

"I've found folks all over these ridges, from here to God's Knuckles," Pronto said. "Keep your head up, eyes open. Now let's move, man."

He led Jack around the shed and through a cluster of pines. They walked twenty yards uphill through pine straw until Pronto halted, dead still, as if struck by some dreadful epiphany. He bent over and gagged. "Fire me, fucker," Pronto said, standing again. "This ain't the time for this. I am too damn blitzed." And then he traipsed back to the cabin and collapsed on the couch, opposite the pastor.

For several minutes Jack stood still in the woods. His impulse was to charge down the mountain, kick in the back door, and punch that quitter Pronto in his nose. But he knew this dilemma was primarily his doing, so he forgave his lightweight allies and focused on his own scant capabilities. Higher on the slope he spotted the round little summit he'd found the first night, and he hoofed hard through the straw, aiming for it. He charged ahead with all his legs could handle, broke a sweat, and let loose a wordless scream. He knew from past fishing trips to be mindful of every S shape in sunny leaves, as it could be a copperhead, and only its curvature would deceive its camouflage. Even the slightest bent straw seized Jack with paranoia, so he decided to take his chances, to keep his head up, pointed almost skyward, as if trying to catch the scent of his vanished kin.

Soon Jack neared the big rock, which was beige and blatant against the forest, like a capsized boat in waves. He wanted the familiarity of that place—any place—and he toddled up to the rock, climbed atop, and prowled around it, gazing into the sunlit valley. It had to be hot down there, he thought, unseasonably hot. He felt lightheaded and weak. He lay back on the rock and closed his eyes. He thought of a time when he and Chase floated down the Chattahoochee on a big raft, both boys in this same relaxed pose, soaking in the summer swelter and what seemed like limitless youth. Then came awful thoughts of Chase in desert fatigues, lying lifeless mere yards away, his skin baked to glazy amber tautness, his emaciated hands reaching out for help that never came. For a minute Jack couldn't purge that image. But soon the heated rock loosened his back, relaxed his frantic head, and he knew he couldn't fight sleep for long. He made a cryptic resolution: *Once I'm rested, fully sober, I'm not going back to the cabin, not going back to civilization, until I find the body.*

***

Chase awoke but did not open his eyes. He squeezed his eyelids shut and saw a kaleidoscope of burgundy amoebas, which made him want to cover his face. When his hands did nothing, he remembered his predicament, and his eyes burst open. The wounds in his mouth and on his neck seemed stiff with thick scabs, but his neck muscles were still responsive, which surprised him. He jerked his head to the left; the sunlight had dotted his vision with purple orbs, now hovering across the valley like alien spacecraft. Tears pooled in his eyes, dripped slowly down his cheeks, toward his ears and lips. He was so parched he caught one with his tongue and felt a tiny relief.

For a second Chase thought he'd entered a realm of glorious light, that maybe he'd died in his sleep and trespassed beyond The Gates. The notion of breaking into heaven nearly made him smile, but his face was too tight. His lips and cheeks felt sunburned, and if not for the earthen scent of mountain dirt and pine, he could've been vacationing at Daytona Beach or Perdido Key. Over his chest he saw the calico of autumn. Closer to him, downslope and to the left, he saw white oaks with wildly twisted branches, the effect of gravity in steep places. The thickest trees had held court there for centuries—for so long the real Cherokee once sat upon their branches. Chase's bones, he thought, would be apt company for such strange trees.

Despite his numbness, hunger gnawed. In Afghanistan, he'd read in survivalist pamphlets how long a man his size could survive without food, but he couldn't recall the answer. Three days? Six? It seemed that dehydration would kill a man first, but he wasn't sure of that, either. He wanted two minutes with the internet. He squinted into cirrus clouds and saw thin white contrails left by southbound planes. Only a few miles of clean mountain air separated bespoke-suit businessmen and cracker-eating kids from this starving soldier.

Then, much lower, Chase heard a sound he knew well: the chug and hush of a helicopter. At first, he nudged his face back and forth with reflexive joy, but he thought for a moment and stilled his head in terror; though his instincts screamed to be noticed, to be pulled out alive, he held his breath, steadied his quivering lips, and waited.

"Don't bank this way," he whispered. "Don't see blood on rocks."

The distant chopper swept into view, flanking the mountain but now drifting toward the valley, gaining altitude. From the body style Chase could tell it wasn't the GBI, or any law enforcement agency, but a smaller chopper with a thin-tube undercarriage meant for either personal or tourism use. That much comforted him. But when the pilot whipped his head away from the instrument panel and toward the mountain, looking down in the curious way a searcher would, Chase felt dizzy and nauseous. He squinted and focused and saw the entire machine had tipped sideways, the pilot leaning with it. He watched for a moment and guessed it wasn't coming within a quarter mile of his location. The ensuing banks and sharp turns were challenges for the machine, simple tests of flying acumen, and the pilot hardly glanced at the ground again. He was joyriding, laughing in silhouette against the sun, some plump rich dude on his day off.

The chopper drifted across the valley, a skiff into the abyss, and soon Chase knew he lay beyond the pilot's sight. The wind began to mask the thwack of blades, and the chopper banked left, vanishing into a backdrop of yellow leaves. "Attaboy," Chase said, resting his woozy head on rocks. It occurred to him his faded camo rendered him invisible, and though he felt desperate and marooned, he knew that, in a way, his clothing was perfect. These desert fatigues had been shipped back when he was shot overseas, but they didn't belong to him, at least not initially, not until he asked for them. They'd been issued to a bucktoothed private second class from South Jersey, Emilio Rodriguez, a sharp guy who'd studied econ in college, dropped out, and then become known for hissing little post-combat tantrums. Some guys, on certain nights, said they hated Rodriguez as much as the Taliban, that he'd become a cancer on the platoon. Chase had last seen Roddy, as they called him, in a chopper.

The fighting in southern Kandahar, a mountain-rimmed flatland of grape rows and poppy fields, had been constant and weird. In places, the vast terrain left soldiers susceptible to attack from long distances, but not one solider from Chase's platoon died in the first five weeks. Still, each night after a firefight, Roddy would weep in the next cot. What Chase mistook for masturbation one night was Roddy curled up and crying. Chase reached over and consolingly squeezed an arm. "What's wrong?"

"Seriously, what are we accomplishing out there?" Roddy said. "Lieutenant says we're casing a compound tomorrow for a Taliban leader he won't name. Nothing based on intel, just a presence patrol. I ask him why, he looks at me and says, 'We're going out there, and we're going to wait until we get shot at.' *Why?* 'So we know where they are—so we can kill them.' That's it. We're fucking pawns here, man. Just puppets."

Chase rolled back onto his cot. "This is war," he said, "and you applied."

Roddy laced his fingers behind his head, crossed his legs, and stared at the metal ceiling. "I'm not going back out tomorrow," he said. "They can AWOL my ass. I'm done. I'm out. Fucking *forget it!*"

The next day Roddy marched to the Humvee as he was told, raised no objections, kept his eyes forward, and went back to the fight. Chase had been watching him and worrying, but he told no one. Some men couldn't handle firefights. Some couldn't bear the mundaneness of routine patrols. They all had the core selfish mission to survive and pretend the weight of living for their families didn't bother them. On some days, they were a company of actors. When Roddy was forced to act as mine sweeper, about a month into his deployment, Chase knew he'd quickly lose his composure and melt down. And he did.

***

A boot to the shoulders, gently nudging. Another boot to his thigh. Jack squinted into sunlight blocked only by Pronto's long face. "He went this way," Pronto said, pointing. "Due north. Get up, bachelor man. Let's go."

Jack touched his cheeks, sunburned and stiff, and he sat up, surprised to see Pastor Rutgers at the base of the rock.

The pastor pulled a water-filled Coca-Cola bottle from a backpack and tossed it to Jack, who said, "You're a godsend, Sherpa." Next the pastor handed Jack an egg sandwich.

"What time you have?" he asked either of them, devouring the sandwich.

"We have a good three hours to get up and back down," Pronto said. "There was a clear path of someone who came north from the cabin within the last week. Someone who broke twigs twice their width. Someone who tiptoed through the straw, who was really moving and ready to get somewhere."

Jack turned the bottle over his head and splashed his face and neck. He drank the warm water until he felt gorged. He looked up to Pronto, who stood at the rock's crest, studying trees and routes. "I like what I'm hearing," Jack said. "You just might earn a bonus."

Without looking back, Pronto said, "I read the note, Jack. I read each line, over and over. I wanna say I'm sorry, because he sounds like a good man, better than I understood before. And it's clear he really loved and admired you, for some reason. But I'll tell you now, just being honest, I don't think we're on a rescue mission. This is all recovery, man. I want to make sure you're prepared for what we'll find."

"I'm a realist," Jack said. "I can handle what I have to."

Pronto stomped off the rock and headed north, toward a stony little ridge, nodding his head for the others to follow, all business. They trod uphill for an hour. With each arduous step, Jack grew prouder of himself. And with Pronto in front of him, he felt shielded, like a skittish kid, from fanged things in the trees and leaves. They came to a small grassy clearing and passed around the water bottle, each trekker still sweating out the previous night.

"Come on," the pastor said. "Which way?"

Pronto turned in slow circles, focused on the branches at chest-level. Jack watched him for a moment, and then stared into his face.

"You're at a loss, aren't you?" Jack said. "You've lost him already?"

"No, this way," Pronto said, changing course to the west. "I think he may have rested here, like us, and moved laterally. I don't really understand, to be honest; it's like he changed course, all abrupt. But I'll figure this out. Just give me a second. And trust me, y'all."

"Oh, we do," said the pastor, in his sweet, oblivious way. "It's an honor to see your ancestry at work here."

At that, Jack accidentally laughed. "You need to upgrade that ancestry," he said, "to a high-speed connection!"

They stomped up musky terrain, around gnarly trees, and through thick masses of glossy-leafed bushes. After a while, Jack caught up to Pronto, nearly tripping him from behind. "You can't shit a bullshitter. Are we lost? Don't lie to me."

"Quiet," said Pronto.

"I'm your employer right now, so tell me the truth."

"Shut up."

The trio cut west in silence.

A quarter mile later, they were deep into a canopied, almost sunless place when Pronto said, "Stop," and started climbing a thin, towering hardwood. He cuffed his boots on the trunk and gained a vantage that seemed impossible to Jack. The tree swayed from the weight of Pronto, waving at the top. From below both men yelled to stop climbing, to avoid dying, and he did. "A real great perspective—and I have an idea where he might have gone," Pronto called down. "Two hills over there's a big outcrop of rocks. I don't recognize it. I could be wrong, but I think I see vultures."

Jack said, "*Vultures?*" and clasped his face. "That's some horrible shit right there."

"Don't see any trails leading there, though," Pronto said. "And I don't know if we can make it before sundown, not with enough time to get our asses back."

"Point the way," Jack yelled. "I'll get there myself!"

Pronto eased himself down, branch to branch. "Hold on, I'll lead," he said. "We'll do what we can do."

They jogged uphill. The slope steepened drastically, forcing them to climb like animals, plunging their fists into the leaves. Pronto lifted the backpack off the pastor and tossed a pair of gloves to Jack. "They'll keep the fangs out your fingers," he smiled. "I can see your city-bitch self about to flip out." Jack obliged and charged ahead but tired quickly, his muscles pinching under his ribs. From behind, Pronto lay hands on Jack's ass and heaved him ahead, and Jack surprised himself by saying nothing to end that assistance. Soon they strayed from the course Pronto had set in his mind, and he shimmied up another tree. "Got it," he said, and the other two trudged on before Pronto reached the ground. When Pronto caught up, he said, dejectedly, "We won't be within a mile of the target before night."

Jack stopped climbing and cuffed his hands on his hips, gasping. "What'd you say?" he asked. "Did you say we should quit?"

"He's right, Jack," the pastor said. "We've got no supplies for camping. It might be warm now, but it gets to freezing before you know it. We've only got an hour before the sun sets, and then trying to get back down, in the dark, will break your ankles."

Clutching a scrawny pine, Jack steadied himself and tried to peer through the forest to the high rocks. He saw nothing. In frustration he ripped the tree from the dirt and held it like a lance. "What happens if I go it alone? What if I take the supplies and make a dash up there right now?"

Pronto and the pastor stepped away, downhill. "Then we'll be searching for two lost brothers tomorrow," the pastor said. "It's not hospitable terrain for you."

Jack cocked back the tree and tossed it downhill, missing Pronto but catching the pastor in the eye with a long branch.

Before Jack could apologize, the pastor grunted, called him a jerk, and checked with his fingers for blood. The dull angry look he gave Jack suggested his passion for the cause was dwindling.

"You're quitters," Jack said. "Go home. *Go the hell home!*"

The pastor turned and tromped down the mountain, Pronto in tow. Jack stood stubborn for a few moments, until he could only occasionally see khaki flashes of the pastor's pants through the trees. A gentle wind pushed in from the valley, and Jack peered up the mountain, trying to spot a tree that might hold his weight through the night or a tall rock the forest beasts couldn't climb. He found neither. So, again, he resorted to screaming his brother's name toward the summit, any summit, casting his voice into sky-bound wind, until he feared his vocal cords would rip.

The screaming reached Pronto and the pastor, halting their descent. They hollered for Jack to come down, to hurry, and without any hope, Jack obliged them, budging reluctantly down the mountain at first, but then galloping. Pronto led the way down, and no one said another word.

***

On his front porch, Chase had loved watching buzzards waft across the valley, but he'd never really seen them, their immense wingspans and hideous turkey faces. Eight of them hovered over his rank grave now. They floated and floated and waited. When one would get brave, Chase worked up the energy to whistle. The shrill sound sent them all fifty feet higher. He would not be pecked to death.

For an hour Chase wondered how he might make himself less perceptible to pilots—and buzzards—to somehow camouflage what he imagined looked like a red cloud behind him. When no ideas came, he closed his eyes, bit his bottom lip, and tried to hold his breath until he died. Against his will his lungs activated. His lips curled back, and his crying was childish, so forceful there was no sound, no breathing, his mouth agape, eyes closed, head wobbling, all in silence. He calmed down and wept in tiny gasps, wishing to rewind time, to have died overseas like bitchy private second class Emilio Rodriguez, clutching an AR15.

The day of his last mission, Roddy had rocked in the rear of the bomb truck near the robots, which were his responsibility. During missions he had become despondent, quiet, and odd. He smiled too much, and especially at Chase, who developed a strange fatherly instinct for Roddy that he'd never felt before. "Back home," Chase had told him, "I've got a brother who was always pretty much a dad for me. I'm feeling like I should return the favor. I'm gonna help you through these months, okay?"

Roddy said nothing. The truck rocked for another mile, then stopped. A sergeant and the driver had noticed churned sand beside the road, little veins of brown in so much beige. Someone else thought they'd seen blue tarp. They stopped the Humvee and dispatched Roddy to investigate. He loaded three charges into his pocket and latched ahold of Chase's arm. "I don't need this fancy robot shit," Roddy said. "The key to finding bombs is eyes, ears, nose—senses, man."

"Get the fuck out there," Chase said.

Roddy gathered his equipment. "You know what? I say fuck it ... if I hit an IED, then I hit an IED."

"Don't touch blue tarps," Chase said. "Keep your head straight. Stop talking crazy."

Roddy resumed his preparations. "I'll mine sweep with my boots, Lumpkin. I'm not going home an amputee. I'm all or nothing." He unlatched the Humvee's back hatch and walked around the vehicle to the spot in question. Abruptly, he stepped back and waved for the truck to reverse about fifty yards, and the platoon sergeant complied. With the truck out of range, Roddy tossed little desert rocks onto the

disheveled dirt, attempting to detonate the device. When
that failed he kicked around for stones, found a flat rock,
and danced in celebration. He lifted the rock and clutched
it in his hand and elbow, Frisbee-like, and then twisted his
torso, warming up like a discus thrower. The sergeant's door
opened and a deep Southern dialect boomed, "Get back from
'air, yeww stewwpid shit!"

Roddy launched the rock anyhow, and the bomb spat a
huge column of sand and rocks. Inside the truck the men
shielded their faces and screamed about Roddy's stupidity.
But the blast had barely budged the truck, and before Chase
looked out the window he knew Roddy had probably
survived. Hands open, as if catching rain, Roddy lay on his
back, his wet teeth reflecting sunshine.

"Is he laughing?" Chase said in the truck. "He is. I'll get
him."

"Hold back," the sergeant said. "We're being watched
now, I think."

Chase cracked his door. "Roddy, you good?"

Roddy said nothing, only smiled. He tapped his chest
and clutched his head, which Chase knew the blast had
likely concussed.

At first, the fast krackle of an AK47 didn't seem real to
Chase. Roddy shivered and grunted. Chase saw errant bullets
hitting the road, all around Roddy, working back toward him.
The bullets bit into his stomach and neck, tossing tiny blood
puddles. When the gunfire subsided, Roddy lay motionless,
his legs bent up. The sergeant hollered to stay clear of the
truck's right windows, and he told the gunner to kneel down
inside the cabin. Chase kicked open the door and leapt out,
using the truck as cover, blindly returning fire toward a low
ridge. The sergeant, barking, ordered Chase back into the
truck. Instead, Chase trained his eyes on the ridge, squatted,
and backed slowly up to where Roddy wheezed in the dust.
He emptied his M16 but saw no one. The gunner, covering

Chase, manned his .50 caliber but did not fire. Chase focused on Roddy, and again he saw war's aftermath, but now in a face too much like his own.

Chase reached down to find a neck pulse but halted; he couldn't bear to touch Roddy's blood. Instead, he latched ahold of Roddy's helmet and yelled into his face, "*Talk.*" Chase dropped the head and clasped the ankles, dragging the big body toward the truck with a few backward heaves. Another corporal sprang from the back, grabbed Roddy's shoulders, and together they hoisted him into the truck. The driver backed up wildly, weaving in reverse, and as the others ripped open gauze packages and unfurled bandage rolls, Chase latched onto Roddy's lower leg, squeezing. It's all he could do to stop himself from reaching back, leaping forward, and punching the body in the face.

12

At the cabin, Pronto and the pastor devised schemes to skip work the next day. Before Pronto tried calling his boss, however, he demanded payment from Jack—in cash. At least two thousand. The pastor said his assistance was pro bono and would remain free until Jack had his brother back. Carrie awoke from a nap, and with a croaking voice cursed herself for sleeping all afternoon.

"I'll have to run to the nearest machine," Jack said to Pronto. "Stay right here." He hustled to his car and drove a mile to a gas station. The machine didn't cooperate, informing Jack his funds were insufficient. He slapped the computer screen and kicked the base. A clerk ordered Jack to leave the premises, so he stormed home at ninety miles per hour, went to the kitchen, and called his bank, whose automated help desk said his checking funds had been depleted.

"That's *impossible*," Jack screamed into his phone. "I must have $15,000 in that account."

An operator came on the line and clicked her computer keys. "Your balance shows *numerous* purchases in Cherokee, Georgia," she said. "The tally I have is more than $17,000. You're borrowing against your credit limit at the moment, and that's being exhausted, too, sir."

Jack hung up and walked into the living room, holding court over the pastor, Pronto, and Carrie. The eye black had smeared into dark clouds across his cheeks, and he looked like a crazed, rotund chimney sweep. "Look, those freeloaders down at the Lonesome—the same people who wouldn't help me yesterday—have apparently sucked me dry, and I'm out of money for now," Jack said, slumping his shoulders. "I know, it's sorry, but I have literally no accessible dollars to my name at the moment. I'm good to pay you, Pronto. I need you on board. I'll be paid at the end of this week, a direct deposit. I could call my agent for money, but he'll tell me to fuck off, because he thinks I'm on the verge of being fired. With what's happened up here, he might be right."

"*You* put yourself in the red," the pastor said. "Not the drinkers. Own up, Jack. Sometimes it's your fault."

Jack hung his head. He was practically bent over now, as if stretching for a race, so slackened by shame.

"What about your savings?" said Pronto. "Can you transfer?"

Jack laughed, but the laughter sounded desperate. "I live too fast—too stupid—for savings accounts. And, frankly, I'm learning the hard way that child support isn't cheap."

"I don't get it," the pastor said. "You're syndicated across the country. A man's earnings are his business, but how could a little country town deplete high-rolling Bachelor Jack?"

"To your earlier point," Jack said, standing up, turning away, "I did much of the depleting myself, but it wasn't just money burned. I bought my mom a house, cash. That poor woman lived in the shadow of my jerk-off dad, and she deserves the best digs in Buckhead. But maybe I should've opted for a rental."

Pronto stood up, and the skin of his forehead tightened. Jack stared into his face, as before, and said, "I know what you're going to say, and just don't."

"We had an agreement," Pronto said.

"How about this," said Jack, "you can keep my car as collateral until I'm able to meet our terms. After tomorrow, go joyriding around the mountains for all I care. If I don't pay you, the 'vette is yours. Gentleman's agreement, right now. Let's shake. Or I'll swear it on that Bible if you want me to."

"That don't do me no good," Pronto said, shaking his head and putting on his jacket. "I don't drive."

"*Come on*," said Jack. "Everybody drives here."

"My license was revoked—permanently—ten years ago by Cherokee's finest," Pronto said. "And up here, man, permanently means for good."

"Fantastic," Jack said, slapping his hips. "How about you just help me then, like the good Christian you are, for another day? Or just a few hours at first light? Don't make me beg, man."

"I missed work, and you said you'd pay me *today*," Pronto shouted. "With our late start, which was my fault, too, I'll take half. But if not, I'm going to need a ride—" before Pronto could finish, Jack threw a fist into his lips, which hardly budged Pronto's head but made a floppy, effeminate explosion of Jack's fingers and wrist. The fleshy little thud made Carrie scream.

Pronto recoiled, his body a cocked weapon, and he launched toward Jack, swung, and missed his face, then grabbed his shoulders and tossed him across the kitchen table and over it, down into a tin wastebasket that jabbed Jack's ribs, leaving him writhing, hissing, and pounding his heels on the floor. Pronto calmly approached his downed opponent, kicked him once in the ribs, and walked out the front door. The pastor knelt to Jack, touched his face, and followed Pronto onto the porch. Jack could hear them bounding down the steps, to the highway. He felt relieved to have them gone, yet desperate to have them back.

Carrie, dumbstruck and doting, finally spoke: "Are you okay?"

"Go."

"That was no way to treat them. They're good people."

"*Go*—please."

"Jack, we're not all going to walk down the highway in the dark. I don't have anywhere to be. I can stay and help you with your strategies. I can call a friend to get these guys."

Jack rolled onto his back and bit his knuckles. He stared into the popcorn ceiling. "Take my keys from the table," he said. "Drive them where they need to be, park the car somewhere safe, and *please* close that goddamn tab."

"Can I get you anything?"

He attempted to push himself up but collapsed. "I just need to think. Keep the car for a while, do whatever. I won't need it where I'm going tomorrow." Jack took several deep breaths, testing his diaphragm for cracked bone. "I need to get serious. I need to put everything I can into this, as soon as the sun comes up. I can do this myself."

Carrie bent down and combed her fingernails through Jack's hair, disappointed in him but not letting on; he was the antithesis of the muscled gearheads she'd dated the past few years and, as such, was refreshing. That Jack wasn't beating Pronto bloody with a pool cue right now could be a sign, Carrie thought, that her tastes were refining, that something more than a quick ticket out of Ash County was at last materializing, that she'd found a man who could make her happy, who could teach her the intricacies of public transit and fine-knit winterwear over plates of Parisian cuisine, or something like that. She flinched and shook her head to expel such selfish thoughts at a time like this. "See you soon," she said, hurrying out the door on tiptoes. "Feel better."

This compassionate side of Carrie was growing on Jack, and in her absence he felt abandoned. Groaning and miserable, he crawled onto the carpet, got to his knees, and like an arthritic St. Bernard lumbered toward the refrigerator. He opened the door, enjoyed a rush of cool air, but then let go, opting to hobble to the back door and stand there with empty hands.

In the Corvette's passenger seat, the pastor sat in Pronto's lap. As Carrie rounded the corner of Marietta Street, nearing downtown, the engine's purr echoed off ancient brick. It was Friday night but late. The streets were empty.

"You both look pooped," Carrie said. "Poor guys."

"I'm too tired to care who sees me on another man's lap," the pastor said. "Just get me to the red truck."

Pronto ran his tongue across teeth-punctured lips. With his fingers he checked his chin for dried blood, and he finally spoke: "When Jack finds that body, I hope it haunts him for the rest of his life."

Carrie parked the car. In silence they all stepped into the street. She barely knew the men but wanted to hold them, to heal them in some human way. Pronto nodded, said nothing, and walked into the night.

Pastor Rutgers limped around the car and briefly hugged Carrie. "He didn't mean that," the pastor said. "It came from frustration, from his not being able to find the missing, for once."

Carrie began to speak but was distracted by footfalls on wood, down the street. She turned to see Deputy McLaren outside the sheriff's department, stepping so hard in fat cop boots she clearly wanted to be noticed.

"Evening," the deputy said, hustling closer. "Since when do you drive such a pretty car, Carrie Matthews? Are tips *that* good these days?"

She said nothing; the pastor looked away, too. The deputy closed in, running fingertips across the dusty hood. She stood a head taller than the squat pastor, looking down on him. But she was basically, physically Carrie's equal. "Where's our favorite radio star?"

"Y'all should be ashamed of yourselves," the pastor said, jabbing his finger at the lawwoman's chin. "Tomorrow you'll have two missing men on your hands. You know that?" He harrumphed and marched, chest puffed like a pigeon, toward the Lonesome Cub and his truck.

"Sorry you feel that way, pastor," the deputy said, peeved by his condemnation but tempering her scorn of a godly man. "Have yourself a great night. And let's save the singin' in the streets for Christmas carols, okay?" McLaren glanced at Carrie's face and arms and asked if she was okay. Carrie said nothing. She opened the door, sat down, and fired up the car. "Just tell me what happened last night, and today," McLaren said. "I want a peaceful resolution to this, like everyone."

"Then do something."

"I wish I could, really," McLaren said. "Can't yet."

"Goodnight, Rhonda," said Carrie. "Tell your drunk cousins their supplier said hello."

"*Wait*," said the deputy, clasping the side-view mirror. "Just tell me what's going on up there with the Lumpkin clan."

Carrie's disappointment now bled toward hostility. She shifted the car into reverse and scowled at McLaren, whose stern face, aglow in moonlight, was starving for details. "I'll try to stop him, as best I can," Carrie said. "But damn it, I think Jack'll seriously attempt a rescue by himself. He couldn't be more stupid to the terrain, or to anything here. We both know he's going to get lost and stranded up there. He doesn't stand a chance."

McLaren stared at the street, as if pouting, an icy sense of ineptitude and cowardice snaking through her. "I'm pretty much hamstrung by the rules, but I'm off the next two days. I'll have more freedom, you know."

Carrie shook her head. "You're a hunter," she said. "Why don't you get off your ass and go hunting?"

"Watch your mouth, girl."

"Of all the decent people in town," Carrie continued, "I'd expect you to be doing everything to bring that boy back alive." She tightened her eyes and leaned forward, weaponizing her glare. "Chase told me one night about the weight he had to carry after the war. Imagine what you'll carry by not doing shit."

Her tone startled McLaren; she dropped her hands and stepped away. Carrie sped toward her cottage on the south side of town, and the deputy watched the taillights shrink and dim like two damning eyes. She turned around and stood there in the street, peering over rooftops, over foothills, over sleepy RV parks with campfires faintly flickering, into the dark crests of mountains beyond.

***

On the mountaintop for a second night, Chase shivered too violently for sleeping, but the arctic air did have attributes: It numbed his aching skull, and the blood that had cooked in the sun behind him did not stink like rotting meat now. He leaned his head up and saw the valley lit gray, another fine night to die.

Something in the woods disrupted Chase's musings— cracking twigs and pinecones. His heart was frantic, but the opportunity excited him. He peered into the woods but heard nothing for a moment. Branches snapped, leaves rustled, and then, again, silence.

Chase wondered if the visitor was apprehensive or if there was no noise at all, only the hallucinatory effects of severe blood loss, starvation, and early phase death. When the woods shivered all at once, however, the visitor was too real, its clean black coat washed silver in moonlight, its clawed paws the size of dinner plates.

***

Around midnight, Jack decided to call his mother and come clean. Or at least he'd give her some shred of truth, something to tide her over, a means to start covering his bases in the advent of the worst-case scenario: that he'd be swallowed by the forest, too. He rubbed ice cubes across his throbbing ribs and worried he would sound injured. He wondered if this would be the last his mother would hear from either of her sons.

In her bed Anne flinched. She didn't understand the sound at first. No one called this late. Then she put down her book and answered: "Yes?"

"Ma, it's Jackie."

Anne sat up, encircling herself with a moat of pillows, a nervous habit. "What is it? You having a late night? Be careful if you're heading out."

"No, staying here," he said. "At the cabin. By myself. I hate to call so late. But we need to talk."

Anne leapt to the hardwood floor, her stomach in free fall. "Where's Chase?"

"Go easy, Ma," Jack said. "No need to jump around. He's just being weird." He could hear his mother's labored breathing.

"You think he's okay?" she said. "Should I come? Yes, I should. I'm coming in the morning, once the fog lifts."

"No," Jack said. "Not necessary. You'd be more a fish out of water than I am. Sit down, on the bed. Relax, and let me tell you something."

Anne obliged, eyeing the ornate golden cross on her bedroom's fireplace mantle. "Go on."

Jack walked to the back of the cabin, took a long slug of water, and breathed until his hands held still. "Mom, I think he's really gone. Left here. Left town. When I was sleeping." Jack inhaled big, and slowly let out. "He could be in Carolina, or California, or Tallahassee by now. Let's hope he has a change of heart, but he might just want to live alone. I found a little note that said as much, that said he didn't want to burden us." He paused for a moment, listening for a berserk reaction but hearing nothing. "Chase said he wants to go off the grid.

He doesn't want us looking for him. With what he's survived already, I don't think we have much to worry about. If anyone can fend for himself, off the grid, Chase can."

Anne pounded her palm against an armoire. "Read it to me!" she said. "I want to hear this, in his words."

Panicking, Jack said, "Shit, Mom," and nothing else. In his nervousness he shuffled his feet and rustled papers on the dining room table. "I was pretty sauced when I found the note, and to be honest, I was so angry, I think I burned the damn thing. Out back, over a barrel."

"Don't lie to me, Jackie."

"I'm not lying."

"Don't do this."

"Don't insult me," Jack said. "I'm up here as crushed as anyone."

"Jesus, Jackie, you're so *thoughtless* sometimes," she said. "That was stupid. I'm calling the police. And I'll get ahold of your father, too. He's got friends at the federal level, with access to databases."

"*Mom*," Jack shouted. "Are you listening? None of that will do any good. I've been fighting the local police all day, pleading with them to do something after I found that note. Chase isn't a criminal. He's not a child, and that's the worst part, for our sake. He has the right to make this choice. They won't expend the resources to find him. I'll elaborate later, but Chase didn't exactly make friends here, either. So I hate to put it like this, but nobody cares, Mom. To them he's a voluntary absconder. He's a ghost, and that's exactly what he wants to be."

She flailed her arms and screamed: "Don't say these cryptic things."

"I'm being a realist," Jack said. "We have to face it."

"I want to come there."

"You'd only slow me down," Jack said. "I hate to put it like that, again, but our best bet is letting me go this alone.

I'll look around some more, find out all that I can, and probably be home soon."

He heard a series of thuds, the choke of his mother's weeping, and the swishing of her slippers on hardwoods. "Sorry, but I have to go," Jack said. "Tomorrow I'll be tying up some loose ends here and maybe going for a hike to clear my head. Just please wish me luck, and know that I appreciate you and always have. You're a selfless, remarkable person, and you always have been. I know that sounds sappy, but I need you to know that, right now, tonight. Okay? I'm going to hang up and get off to bed. Okay? I have to come home soon, to get back to work. Everything will be good. I'll be there with you soon."

Jack's hand trembled as he killed the call to end the sound of his mother's wailing. That harried tone brought him back to the day he'd been most proud of his mother, back twenty years ago when they'd finally arranged a family meeting to discuss the problems of little Chase. Jack had insisted that his brother be present for these talks, which happened to fall on Easter. Their grandfather, Henry, agreed to host in his meticulously restored Tudor. The boys' father arrived on time, still dressed in his church best.

Charles chose a seat at the dinner table's head, three chairs down from Chase, then in sixth grade, with Anne sitting between them. After awkward greetings, they dined on ham and sweet rolls in silence, until Jack nearly made his father choke. "Dad, have you given more thought to buying Chase a shrink?" Jack had said. "Not to be a rat, but he's been cutting school. Like last year. And he's averaging a D in three classes."

Charles picked bits of ham from his teeth with a fingernail and bent up his collar-stays with the other hand. "Funny you should bring that up," he said, looking at Anne. "I've been researching a prep military school up in Virginia. Tom at the office has a nephew there. It's effective. And you love the military, right, Chase? How'd you feel about a school that'll make you a great candidate for any branch you want?"

Chase picked at a roll. "How far is Virginia?" he said.

"Just up the road, and it's a beautiful state," said Charles. "You'll love it. I've got some paperwork started already."

"Oh, come *on*, Dad," Jack said. "This isn't what we discussed. This shit is crazy."

Henry shushed his oldest grandson. "You won't talk to your father like that here." And then he went back to open-mouthed eating.

When Chase clutched both hands over his face, Anne whipped her head toward her ex-husband. Her breathing was heavy, and her jaw jutted like a bulldog's. "This isn't *for* him, Charles," she said. "It's to *export* him, to get rid of him. And you know it."

"She's right, Dad," said Jack. "You're doing this for you—"

Before Jack could say anything else, Chase lunged, snatched a water glass, and launched it sidearm across the table. The glass clipped a tulip in a centerpiece vase, scattering petals, and struck his father's chest with a deep thud, the sound of a kicked cardboard box. Charles grimaced, exhaled, stood up, balled his fist, and then raised it like a mallet, charging at Chase.

His retaliation halted when Anne shot up between them, grabbed Charles by his collar, and slapped him twice across the cheek and nose, unleashing into his face a word-less scream.

Bent over in retreat, with his hands flailing, Charles said he was finished. "Done," he shouted, "absolutely done!" He said Chase wasn't his problem after that day. That Chase was dead to him. Around the table, nobody said a word in response, all of them so eager to have Charles gone. Stomping out the door, Charles made stinging, empty threats about calling Atlanta police on Anne and Child Services on Chase, but he otherwise followed through for the next two decades, cutting ties with his disrespectful and damaged boy.

***

Black bears occasionally made the Atlanta news. Sometimes they ambled into the northern suburbs and devoured a bird feeder, ripped into garbage cans, or ate a Dachshund. In news clips lost bears seemed daffy, almost huggable, so misplaced they were funny. And Chase felt sorry for the bears killed on interstates, their oversized paws no match for semis. He'd taken solace in the same statistic, rehashed in almost every attack article: Across America, black bears kill less than one person on average per year, with all the killings happening not in cushy suburbs but in remote areas where bears didn't understand the encroachment of people. Only two fatal black bear attacks had been recorded in the entire Southeast, and none in the history of Georgia. But elsewhere in the world, Chase knew, these predators had broken through cabin windows to eat elderly men, charged and mauled triathletes, ripped sleeping boys from tents.

The bears that made the news were never half as big as this. It was curious and grumbling, either licking at nothing or tasting the airborne prospects of flesh. Chase held his breath. Despite his desperation, he hoped the animal would pass. The head and neck were so thick, so impossibly stout, he would have felt helpless, even with all his faculties, even with his gun. The ears were not threatening, just rounded nubs atop the great head, giving the illusion of friendliness. Chase didn't know how, exactly, but he could sense the bear was female, maybe foraging in rhododendron for her wayward cubs. It lumbered over sharp stones and halted when it saw Chase's face move. Not ten feet away, the bear cocked its head, crouched, and licked its top lip. It inched toward his head and, slowly, reached out across the rocks, cautious as a child. With its claws it peeled a flat stone flecked with blood from the rock pile, corralling it with a sideways paw. It ran a long tongue across the stone until it shone beige.

Now there was a dilemma: Chase could scream with all his throat had left—and from what little he remembered of Boy Scouts lessons, he knew he might succeed in spooking the bear—but lose a chance at quick death. The bear took another stone, licked it, and Chase feared she might begin with his neck or face, and that he might feel it. He lay still and closed his eyes, trying to think of anything else.

A minute later, he was sure the bear was preparing to feed. Wind pushed in from behind it, and its scent recalled the soiled sleeping bags in Chase's grandfather's shed: leaves and dirt and acrid summer sweat. When the bear nudged Chase's chest with its nose, he couldn't help thrusting open his eyes, and with the burly mass over him, eclipsing all western stars, he inadvertently screamed. Although it was a sickly, almost quiet sound, the bear flinched so quickly its coat rippled, and Chase realized it must have thought the meal of him was already dead. It swatted Chase's midsection and leapt over him, dashing for the cover of larger rocks to Chase's left. The big head peeked over the rocks, looking back, and it seemed younger and more foolish than before. "No!" Chase gasped, unsure of what he meant. "No, no, *no*."

The bear bounded toward the woods, and Chase watched solemnly as it fled. It took one sweeping glance back, licked the air, shivered, and vanished.

In frustration Chase called the bear a pussy. He rolled his head as much as possible to see his chest and stomach, hoping the claws had brought out entrails. From nipples to belly button he'd felt pressure but no pain. Now he saw the paw had torn into the jacket and caused bleeding, but probably not enough for death by bear tonight. The adrenaline ebbed as Chase rested his head, disappointed and contemplative. Did he scream because he wanted to live? Or was living longer his penance for trying to die so young?

Part III

13

At daybreak, Jack awoke to a tiny metallic sound, like a ball-peen hammer on a bowling ball. He went to the front door, hoping to see a deputy.

Carrie had brought him a grease-spotted bag of breakfast. Jack flung open the door, and they kissed in the foyer, in the sun. Still standing, Jack devoured a mound of biscuits and gravy and balled the leftover trash in his hands, laughing, "Now *that's* how a mountain man wakes up!" He traipsed back to the bedroom, returning with muddied boots and a backpack.

She was sitting cross-legged on the dirty carpet. "Do you have a specific goal?" Carrie said. "I mean a goal for today?"

"Your concern," Jack said, "is adorable."

She gave a facial expression both morose and distraught, and to Jack it all looked genuine. "I want to come *with* you," Carrie said, excitedly. "I'm dressed for it. I've hiked this area all my life. And judging by the display here last night with Pronto, I seriously think I'm tougher than you."

"Absolutely not," Jack said.

"*Why* not?"

"Because what sort of asshole would subject you to what I'm doing?" he said. "Just be on standby, please. You'll be a terrific reason for making it back alive."

Carrie deflected the treacly charm in that sentiment, extended her legs in front of her, and stomped her hiking boot. "I'm worried you don't know enough to survive."

Jack moved closer to Carrie and took a knee beside her. He tucked an errant bang behind her ear. "Look, I'm better off today than yesterday, when I was saddled with those two bumblefucks."

She frowned, exaggerating sadness.

"Sorry to talk about a pastor like that," he said. "But I know what to aim for now—a white cliff about three mountains west, or north, or whatever." He laughed; she didn't. "If it comes down to it, I'm not afraid of curling inside a blanket, snoozing for one night up there. I have a big knife, and I found a can of pepper spray in the garage."

"Do you want a gun?" she said. "I can get you any gun you want in an hour."

"Look at my little *arms dealer!*"

"I'm serious," she said. "I have uncles."

"No guns," he said. "They scare the hell out of me. They warped my brother."

She leaned closer. "Swear to me something."

"Sure."

"Swear that you'll tell me all about Chase sometime."

Turning away, Jack said, "It's a little early for 'sometime,' isn't it?"

"You're a jerk." Carrie got up and went toward the door.

Jack slinked around the foyer and stood in front of her, lifting up her chin with his index finger. "I'm sorry to talk like that, really," he said. "Bad habits die hard. I've just always hated the feeling of being pinned down. But I think that little kid in me is finally growing up."

She squeezed his wrist. "I don't really know—and don't really care—who you are in the city," she said. "But I see someone who could use a little balance."

"And *that's* what I'm afraid of," Jack said. "Balance takes my edge away."

"Excuse me?"

"Nothing," he said. "It's that child, that gibberish. Sorry. But anyway, Chase can tell you all about him himself."

They stood still for a contemplative moment as the sunrise lit the living room. Jack shook his wrist free, pulled his hand down to her ribs. "I need to get moving," he said. "I'll walk you out." He touched the small of her back and gently pushed. "I'll call tonight, or in the morning." He massaged his fingers in tiny circles beneath her waistline, awed by the vitality of her youth. "Keep the car as long as you'd like today, but be gentle. You're insured, right?" She hunched her shoulders to make him wonder; she was enjoying his touch. "I'm kidding," he said. "Hell, go for a mountain drive. Keep the damn car. Enjoy your day off." Jack thanked her for the breakfast, and they kissed on the porch beneath a slanted eve. Then she danced down the stairs.

"Is there a chance my phone will work up there?" Jack said. "In case I find something promising and need a hospital helicopter to come get us?"

Carrie took two slow steps toward the driveway. "If you won't let me help you, I recommend you wait until tomorrow," she said. "Wait for the pastor and Pronto. You'll be safer if you make amends and go together. Last thing they'll do is get lost."

"That's ridiculous," he said. "I can't even afford that—"

"Plus," she pleaded, "it's the only way you'd lug someone back if you need to. Have you even thought of that?"

Jack rubbed his face. "How about this," he said. "If you don't hear from me by tomorrow, call the sheriff's department and say your hiker friend is lost in the woods. It's what I should have done in the first place, but I was clueless. I'll do everything I can to get back and call you, unless I find Chase. In which case I'll need you to call out the cavalry."

"You want me to lie to the sheriff's department?"

"It's not illegal to fret about a boyfriend lost in the woods."

"I'll do it," she said. "Boyfriend."

Now Jack was petrified but laughing, a strange diaphragmatic release that felt so good, like a relief valve hissing. It'd been days since his laughter was so genuine, and eons since talking to a woman filled him with this benign, crackling sort of chemistry. "Call me whatever you want," he said. "Just demand those bastards put a chopper in the air if you don't hear from me." He blew a kiss and winked and walked inside the cabin.

***

McLaren lived on the outskirts of Cherokee, near the highway, in a 1911 bungalow she'd restored by hand, with occasional assistance from her husband and retired-cop father-in-law. For years she'd resided in a pine-shaded cabin in the woods—a vastly upgraded dwelling from that of her miserable youth but equally remote—until the long commute of muddy roads and blind curves became too much for her banker husband. The bungalow had potential, and they knew its land would fetch a high price when the scenic hills around Cherokee filled with second-home seekers from Atlanta. For two years McLaren had toiled within these walls, scraping and lacquering the heart-pine floors to a gleam, ripping out paneling, and transforming the old porch into a handsome brick arrangement, with views of distant mountains near Big Canoe. Friends had called the resulting home "magazine worthy," its owner's arms "chiseled" by hard labor; McLaren would smile in knowing both compliments were triumphs over the ravages of poverty, the dark past that lurked quietly behind her, shadowed and waiting, like a pack of famished coyotes.

In her kitchen McLaren stood straight and ready, admiring the home's craftsmanship and sipping local coffee. The window above the kitchen sink had the best view, capturing lumpy calico mountains in the way a painter would frame them. McLaren often found herself standing there before her husband and daughter awoke. She'd watch dawn unveil the forest, longing to be out there, shin deep in tangles of ferns, exploring gullies and lost caves like she'd done with her brother. She yearned to be free of societal duties, at the mercy of the wilderness.

"It's cold, dummy."

That broke McLaren's trance. "What?" she said.

She glanced back and let her eyes adjust from the bright backcountry to a kitchen of shadows. "It's not that cold out," she said. "Not yet."

Her husband, Marcus, blond, soft, and studious, bit his lip. "Your coffee, I mean," he said. His lips shined with balm, ready for talking all day behind a desk. "I've sat here for two minutes, watching all the steam rise off, and you haven't even tried it. It's Costa Rican grade, babe, they said. Grown by some college students up the road."

"Ah, yeah." McLaren inspected her cup and downed a gulp. "It's cold, but great."

Marcus wore a striped gray suit, his salty beard precisely shaven and hair backswept. At his bank that day, he'd have to meet with four clients about their underwater mortgages. He'd consulted with three families wrestling similar dilemmas the day before; Cherokee had not rebounded from the Great Recession like larger economies, and half the town was pinned to homes they couldn't leave until the carpet factories started hiring again—resulting in enough paperwork that Marcus was forced to work one Saturday per month. The misery of good people, something Marcus had dealt with every working day for several years now, had begun to weigh on him, to the point it infected his dreams; lately he'd been waking up clammy, shaken by nightmares of hollow-eyed folks literally wearing blue collars inside burning homes, unable to force open windows and doors. Seeing the slumbering chest of McLaren next to him—where she'd been for twenty years, since they crossed paths at Cherokee Community College, he studying accounting and she criminal justice—was usually an immediate wee-hour elixir for Marcus. Seeing McLaren now, strangely agitated and uptight for her day off, Marcus thought himself lucky to be sharing this charming old home with a woman so dependable, honest, and naturally inclined to be a wonderful mother. Beyond that, Marcus cherished how McLaren had forgiven him for constantly fucking his boss a decade ago— and how she *didn't* shoot dead a respected Cherokee bank vice president in the motel bed. That required restraint and honor. And a year of couples therapy.

Marcus plunged his skinny hand into a Halloween bucket and bit into a mini candy bar. In the morning light his wife's eyes still had that sharp, rugged fierceness. Her physique was still refined, he thought, like sportswear models and show ponies at the Ash County Fair, which prompted him, without planning it, to reach over and cup her right ass cheek. He squeezed and rubbed. Without looking back, she snatched his hand in a blink and tossed the intrusive member across the kitchen. "What are your plans today?" he said, smirking, recovering. "Besides helping me with raking all these damn leaves?"

McLaren vacantly touched his shoulder and turned back to the window. Her eyes searched the high country again. She could hardly look at her husband without welling up with cold guilt, a shameful feeling borne of having almost no physical attraction to him anymore. After so many years, McLaren still adored her husband's perky disposition and chipper voice; and she adamantly wished her ovarian eggs were as receptive to his seed as they once had been, that her insides had persevered into her thirties as well as her exterior, that she could gift them both the baseball practices and other boy things they pined for. But she was so repulsed by the thought of even kissing Marcus, her glimpses at other men had terrified her as being preludes to real adultery. Though she tried not to look, she found Cherokee's latest rookie firemen crop especially appealing. "I can rake those leaves tomorrow," she said finally. "They'll be there." She turned to face her man. "Today, I was thinking of hunting. Or at least scouting some sites, up north of town. I'm just kind of itching to get out there in the woods." She looked back out the window, squinting.

His mouth full of chocolate, Marcus looped a leather backpack strap over his shoulder and wrested car keys from the clutter inside. "How are your hands?" he said. "They healed up yet?"

She didn't look down. "Maybe taxidermy isn't my thing."

"It's funny, you and a hobby like that," he said. "You'll bleed for a little rodent and go blast a buck through the heart."

"Not much meat on a chipmunk, Marcus."

"It's kind of like the prettiest girl on campus," he said, "going off and becoming a sheriff's deputy." He moved close again.

"Life's ironic, I guess," she said, her back stiffening. "I think you've had enough caffeine."

"I have a little time."

"Shouldn't you get moving?" she said. "Because I need to. All those pretty mountains out there, calling my name."

"That's my hard-ass hunter chick," he said. "Getting a jump on that freezer full of deer meat."

"Yep."

"Who else is off?"

"Nobody, that I know of," McLaren said. "It'll just be me, how I like it."

Marcus whipped her around and jabbed her lips with his. She continued her clockwise revolution back to the window.

"Won't be anything too intense," she said. "Just poking around, seeing what's out there."

"Right," he said, quickly losing interest, hustling to the door. He glanced back and was struck by the crisp morning glow enveloping McLaren, illuminating his woman, which he thought was the manifestation of her piousness. "Enjoy yourself, Danielle Crockett," he said. "Don't get lost up there."

***

"Fresh. Warm. Socks."

Jack was talking to himself, nervously repeating his most basic needs and fishing for them around the cabin. He put on three pairs of pure-white socks and squeezed his foot into Chase's oversized boots. The mud on them was too tan for Georgia, so he thought it had to be the mud of war. The calf-high boots, he realized, could ward off copperhead bites. "You're welcome," he said to his legs. While fetching his backpack he had another idea, and he walked to the kitchen. He would lug some booze with him, but only as a make-shift painkiller should he find Chase injured. He rummaged through the cabinets for something stronger than beer but found nothing. He unzipped the backpack and counted as many Chuck's as he thought would fit. Four beers, he decided, would suffice. "Okay," he amended, "six beers." He emptied the last slices of a wheat-bread loaf into the garbage and used the plastic sleeve to hold the beer and two handfuls of ice. He wrapped that within a T-shirt and stuffed it all into the backpack, along with two sandwiches, a small bag of pretzels, trail mix, two apples, a canteen of filtered water, and a boxed MRE he'd found in the garage. He chuckled at the thought of eating soldier food in soldier clothes in a fake solider march.

Prepared but apprehensive, Jack toured the home once more, in search of some other weapon to complement the knife and pepper spray. Something simple, something quiet, something he could operate with a swing of his hand. In the garage he opened a rusted toolbox and hollered, "Jackpot!" upon finding a hatchet. Beneath it lay three bungee cords, still in the package. He packed the hatchet, bungee cords, and a screwdriver into the backpack and started to turn off all the lights but opted to leave them on, a bluff to ward off meth-addled backcountry burglars. As a last step, he hustled to the bathroom to urinate, and it occurred to him he should search the medicine cabinets, which unveiled gauze packets, a half-bottle of peroxide, stretchable bandage wrap, and medicines galore: aspirin, antibiotics, Neosporin, even expired narcotics of some sort. He crammed the loot into his bulging backpack, took one last look around the living room, locked the front door, the back door, and set off across the yard, feeling dignified but unmoored.

By now the first stretch of woods seemed familiar, this steep zone of folly and failure. In the leaves and duff Jack could see the path the trio had trod the night before. It invigorated him to know, for once, which direction to take. And in the real army boots he welcomed copperheads, which he hoped to stomp into mash to exert his human might and feign some modicum of power. The sky seemed a cleaner, wintrier blue. Jack watched the thick forest and felt both fear and love; the place was too beautiful to hate. In the valley he looked for the outline of Cherokee, where Carrie had gone, but in the bright day the town was not there.

***

McLaren rode high into the mountains in her vintage Jeep Wrangler, stirring white dust. Near her former cabin she veered onto a logging road, which had regressed that summer into vaguely striped paths. She recalled the morning, still woozy and deflated, when she and Marcus had driven home Sky, their three-day-old daughter, on this same inhospitable corridor. Marcus' knuckles were white on the wheel, as she hovered paranoid over the car seat as added protection should their Jeep hit a rut and roll. Now the Jeep maneuvered over logs and wind-broken branches until McLaren had the vantage she'd been hoping for: a view across the valley to the far slope where Chase's cabin sat. She parked in a clearing, unpacked her muzzleloader, locked the Jeep, and walked away. A few minutes later she returned to the vehicle. The season for primitive weapons like muzzleloaders had passed. It wasn't like her to err like that; her mind was preoccupied, shaken by the notion of a sibling in grave distress. She swapped that gun for a rifle, a beautiful Remington with a polished walnut stock, and again locked the vehicle. She loaded one bullet and climbed a pile of rocks.

These mountain vistas comforted McLaren, lending with crisp leaves and infinite ridges something that felt like an embrace. She'd bragged of knowing each crevasse, each foot-hill, each slithering stream for ten square miles. A long flat rock at the end of the pile offered the perfect seat for strat-egizing. She charted in her mind possible routes the Lumpkin brothers could have taken from the home. Through her scope the mountains were short and bright. In the vicinity of Chase's home, she looked for signs of life—a wisp of smoke, a drunken sunbather on the roof—but saw nothing. Holding out her finger and thumb, she estimated a mile's distance and extended that seven times in several directions, beginning at the Lumpkin home. Seven miles seemed a good approxima-tion of a novice hiker's best uphill day, even at a desperate pace. McLaren breathed deep and concentrated, trying to reconcile the vastness of her surroundings, before obliging her one vile habit. She tucked a slim pinch of chew into her lip, so far removed from town her city-bred man had no chance of catching her again. Her cheek warmed and stung. She grew lightheaded but satisfied. She fired off a dollop of minty spit.

The makeshift ruler showed several potential destina-tions: plenty of remote little nests where a down man might choose to die. She saw the gray blips of distant farmhouses, a leaning horse barn in the valley's middle distance, a craggy outcropping on a peak she didn't recognize. She stood up, bowed her head, and said a prayer.

Bulbous clouds dragged ship-shaped shadows across Cherokee, toward the immense, hazy ridges of North Carolina. McLaren felt a small intuitive nudge. She needed to be at lower altitudes, in the thick of the valley, her gut or God was telling her. She went to hop off the rock and tromp downhill but halted. Doubting that her phone would work, she nonetheless dialed her husband's direct line at the bank, hoping to tell him she might be out later than expected, that she might have found a deer trail too promising not to follow, that if it came down to it, she'd walk home beside the river and leave her Jeep in the safe, remote place it was parked. But her phone had no service.

She checked the Jeep again, locking spare bullets in the glove box, pocketing an extra rifle cartridge, and then she jogged downhill, to the rural flats.

***

Jack gnawed his turkey sandwich and eyed the cloth-wrapped beers. He zipped his backpack to keep himself from drinking one, and he gulped what he guessed was a healthy amount of water. For the next leg, he would try to trace the general direction Pronto had traveled. "One foot before the other," he said, hoofing upward, "and if shit hits the fan, climb a tree and scream." He dug the toes of his boots into loose soil. His legs burned, his mind raced with lurid scenarios, but he kept going. Soon he broke a sweat, shed his jacket, and wrapped the arms of it around his waist. After an hour he felt substantially higher on the mountain, the cooler air like peppermint breath. He guessed it was still early afternoon, and in case he was wrong he didn't glimpse his watch.

Twenty more minutes passed with Jack grunting and climbing and bitching at his burning legs until he had to stop. He twirled helplessly, contemplating each direction. He was lost in a level shelf of dense woods, unsure which direction led to the peak. Shedding his backpack, he found a sturdy pine and lumbered up it, his hands pinched by flaky bark. The dread returned; Jack knew he'd picked the right tree to climb, even before he could see beyond neighboring pines. He spotted the place, the rocky summit, where Pronto's intuition had pointed, and once he saw it he knew he'd have to be there as soon as possible, despite what could be there. He climbed higher, until the wobbling tree could take no more of him.

From the top he saw a different angle of the same rock formation. It seemed more beige than yesterday. A few yards downslope from there, he spotted a clearing, a long brown rivulet among the foliage, like the path of a short-lived forest fire. Reaching that would put Jack within a quarter mile of his goal, and from there, passage would be easy. Now he had a real plan, and he felt wise to the wilderness.

Climbing down, he caught his elbow on the sharp nub of a broken branch, and he bled, yelping and cussing but quickly shimmying all the way down. The blood had webbed to his fingers before he noticed, and while clinging to the tree he frantically licked his arm to stem the trickle. By the time he reached the ground, his cheeks and nose were smeared red. He could feel the blood drying across his face, stiffening his skin. Surely it would put him on the radar of hungry bears, he thought, so he dumped half his remaining water over his face and arms, before realizing the stupidity in that. He cracked a beer and doused himself until froth and blood congealed on his skin. He sponged it away with his shirt, removing everything but the dull copper smell, the aroma of bar fights. He downed the last gulp of lager, tossed the can aside, and set off for the clearing.

***

Beside a creek McLaren eyed higher elevations through her scope. For a moment she thought she'd made a mistake, that she should've rented a helicopter from the parks service, privately, and paid a pilot to swoop around these valleys. But the sheriff, she knew, would fire her for a protocol violation so severe, despite her tenure. And McLaren wasn't losing her job over some city punk and his rich brother. She'd give a day to this cause, but not her career. Her daughter would enjoy indulgent beach vacations, meaty stews, and the softness of firsthand clothing—period. She hiked into a sunny meadow.

A rescue didn't seem likely. She expected to recover one body, and she tried to fortify her mind to that concept. Finding two bodies would haunt her as a personal failure. She barreled back into a dense gathering of sycamores and crossed the creek at a shallow bend, tiptoeing in steel-toed boots on wet stones, over swirling pools, and along the idle banks where brown trout rest. If her memory served, this was the side of Upland Creek the Lumpkin cabin was on, about ten miles south. From years of fishing the creek she knew this was the shallowest stretch, the long bend before its meandering jaunt through town. It was five feet deep, at least, on the other side of Cherokee. Under no circumstances could she envision either Lumpkin brother swimming across the creek in October. And the creek bisected the county. So they were somewhere on this side of Ash County, with her. She felt closer already.

The farther west McLaren went, the steeper the terrain, and she realized she was climbing a mountain without really aiming to yet. She unzipped her jacket to let cool wind across her chest. The trees thinned out, and she stepped into the yard of an old hand-hewn log cabin. Moss had climbed the foundation and coated its thick base logs. The aluminum roof was covered in leaves and branches that hadn't fallen naturally. A tall gruff man, wearing a camouflage T-shirt and jeans, was tending an outspread deer carcass, knifing out the innards. The animal's face—stupefied by death, tongue dangling—watched McLaren. The sight of pink flesh made her hungry.

McLaren coughed as softly as she could to announce herself without startling the man. When the man didn't respond, she coughed louder, sniffed her nose, stomped her boot, and finally the man spun around to face her, the jack-knife in his outstretched hand.

"Afternoon," McLaren said.

The man exhaled, cracked a smile. "Sweet Jesus, honey. I'd have just about stabbed you if you'd been closer."

McLaren chuckled, but not in a way that invited him closer. "My lucky day then," she said. "I come in peace."

The man half-smiled. To McLaren he seemed anxious.

"Won't bug you long," McLaren said, spitting on leaves. "I've got ground to cover."

"You up here all alone, hon?"

"Probably not," she said. "And I only let my husband call me that. So stop."

The man sensed something in her tone and stared, awkward and dumb, into her camouflage. "If you're DNR, I've got permits for everything," the man said. "Killed this with a rifle, way up the mountain. It's legal." He touched the dead animal's face. "I'm nowhere near my antlerless limit, neither."

"Not about that," McLaren said. "I am a deputy, but I'm not on duty, and that deer's none of my concern anyhow." She peered around the man to the carcass. "But I've got to say, from one hunter to another, it's obvious that doe's been shot through with an arrow. I don't appreciate you lying to my face."

The man plunged the blade into a block of wood. "Damn bullets is expensive," he said. "You *feel* me?"

With roaming eyes McLaren searched the property for trails, paths that mountain wanderers might have taken. "You seen anybody pass through here lately?" she said. "Anyone who seemed lost in the mountains, like they belonged in Atlanta?"

The man recoiled his lips and rolled his eyes, an exaggerated state of contemplation. "Naw, ma'am," he said. "Can't say so."

"Heard anything suspicious?"

Same facial expression; same response.

"All right, then," McLaren said, deflating. "I think some pals of mine might've gotten off track while deer hunting up here. Couple of city guys, friends of my husband's family. Haven't heard from them in a while. If you see a younger guy—or two guys, one tall, the other not—let them know a deputy is out here trying to find them, to help them."

"You got a name?" the man said.

That rubbed McLaren wrong. "They'll know it's me," she said. "Just make sure you say deputy, and specify that I'm a woman, obviously. Whatever you do, don't say sheriff. You hear me?"

"Not a problem," the man said.

McLaren nodded and started to hike away but stopped. "By chance, you have any spare deer jerky?" she said. "I brought a few bucks I can trade you for. I didn't pack much protein. Looks like I'll be tracking awhile."

The request seemed to bother the man. McLaren saw his eyes jerk around as he nodded and ducked into the cabin. In a minute he returned, wrapping salted meat in tinfoil, squeezing it tight, and then tossing the package to McLaren. "Come to think of it, when I was getting the deer this meat come off of, I was up higher than I usually have to go," the man said. "This was, what, Thursday? Yeah, that's right. Maybe Thursday morning, whichever day was sunny and cold. So I hear what I think is my mind fucking with me, you know, and I ignore it. Thought maybe I hadn't had enough breakfast. But then it happens again and again. Just a horrible, wicked sound, like a banshee scream. I tried for two hours to find the source. I finally got too hungry and gave up."

"Okay," said McLaren, tensing her shoulders. "*Okay?*"

"Okay, what?"

"Well," McLaren said, "go on."

"I'll tell you, deputy, I'm 90 percent sure the voice was a man, but I haven't ruled out an injured mountain lion, maybe a bear cub, or some sort of—"

"Point the way," McLaren said. "Be precise."

The man turned his thick shoulders. "I can't promise it was anything worth investigating, but it came from that general area, where the trees fall back and that mountain juts up. A good view from up there, at very least, if you go. I've camped near there before, years ago."

McLaren nodded and took a few steps uphill, squinting skeptically at the distant summit. She opened the package, smelled its contents, and stuffed a handful into her mouth. "What do I owe you for the jerky?"

"Nah," the man said. "Repay me by keeping the arrow a secret."

"How about you do me one more favor?" McLaren unscrewed her canteen, drank from it, and swallowed the meat. "Cut out all the marijuana plants around this property, add them to the pile in your shed, and burn the whole supply. What you don't cut down, the helicopter rangers will spot tomorrow. They'll know exactly where to look. You feel me?"

The man dropped his head. "Yes, ma'am."

"And you never saw me today, okay? No deputy was here, if anyone but a lost man asks."

"Never saw nothing," the man said.

"Good," said McLaren, turning uphill.

"Sounds like we both have secrets."

McLaren smiled, chewed another wad of meat, and said, "It's a good thing these mountains don't rat."

***

Jack had wiped himself clean, he was sure of it, but the smell of beer stoked his craving for more. As he hoofed over roots and rocks and around the evergreen underbrush he slapped his face to distract himself. The pain angered him, and the anger made him resolute, even cocky; and now he thought he could forget the beer and summit the mountain within the hour.

In a minute he was breathless and mortal again. He bent over and latched hands on his knees, spitting into the soil, gasping. The bags beneath his eyes cradled sweat. For motivation, he tried to concentrate on some vague image of Chase, younger, in trouble; instead he remembered a phone call on the day, in his estimation, it'd all started to go really, irrevocably wrong: when Chase called Jack in Miami to ask how his first peon radio job was going—and suddenly dropped the bombshell that he was committed to the army and headed to Fort Benning for basic in two weeks. "Wait, man, *what?*" Jack had shouted into the phone that day. He reminded Chase how taking orders wasn't exactly his strong suit, suggesting he channel his energy into some other dangerous job. Like forestry. Or policing. Or diving from burning trucks as a stuntman. Chase could prove his manhood and value to society, his brother said, in less internally damaging ways.

"It's a done deal, Jack, and I think it'll be good for me," Chase said. "I can't just fall in line and do a daily job. Not without doing this first."

"Look," said Jack, "you don't need the military to get your head right. You're not all that different. The more people I meet out here in the real world, the more I know that everybody is insane. Nobody is normal. There is no normal. Anyone you think is normal is just a good actor. My high-powered station manager likes to cry in the office bathroom.

Can you *believe* that? Dries his tears with the sleeves of
Armani suits, a total con artist. Everybody can hear him, and
when ratings dive, they secretly call him Wally Wet Sleeves.
Now, sure, you're at an elevated degree of abnormal, a real
batshit macho man sometimes. But it's nothing a shrink
can't mend. I've been saying that for years, and nobody's
listening but Mom."

"I'm going, Jack. The ink's dry. That's all there is to it."

"And besides," Jack said, ignoring his brother, "there's
no way I can intervene and save your ass from 10,000 miles
away."

"It's my calling."

"It's risky."

"It's my *calling*."

"Goddamn it, Chase. You don't know what you're doing.
I understand your motivations, and I'm proud to call you
brother, but you're jumping right into the teeth of really
harsh shit."

Jack flinched as he heard Chase hang up.

Just one short call came from Chase's time at basic
training, during which he told Jack that drill sergeants were
actually fond of a no-nonsense bulldog like him. It was the
last time the brothers spoke before deployment, before Jack
started volleying naughty emails across the world to cheer
Chase up, before Chase's battle buddies started falling. On
the mountain, Jack struggled to comprehend warfare, to
imagine being his brother in combat, realizing his morbid
destiny. Once Jack had failed as always to do so, he laughed
in thinking that modern war must be a cakewalk, at least
compared to mountain treks for overweight lushes with
irrational fears of nature.

At this altitude, Jack noticed, the trees were knotted,
misshapen. The sunlight seemed clean and sacred, but the
place felt forbidden, unnerving and alien in its silence. "Focus,
focus," Jack said. "Get your head right. Get fucking mad."

He tromped over stones and kicked branches, convinced he was beyond the climbing capabilities of rattlesnakes but sending warning vibrations if not. With his dry tongue and lips he whistled as loudly as he could. The more noise the better, he thought. To his right he saw a deep and rippled valley and a thin blue seam where the sky met foothills. He squinted as he walked, and beyond the farthest hills he saw, for an instant, a gold flicker off the ornate crown of the One Atlantic Center skyscraper in Midtown Atlanta, a fleeting transmission from another life.

He used small stones to stairstep around and over a high mossy ledge. He pushed himself into a standing position, careful not to place his hands close to crevasses, and suddenly he could see the rim of the clearing. A few dozen yards away, this grassy scar of mountainside was no longer than two football fields, studded with rocks bleached white by unimpeded sun. Jack cracked his fingers to alleviate the numbness in them. Beyond the clearing, only a thick bank of pines separated him from the rocky summit.

Despite the fatigue in his thighs and feet, despite his thirst, Jack held the straps of his backpack tight, and he started to run. He kicked up slate and puddled rain. Wind pushed back his hair, and in that invigorating moment he felt tethered to nothing, not the earth, gravity, or his physical self. He felt gigantic. He leapt over stones and heaved up to the edge of the clearing, which lay before him now like the manicured meadows of Piedmont Park. Hands cupped around his mouth, he screamed his brother's name until his voice cracked and quit. The desperate tenor of his yelping sounded like Anne when she was distraught, Jack realized, and he felt duly motivated to bring Chase back for her, to complete the rescue they'd been attempting for more than twenty years. Intuitively, Jack knew he was almost there, that he'd almost done it, and his elation trumped thoughts of what might be beyond the trees. He shouted for Chase again, louder this time, and then again. It was a distress call and joyful outburst in the same breath, a distinctly boyish sound.

14

McLaren stopped climbing for a moment and sat down on a felled sugar maple. The tree, seared at its top, had clearly been struck by lightning. It must have plummeted like a blazing matchstick into the duff. Nothing else had caught fire around it, McLaren noticed, because the summer had been so tropically wet. She wondered if she might lift the tree to unearth some pool of captured rain. The jerky had dried her mouth, and her canteen had only three or four more swallows. Her husband usually begged her to better prepare for these stubborn mountain treks, but his haste to get to work—combined with his typical morning horniness—had distracted him. As a last resort she could turn back to the creek, but she wanted to keep climbing, to reach a respectable height by 4 p.m., allowing herself two hours to bound down the mountain, cross the creek, and tear away in her truck before nightfall. By not turning back, she knew, she was putting herself at risk, and for no reason but to help these interlopers from the city. The thought first struck her then: She might sleep up here tonight, well-armed and enraptured by the nocturnal mountain sounds of her girlhood, because she might not be able to stop looking. If she found nothing by noon tomorrow, she promised herself, she would retreat. En route home she would raid the scofflaw's cabin for all the food and water she wanted. When she didn't come home tonight, Marcus would think she downed her buck and called in an underling from the sheriff's department who owned an ATV to help her haul the carcass out; or he'd assume she caught a fresh deer trail and could not abandon it. That had happened the previous deer season and several seasons before that, and each time she'd built a nest of branches and slept soundly in the pines. McLaren almost never came home without a kill, and all winter they feasted on deer steaks at no cost to the family. The McLarens were very carnivorous in winter.

A falcon glided down to investigate her, leaning sideways to slow itself midair. McLaren peeked through her scope to examine the bird, and it cut away fast. "Smart girl," she whispered. "What a peregrine beauty you are." She took a long gulp from the canteen, too long. The lightness of it made her nervous; she vowed not to spit, and she emptied the hockey puck of a canister in her pocket to avoid nicotine temptation.

She was here, she concluded, because she would not sleep well at home tonight without expending her best effort today. In Chase she'd seen a glimpse of her younger patriotic self, though she'd served in peacetime and avoided postwar horrors. The only aftereffect of her service was the minor tendinitis in her left knee, a result of repeatedly parachuting into hard fields. She'd been discharged from the army with honors, unlike her wicked, vanished father. In fact, she left the service with such a clear mind she felt guilty for it, almost shortchanged. Her daddy, according to her uncles, had come back from South Vietnam with gargoyles in his head, and the choking of his wives and disappearing to ride motorcycles in American deserts was, per his sympathetic siblings, an endless attempt to shake the crazy shit out. So maybe, McLaren thought, her being on the mountain was some kind of retribution, an effort to right a family wrong. Or maybe she was climbing to atone for being a fraud.

McLaren stood up again, and she knew she'd reached a fork. There were two summits she could make by nightfall. The pot harvester had suggested she head to the rocky summit, but that advice could not be trusted. The wiser destination, McLaren thought, would be the lower, tree-covered summit next door. It was a much easier target, and one canopied enough to conceal a man who wished to privately die. Still, McLaren's instincts nudged her toward the rocks. She pulled a little cowhide purse from her jacket pocket, shuffled through the buck lure and old birdcall, and fished out a quarter.

"Heads trees," she said, "tails rocks."

Heads.

She felt relieved. The easier route, with its lower altitude, was more suitable for her limited supplies. Or maybe she was a coward, no tougher than a thin-skinned city kid. The goal of being here, she thought, is to try. "Rocks, trees, whatever," she said. "God knows it's all trying." She shouldered her rifle and canteen and climbed the steep, loose mountainside into woods so thick they rendered her invisible.

***

At the edge of the clearing, Jack stopped his hollering and stood still, paralyzed by apprehension. After several long, controlled breaths he charged ahead for a hundred yards, and then two hundred, humming and thrusting his knees until he abruptly stopped. The piled rocks were so close they frightened him. They lay just ahead, dusty and huge, visible through gaps between the hardwoods.

Jack slugged some water, careful to leave enough to wet two palates, and he inched into the trees, croaking, "Chase ... Chase?" The lack of response relieved him—maybe the kid wasn't here. "Hey, dickwad," he said to the rocks. Still nothing. A few steps at a time, he came closer, until the pines and red oaks ended, and he could no longer cower in the shadows. "Chase, you up here? It's your brother. Ash County's most clueless mountaineer." Jack saw a small round rock spit downhill, between two boulders, and he yelled.

"Say something, damn it!" he pleaded. "I'm armed. If you're not Chase Lumpkin, I'll kill you."

The sound didn't register at first, didn't make sense, didn't seem possible. It was faint, like the distant moaning of a city bus. It came again, louder, and struck some sentimental nerve in Jack. He was listening to Chase groan—a pitiful, wonderful thing. It was Chase in pain, a sound he'd always known, an emotion he'd frequently ridiculed in his role as dominant sibling. Jack heard the boy who'd fallen off a slide, slipped from monkey bars in Candler Park, caught his pinkie finger with a stapler. The boy pissed at his father. The angry boy always punching above his weight but not connecting. The very little boy stung by jellyfish off the Florida coast, surrounded by lifeguards who clumsily splashed him with meat tenderizer as a cure. Jack sprinted up the last small hill, latched ahold of the closest boulder, pulled himself around it, and came to a maze of immense white rocks.

"Chase!" he screamed. "You up there?"

A few yards away, near the steep stone wall now glistening in the sun, Chase awoke. His sunburned face was stiff, lips raw and sore, mouth arid. From his position, and in his state of mind, the other voice was muffled, like underwater shouting. It didn't make sense to him, either. He dismissed it as a trick of his mind or the onset, at last, of death. To make sure, he attempted to lift his head but could only quietly groan. When he saw the silhouette—a dumpy, huffing man standing over him, blocking the sun and girded by magnificent blue—Chase wondered if the visitor might be real. He focused hard and saw Jack's face. And then he knew for sure he was dying.

Chase whispered, too softly to hear, "You dead too?"

Still winded, Jack looked down and barely could think, seeing what he'd dreaded most but not really seeing it; he glanced at the body but not the face. Chase was fully reclined, his belly raised by the rock on which he'd chosen to sit. His arms stretched outward, palms up, as though prepped for surgery or death by lethal injection. At his ribs three small streams of blood had trickled down and dried across the rocks. Jack recognized the boots, the chunky ones Chase had refused to take off once he came back stateside, the boots he used to wear on Anne's breezy porch, staring blankly into the cul-de-sac as Jack tried to lure him to bars, back to foolhardy American normalcy. White dust had settled across these boots and camouflage pants, and Jack could tell this carnage was not fresh. He avoided looking at the head, though from the corner of his eye he could see a grisly maroon splash above it. The smell could only be described as gothic.

Jack fell to his knees, landing hard on brittle stones. Pain shot from his kneecaps, through his thighs, to his hips, and he fell onto his hands, as if in prayer. "No," he said, quietly at first, and then louder, angrier: "Fucking *no*." When Jack's hand brushed the barrel of a gun, he gasped and leaned away, trembling.

Without the eclipse of Jack, the afternoon light washed back into Chase's face, and he squeezed shut his eyes, concentrating. He'd never heard his brother so frenzied, so sober. Even at funerals or when their grandfather lay tube-swollen and withered in the cancer hospital, Jack had kept in his voice the madcap buoyancy that made him famous. But here, Jack seemed exhausted and anguished, almost sick, emitting a bleak wheeze borne of catastrophe. Chase managed to swallow some saliva, confirming his consciousness, and he knew this was no hallucination. His wild brother from the city had somehow found his secret gravesite.

Chase whispered, "Jack?" and then resumed his motionless pose.

No reply. Jack was transfixed on the gun, beholding it like a live grenade. Reflexively he snatched up the barrel and flung it spinning into woods below. Wherever the gun landed, it was soft, as the impact made no sound.

Chase slightly shifted his head, now pointing his face at his brother. "Jack?"

Startled, Jack stood up and dusted off his jeans. "You breathing, man?" he said, still unable to look. "A real miracle, if you are."

"Jack?" came the whisper again. "Oh God, oh God ..."

"Speaking of," Jack said, over the panic, "I swear to Christ I tried everything to get here sooner." From boots to chin Chase's body slowly came into focus, and Jack nudged his eyes a little higher, inches at a time, until the face was there: Two cracked red riverbeds ran from the corners of Chase's mouth to the earlobes, a big macabre smile. The eyes were bloodshot and exhausted. Clumps of dirty blood had gathered at the nostrils, ringing them black and foul. The eyebrows were seared, nearly to the skin, and his blond hair was tousled and dirty, caked with blackened blood and hardened soil, longer than Jack had seen it in years. Beyond the hair, blood and tiny bits of putty-colored matter lay everywhere, baked hard with sun and decay. Dizzy, Jack heaved for breath like an asthmatic, unraveling, coughing, and lunging behind the nearest boulder.

"That *you*, Jack?"

Jack regained his balance and emerged sheepishly from behind the rock. In the downed red face he saw total disbelief. He dropped his shoulders and tried not to collapse. He rested a hand against the rock and collected his thoughts, gazing up, struggling to suppress his fallback defense: humor. "A thousand apologies," Jack said. "Would've been here sooner, but the cabbie took a wrong turn at 4,000 feet." Jack threw his hands aside, as if miming "ta-da!" in a Vaudevillian performance. "I have to say, man, you look like something undead, like a zombie," said Jack. "Don't hate me for saying that. Blame it on the shock. Maybe we'll both wake up from this."

He reached out and clutched Chase's open wrist, finding a faint pulse. "I don't know what to do," Jack continued.

"You're in a really shitty way, man, and I couldn't be more out of my element here. How do we get out of this? How do we *fix* this?" Jack let go of the wrist and squeezed a leg. "Jesus, man, you look rough. It's bad, *so* bad. You can't die, Chase—everything is still ahead of you. This can't be fucking real."

Chase's eyelids burst open, and he rubbed his lips together. His Adam's apple bobbed, trying to swallow, his tongue turning circles. "Water," he said.

"Ah, sorry," Jack said, smacking his face and exaggerating the impact. "Basic needs first." He took two steps toward Chase, but then slowed down, terrified of seeing the damage up close. "Here," Jack said, dangling the canteen. "Just take it. Take it all." He turned his face away, arm outstretched. "They say not to drink too fast." He watched Chase's open hand and cocked his head. "*Take* it, man." He glimpsed at the face, which was pained and frustrated. "Shit," Jack said, "you can't move your arms at all?"

A somber wheeze: "I fucked up."

Jack unscrewed the canteen. "It's all right," he said, again falling to his knees. "We'll figure this out. Just open those ashy-ass lips for me and take some sips. This'll be heaven in your mouth."

Jack pressed the canteen's rim to his brother's lips, watching the eyes alight with the relief of water. Chase was careful and slow, merely licking at the canteen. With his tongue he painted his mouth wet. When his jaws opened, Jack saw a raw blackened splotch between the back upper teeth, stretching halfway across the roof of the mouth, back into the tonsils, and he quickly looked away. Chase gulped, and then came a phlegmy gargle. "My throat," Chase said.

Jack could already smell infection. "When'd you last eat?" he said. "How many days you been here?"

"I'm fine," Chase said, his voice small and ragged but stronger.

"To hell you're *fine*," Jack said, digging into his backpack. He ripped off a chunk of sandwich and balled it tight in his fist—and then he recalled the medicine. Quietly he opened the pill bottles, unpacked the balled bit of sandwich, and planted in it a collection of clear-coated antibiotics and pills, including what looked like Vicodin. When Chase's lips parted again, Jack squeezed the concoction tight and pushed the wad of bread, turkey, and drugs into his mouth and pinched his nose. Chase writhed for a moment, budging his face, but then he relented, pleased with the taste, albeit faint. He gingerly chewed and tried to swallow as Jack said, "There you go, there you go. Take it on down. It's sharp cheddar and painkillers on wheat."

"Water," Chase whispered, before asking for a second and third bite. He stopped eating when the scabs ripped loose and blood filled the gaps of his teeth. Jack carefully tipped the canteen to wash the blood down the throat. "I swear to God, I think I can remember feeding you a bottle of formula like this, back on Grandpa's paisley couch, when Mom was out gardening in the yard or something," said Jack. "You may have been, what, six months old? Not walking yet, but not a helpless nugget. I was sitting there, telling you to hurry up, and I had these huge scabs on both knees, which you kept touching. You were always fascinated by scabs. Anyhow, I remember thinking, sitting there with the bottle, how you were mean as shit, and how I resented you for taking my mom. I'm not kidding; that's coming back to me right now. Funny what they say about full circle. Funny how the mind works in crisis."

The stench became too much for Jack, and he felt the need to be brash. His head spun, face tingled, and to his eyes the valley's dying light undulated. He clamped his hand on Chase's jaw, leaned in, and screamed into his face, losing what composure he had left. "Why didn't you *tell me?*" Jack yelled, their noses almost touching. "You know what this is?

You know what you did? You went the fucking easy route."
Jack leaned back a few inches. "All of this, right here, is a
permanent answer to a temporary problem. This is cowardly
shit. And now you've got us both here, Chase. What are we
gonna do? Tell me that, soldier. Take charge. Think of something, because I sure as hell don't know how to stabilize you.
And I'm not going to leave you alone."

Chase closed his eyes and wrested his jaw free. "Leave,
Jack."

"Excuse me?"

"Fuck off."

"What?"

"*Go*," Chase said.

"And to hell with you for saying *that*," Jack said. "I *should*
leave, though, the way you're acting. If it wasn't for Mom,
I'd pretend I never found you. I could live with it. I could
face that. You obviously aren't going to last much longer
without my help."

Chase asked for water, and Jack tipped another sip into
his mouth. "This isn't your problem," Chase said, a bit louder
now. "It won't be long. Probably tonight."

Jack jerked the canteen away. "How do you know?"

"I'm slipping, like I'm pulling out of my body," Chase
said. "I got numbness in my face and neck. Wasn't like that
yesterday. I stopped the bleeding at the back of my skull by
accident, but it must be rotten now. Infected. We can both
smell it. And there's a big black bear up here, no shit, that
should get the balls to drag me in the woods tonight, rip me
apart."

"*What?*"

Chase paused, short of breath. "My scent drifted all over
this mountain," he said. "You should leave, but if you're going
to hang here, you'll want that gun. That bear will come back,
and she'll feed. They say their sense of smell is ten times a
bloodhound's."

Jack rolled his eyes. And though he tried not to, he peered into the woods, estimating where the pistol may have landed, how far down it may have bounced. "You're hallucinating," Jack said. "Bears are hibernating by now." Jack sipped from the canteen and tried not to think about the beer. He thought about the beer. "But it makes sense, because you smell like roadkill," he said. "Like a backwoods appetizer."

It pained his mouth and head, but Chase began to laugh. He dragged the laugh on, pushed it out, until his neck veins bulged, and the chuckle grew blatantly fake. "The hell's wrong with you?" Jack said. "Shit wasn't *that* funny." Jack couldn't help but smile, too, though he was fighting it, and suddenly they were two dissenting boys, staving off forbidden giggling at a dinner table.

Chase lay back his head and closed his eyes, the satisfied demeanor of a sunbather. "Can't tell you how sorry I am," he said. "About this. About everything before. About the fishing trip."

With the toes of his boots Jack nudged some stones, thinking of how best to verbalize a swelling anger so intense his fingertips twitched. "Was there ever going to *be* a fishing trip?" he said. "Or was I the fish?"

Chase kept on, as if he hadn't heard the question, "... and I'm sorry about leaving you and Mom in the dark for so long, about so many things, when you deserved to know everything—everything I've done—a long time ago. I've been up here, doing some thinking, looking back."

Jack hoisted himself up. "You *didn't* forget the fishing trip, did you?" he said. "There never was a trip. You needed me at the cabin. You needed an errand boy to get your affairs in order, to have your home sold and all that. You arranged me there to wipe up after you again. Didn't you?"

"Never thought you'd come into the woods."

"That's offensive," Jack said.

"I wanted the money from the house to help you and Mom."

"You're really considerate," Jack said. "So everything you tried to do has backfired?"

"Yes."

"And so here we are."

"Yes."

"You roped me into this," Jack said. "You think I'll ever be able to get this out of my mind? You think this isn't traumatizing already?"

"Listen," Chase said, as forcefully as he could, though it was merely a growl, a smoker's croak, "I want to make amends; I want to know you'll take care of Mom. I couldn't leave my family in the dark. And last thing I wanted is Mom up here tromping around. She'd never leave without answers."

"I lied to Mom already," Jack said. "I told her you're okay, but that you've run away for good, gone off the grid. How you like that? Lying to a woman who can't leave the house because of your shit—"

"Mom struggled way before me," Chase said.

"Right," Jack shot back, "but your choices have done nothing but exacerbate her bullshit."

Chase wormed his tongue across dead lips and bunched the skin between his eyes. His crow's feet swelled like deltas after rain.

"Relax," Jack said. "Last thing you need, with a hole in your head, is high blood pressure."

The chill of high-altitude night came early, and Jack stared into the dying sun, his face brightening with an idea. He stomped into the fringes of the forest for a moment, made a commotion of leaves, and returned with a flat, jagged slab of wood from a felled ash, about the size of the fraternity disciplinary paddle his father had used on him. "Tell you what," he said, leaning down. "I'm going to use these bungee cords, and this piece of wood, to stabilize your neck as much as possible. Then I'm going to hoist you on my back and carry you out of here, while we still have some light. I'll wear you like a backpack. We've got a good hour before it's totally dark, I think. And going downhill the whole way, I think this shit is possible." Jack studied his brother, who was shaking his head against the plan. "We have to get medical help, right now. There's no other option. Phone calls won't transmit here, and I don't see any rescue choppers swooping down to save you—"

"Don't touch me."

The directive startled Jack. "I don't want to rile you up, Chase, but if you think I'm letting you rot and die up here—"

"Tell me something," Chase snapped.

"Yeah?"

"Who're you really here for?"

"*What?*"

"This isn't you," Chase said. "This isn't Bachelor Jack."

"Stop."

"Pulling me out of here would go a long way toward repairing your image or whatever," Chase said. "Alcoholic radio man saves his Purple Hearter brother."

"Swear to God, keep talking like that, and I'll punch you in the nuts."

They said nothing for a few moments. And for the first time it occurred to Jack that maybe this expedition wasn't for his brother's sake at all. Maybe in Jack's subconscious he did long to be a savior. Maybe Chase was right; it would be sensational news at each syndicate that carried Jack's show, and it could help atone for his bad-boy antics, endearing him to new demographics—older veterans and respectable women—while softening even the sternest superior-court custody judge.

"Listen, fuckface, I came here to go fishing, and then shit got weird," Jack said. "Don't play your war games with my head."

Chase moved his face away from Jack and swallowed hard, the hot spit like a throatful of busted glass. Again his eyes closed in a slow, pitiful way that reminded Jack of watching pellet-shot pigeons die. Then Jack stiffened, his back straight, bracing for something beyond his control; he could not wait here through the night, could not let his kin die that much more. Before it fully occurred to him what he was doing, he'd stepped over Chase, worked the wooden slab behind his head and neck, and then looped a bungee cord around his forehead and another across his chest, pulling tight. With Chase securely fastened to the wood, Jack latched his arm timidly around the back of Chase's shoulders, roped the limp arms over his own chest, and leaned forward with all the leverage he could muster, pulling the larger man into a seated position, and then wearing his arms like a collar. Facing the slope, Jack heaved twice, leaning over, and finally worked Chase off the ground, standing up wobbly with his brother's feet dangling behind. Jack imagined he looked like an old-time trapper with a fresh, enormous Kodiak skin draped over his back. Immediately Chase began to howl—a series of pained, empty threats about choking and punching and ripping Jack's hair out, which Jack tried to ignore. Together they started to move downhill, leaning like an old bulbous pine in the wind, with Jack staggering to keep balance; yards later, they were two conjoined novices on a ski slope. On the ground, around the rocks, the backpack caught Jack's eye, and he considered leaning down to pick it up, but instead he whooped, "Onward!" and they barreled ahead, faster than he could maintain. He wobbled left, toward South Carolina, but corrected. He turned his body right, and now he could see the clearing, the path toward the cabin, his footprints in the leaves, the route to all the miracles of modern neurosurgery. Jack was so enthralled with their progress he'd grown deaf to his brother's screams.

The pain at first was surreal for Jack, a hotness in the distance, a sensation he didn't fully understand, possibly what football players referred to as a stinger in the neck. His first thought was that he'd pulled a muscle, a consequence of the heavy passenger. Two steps farther, Jack knew his neck was being deeply bitten.

Still screaming, Chase had clamped his jaws on the thin trapezius muscle running up Jack's back to the base of his skull. And though the skin broke, Chase bit deeper and did not relent—not until Jack crumbled and fell headfirst into a bed of loose stones, still careful to keep his brother stabilized throughout the crash. Jack pulled his right arm free and, as if curling his biceps at a gym, repeatedly reached back and poked his brother's face with his index finger. When that failed to unlatch him, Jack broke his left hand free and plugged his thumbnail into an eye socket. Finally Chase thrust back his head and gasped for breath. Jack quickly but carefully flipped him over, onto his back, and there his own blood glistened on his brother's lips.

In a swooping, side-armed motion, Jack punched Chase in his groin, a hysterical reflex he immediately regretted. "You animal! *Fuck!*" he screamed, jumping in place, taking short, pathetic flights as a salve against the pain. "I don't care if that did more damage." Jack pressed hard against the back of his neck, grimaced, and dabbed the blood with his jacket sleeve. "For all I care you're bear food now." Jack stomped back across the stones and hoofed downhill toward the clearing.

***

Hustling to beat nightfall, McLaren reached the summit opposite the rocky one, winded and hungry. She dragged her hunting jacket across her sweating forehead and flapped it for ventilation. She was thirsty but refused to drink for now. It was best to wait until after dark, she thought, when the creeping chill might naturally quell her thirst. She scanned the thickest tree she could find for an appropriate perch, a place she might comfortably rest her damp back on a branch she wouldn't fall from. She needed to be high enough that a climbing bear would give sufficient warning for shooting it in the brain. The mountain night had always made her paranoid, an uneasiness that dated back to one sorry Christmas, at age four, when instead of Santa on the shack's porch her little pink flashlight found a cougar, face-deep in a raccoon's intestines. She'd known high country hermits who'd seen rabid bears, too, and they recalled horrifying, unyielding beasts—snarling economies of muscle, snapping at thin air.

With her head pointed up the tree, planning her climbing route, McLaren halted: On the wind, faint but masculine, she could have sworn she heard shouting. And then another, clearer sound ... a frantic scream. She spun in circles beside the tree, pointing her ears in each direction, wishing for another hint. She held still for several moments but heard nothing. Through her scope she watched the neighboring summit, wishing for a flashlight's flicker, a cigarette's spark. After three minutes she stopped looking, disappointed. The lilac sky went black.

McLaren gathered what limbs she could see, ripping them from low branches and dragging some from nearby brush. In her jacket she found a long thin bag with the string she used for keeping live bait when fishing; though the bag reeked of shad innards and bluegill scales, a siren's song for carnivores, she packed it with leaves and had herself a pillow. She climbed to the tree's thickest branch and saddled it, tucking the pillow behind her back. She set her rifle in front of her, nestling the stock between a thin V of branches.

Next she broke two small branches on each side of her. Her jacket had a drawstring at the waist, as did her hunting pants. She pulled the elastic strings tight, reached behind the tree to the left, hooked the string to the branch nub, and repeated on the other side. Fastened to a tree and heavily armed, she felt immaculate, like an Appalachian warrior princess in her goddamn prime.

At the mountain's dark base, she watched the circuitry of Cherokee ignite. She raised two fingers to her lips and sent her husband and child a goodnight kiss, a silent apology for her absence. In a few minutes she slouched, chin to sternum, and drifted into rhythmic, delicate snores.

***

Jack had reached the middle of the clearing when he sat down to contemplate the situation. In his jacket he found a tissue—however old, however hard with mucus, he didn't care—and pressed it on his neck wound. Drying blood held the tissue in place. He winced at the sting and wondered if the scar would be an inexplicably weird bite mark.

In the night Jack feared he'd break an ankle in the woods, should he really try to hike down, so instead he watched the pearled sky. He was in awe. For several minutes there was absolutely no sound, only gauzy silence. When the wind did rustle leaves, the forest seemed to breathe, like one enormous organism. Silhouettes of wind-blown leaves trickled down in constant cascades. Newly bare branches, dark and sharp among stars, bowed in the wind, as if conducting a bucolic symphony. Against the wilderness Jack was nothing, nobody. He felt both temporary and divine.

Quietly Jack crept back to where his brother lay, eyeing him through a wall of pine needles before moving in to help again. Chase's dying had a kind of gravity now. He lay facing Jack, breathing heavily, his eyes closed.

"You up?" Jack said.

Nothing.

"Hey, Pacman, you die yet?"

Jack eased the cord back around Chase's forehead and brought him to a seated position. Then Jack looped his arms underneath Chase's and laced his fingers over the ox's chest and slow-beating heart. "We're getting you up higher, away from these little trees, because I can't see through them," Jack said. He could hear a faint reply.

"Rhododendron."

"Right on?" Jack said.

"Rhododendron."

"Right on."

Grunting with the weight of Chase, Jack heaved backward, up the slope, using his thighs in the way movers hoist stoves to apartments. Each time he lifted up, the smell reminded Jack of ribeyes he'd forgotten on his balcony for a week the summer before, a tangy gray stink. Near the shooting location, Jack said it was time for a breather, and he took a seat on a flat-topped boulder, holding his brother between his legs. Jack had yet to clearly see the back of Chase's head, but the wound's odor worried him enough that he thought he should. He dug around his pocket and exhumed the cigarette lighter he'd found in the cabin's garage. After two failed strikes the flame jumped, and Jack gasped.

"Jesus, Chase," he said. "Maggots are in the blood. They're everywhere. Can you feel them?"

Chase said nothing. Jack budged his limp body, careful not to let the infected head fall against him again. "I'm going to get the water to clean up your head," he said. "It doesn't look good, but I don't think water can hurt." Jack set his brother against the rock, found the canteen and backpack by the light of the flame, and shook a few drops into the rank gash. He could see the bugs squirm, but the treatment didn't seem effective. He held his breath and scooped his fingers gently over the wound, cleaving through the whitish frenzy, until Chase snapped, "*Enough.*"

For a while Jack stared at the drying, infested gap, still bothered by it. He felt Chase begin to relax and nod off. "You've probably forgotten all about it, but this isn't the first time you've bitten me," said Jack. "Not the first time you've drawn blood either. You remember the first?"

From Chase, nothing.

"Well, it happened at Lenox Square, in maybe 1990. A long time ago, man. Back when all the pretty girls in grade school had poodle hair and big chunky braces, and they wore layers of florescent things." Jack emitted a soft, sentimental laugh. "It was a sweet time, man. No internet, no Taliban, right before the Atlanta Olympics, when everyone knew the city was about to explode. You remember?"

"Not really," Chase whispered. "I was like five."

Undeterred, Jack continued his yarn, detailing the afternoon Charles the Lawyer had put him in charge of Chase at the mall while the recent Emory Law grad had a suit cut. Charles gave them a fresh $10 bill, and Jack recalled the feeling of it between his fingers, so crisp he thought it might crack. Both brothers felt powerful with such wealth, and Chase asked to hold the bill, but instead Jack bought frozen Cokes and soft pretzels. Then he bought cookies for big-haired girls he knew from Buckhead Elementary, and Chase wouldn't forgive him for it—for giving away that precious thing from Dad. Chase flailed and screamed by the escalators, and as Jack tried talking to shy preteens, he stuffed a wad of pretzel in his brother's mouth, a muzzle. Chase spat out the food and latched piranha-like to Jack's wrist. This caused Jack to scream, which attracted an off-duty EMT and a bumbling wave of mall security. Now Jack rubbed his right wrist at the memory.

"Remember Dad saying we embarrassed him in front of his tailor, in that condescending way of his?" Jack said. "That day sucked. It was the beginning of what we have here, I think. At least the first bite never did scar."

The maggots distracted Jack again, their squirming so frenzied and blatant it appeared the wound was bubbling. "Brace yourself for a second," Jack said. "I have to do this."

With the flame at full-torch, Jack brought the lighter against Chase's head, slowly back and forth, burning the wound but also igniting his hair. Jack cuffed his hand in his sleeve, rubbing his forearm across the skull, and Chase's mouth fell open in silent agony. Jack flicked the lighter again, happy with the wound's fresh char. He splashed it with water and moved the flame to his brother's clenched face. "Stupid as that was," Jack said, "I think it worked."

When Chase calmed down, his breathing stable, Jack dragged him to a slope beyond the odor of the initial scene. He could hear Chase stutter with coldness or crying. "If you can eat more, even some bits of bread, you should," Jack said. "Either your stomach's growling, or air's escaping the bear wounds." Jack fetched the blanket and unzipped his jacket and laid them across the quivering chest. He asked if Chase could nod to where the gun might have landed, but there was no response. Cupping his hand, Jack wetted a sliver of bread with water, inserted more antibiotics, Aspirin, and Vicodin, and pressed it into mush, which he slid between Chase's lips. The bread settled into Chase's cheeks, and Jack watched him slowly, stubbornly swallow. As he lay still Jack wetted the skull wound with his bottle of peroxide, then emptied the entire little tube of Neosporin onto the gash, save for a small dose he injected into the mouth, which Chase didn't seem to mind.

"Now, give me pointers on starting a fire," Jack said. "I know you learned how to on those dorky Boy Scout expeditions."

No response.

With little hope of finding a gun in the dark—and no desire to approach the woodline—Jack sat at Chase's feet and gathered stones small enough for throwing. He arranged the knife, pepper spray, screwdriver, and hatchet at his feet, too. His voice felt like company, so he kept talking to himself, rambling about the aerodynamic importance of spherical stones. He put the sweatshirt on and stacked the rocks in a pyramid, where he could grab and launch them in less than one second. He cracked his neck and took a crouched position, ready like a catcher.

"Just sleep for now," Jack said. "I'll guard."

***

Cold wind awoke McLaren on the neighboring summit. She shivered hard enough to shake the rifle's butt. She tried to think warm thoughts. Erotic things, even. She searched her memory for the right reminiscences—natural, permissible, and sinless memories that would nonetheless make her pastor blush.

Chiseled, oily, blond lifeguards bounded to life in McLaren's mind. She'd seen them in Florida last July, during her twenty-year anniversary trip with Marcus. They ran across the sand during training exercises. They punched shoulders like boys and splashed through curling waves and rescued a limp, buoyant dummy. McLaren watched their hard backs as she floated in the Gulf of Mexico, floppy, smiley, and thoroughly drunk on three lite beers.

Being a godly woman, she felt guilty for doing it, but she'd filed the young men's figures and physical capabilities into her memory for use on boring warrant-serving escapades and lonely hunting trips. Now it all came back: the salt on her lips, an ocean's persistent nudge, the sentries of condo towers stretching the horizon. The beefiest lifeguard boomed rip-tide warnings in breezy coastal dialect, and McLaren lay buzzed and floating, ignoring the dimpled white banker on shore, wishing she was that dummy.

***

Nervous, alert, and absolutely berserk, Jack launched rocks at every falling twig and pinecone. When his pile dwindled, he aimed the pepper spray at nothing, unleashed some into the air, and crept uphill to fetch more rocks, as plentiful ammunition lay all around him. He decided to throw at least one stone per minute—preemptive strikes—until first light, when he planned to reclaim his jacket from Chase and rest.

This lasted several hours, until Jack's arm throbbed; he hadn't warmed up, and he hadn't made such violent sidearm movements for twenty years. Each time he became groggy, he thought of being mauled, clawed open from throat to navel. That revived him for a bit, but the tactic lost its power as night dragged toward faint morning. Jack stood up, stuffed rocks into his pant pockets, and decided to walk the perimeter, unleashing clouds of pepper spray around him like mosquito repellant.

"Get a whiff of that shit, Teddy."

He flicked his lighter, watched his brother's face, clasped the neck, found the proper vein and within it a faint thump, a pulse. Satisfied, Jack tucked his jacket underneath his brother's chin and walked to the wood line, the flame lighting his way.

***

Above the mountains McLaren saw Orion, the legless batch of supergiant stars, The Hunter. She smirked. The worship of astronomy, and the charting of constellations, had always struck her as ridiculous. The stars were moving, their alignments temporary, their meanings manmade. At her core she believed the stars had been purposely arranged, merely to amuse humankind for now.

"Get on with it," she whispered. "Been hunting for eons, and what've you bagged?"

She leaned forward and let the elastic straps restrain her weight. When the setup worked again, she felt coddled by it, proud of her ingenuity. Tucked between two branches, the rifle aimed at the forest floor, she did her best to look beyond the stars, to see some confirmation that her path was righteous. Instead, she fell asleep, her right hand still buried in her pants.

***

The recesses of the forest terrified Jack, and he hustled across stones, nearly jogging. The weapon, he remembered, had landed with a soft thump that could not have been steel on stone. It lay on pine straw or fresh leaves, somewhere in the trees. He pulled his hot thumb off the lighter, resting before going headlong into the pines, guided by sideways columns of moonlight.

When his thumb cooled off Jack flicked up another flame. Not two steps into the woods he saw the gun, wedged beneath the thick fallen branch of a mountain ash. The steel barrel tip reflected the flame, and instinctually Jack ducked, as the gun was pointed at his face. He circled behind it and smiled: "Goddamn miracle!" He gripped the weapon, held the lighter to it, and engaged the safety button. Immediately he felt invincible. "Found the gun, Chase!" he yelled uphill. "Fuck that bear!"

Jack climbed back to Chase and watched him breathe. He emptied his pockets of the rocks but kept them close by. He stole a sip from the canteen and sat down, though he knew that was dangerous. His first yawn prompted Jack to stand again, and he lightly slapped his face to whip up adrenaline. The exhaustion, though, was intense. He unlocked the trigger, laid the gun at his side, unleashed more pepper spray into the wind, and huddled next to his sleeping brother, slipping his free arm into his own shirt for warmth.

The sky was a planetarium now. Several constellations shone clearly to Jack, though he recognized only The

Hunter. For a moment he fancied *himself* Orion, having tracked down his target against such odds. After one more visual check of the perimeter, one more glance to see the clouds of Chase's breath, Jack set the gun on his stomach and gave in to sleep.

15

Faint sounds of morning awoke McLaren in her perch. Jolting upright, she realized she was not in bed, not nestled with her husband, a dashing lifeguard, or greenhorn fireman, their arms not entwined like a child's braids. Instead, she was wrapped within her own arms, shivering. She opened her eyes to a strange cold place, forbidding on all sides, and as she sprang forward, she tipped the rifle's butt up and over. The weapon leaned into a dive, slid down the branch, and fell, barrel-first, like a dart, toward the dirt. The gun seemed to drop in slow motion, and when it landed, it planted itself, erect like a fence post. McLaren winced in anticipation of an errant bullet. When none came, she relaxed, leaned back, and drank in the most immaculate sunrise she'd ever seen.

The sky was a blend of orange peel and salmon flesh. A pink burst lifted from the farthest ridges, then faded into light blue overhead, a color like the drapes of her spare room, meant for the son they'd tried to, but couldn't, conceive. Behind her, the most stubborn stars still winked. A clear sky to the east and west, but overhead sat a cottony warship, blurring at its edges, burning away slowly in the rising sun. McLaren arched her back, cracked her neck, and opened her arms. She could see a miles-long fog still nestled in the valley. Nothing of the town poked through. The tallest mountains walled the fog in, corralling it like the edges of a swimming pool.

Unhooking her jacket, McLaren twisted at the waist to work the stiffness from her back. She latched her hands on a high branch, did a pull-up, and another, and another, until her heartbeat accelerated, as if she was caffeinated. That her gun did not fire or break in half meant this day would be lucky, she told herself.

She climbed down the tree and leaned against it, pulling a long finger of jerky from her pocket and folding it into her mouth. She thought of excuses to give Marcus, explanations for her deer-less return. Maybe it was time to go home, regardless. Maybe she'd had enough of this poking around in someone else's tragedy. This was her last day off, and with the tourist hordes coming for Oktoberfest, the week promised to be hectic. The notion of a downhill walk and short hike to her truck appealed to McLaren in a way she didn't necessarily like; she counteracted that with thoughts of lifting her squealy daughter up to her face and doing the Eskimo kiss with noses. She felt sorry for Chase's mother and brother and friends, but she was also aloof. It would be healthier to care less. She had her own dilemmas: the miscarriages, her workaholic husband, and her frozen salary in a region of economic stasis.

The jerky was badly oversalted, and McLaren winced at the taste but couldn't bring herself to spit it out. She fetched her rifle and blew a geyser of dust and soil from the barrel. She closed one eye and put the other to the hole, diagnosing: "Clean enough."

She loaded the rifle again, held it at hip level, and playfully swept its aim around the woods. This was her time, and she would do with these free moments as she pleased. Then, looping the gun strap over her shoulder, she knelt to tie her boots, tight enough to hinder blood circulation, the better for protecting her ankles as she charged downhill.

Curious, McLaren aimed her scope at the neighboring mountain and scanned between the rocks, searching for movement, animal or otherwise. With this new daytime perspective she inspected the surrounding woods, too, from the treetops to impenetrable brush. She was satisfied;

the sounds she'd heard last night were mental tricks. She decided hiking to the rocks, burning away her morning, was not worth the effort. If she hurried, she might get home in time for eighteen holes at Crooked Stick or a meandering jog through Cherokee's military cemetery. Maybe a blissful autumn ride on the Harley Sportster she had built from parts, if not a walk with Sky, chatty and pulling, to the downtown ice cream parlor, once the girl got home from her grandfather's.

Still, she watched the rocks through the scope and with squinted, naked eyes for five more minutes. Nothing.

She turned her shoulders and ankles in unison, as if in military file, and marched downhill, toward the grower's cabin. The course seemed wise, but she felt the pang of failure. One swing of her seven iron or a sweet-voiced request from her child, she thought, would cure this silly guilt.

***

"Hey."

Jack didn't budge. With the warmth of day his shivering had ceased, and in his sleeping he felt luxuriously cocooned. His lips, no longer blue, bent into a clueless smile.

"Wake up." It was a hoarse whisper at first, but then came a stronger, more motivated voice than the night before. "Come on, idiot."

Now Jack heard his brother, but he told himself the sounds were dreams, echoes from a trout-fishing excursion with their grandfather, Chase being the impatient early bird, and Jack attempting sleeping-bag hibernation.

"Damn it, Jack," and he was louder now, aggravated. "Take back this jacket. You've been shivering like a bitch." Chase filled his lungs and blew hot rank breath across his brother's face, into his hair. "Take the jacket and blanket and sleep. I don't want it. I don't feel the cold but for my face."

Their plight dawned on Jack again, and his empty stomach sank. The awful reality set in. He squinted up toward his brother. "*Jesus*," said Jack, "you're ghost-white, man."

Still restrained by the bungee cords, Chase set his head back, relaxing his neck, and said nothing. Holding his breath, he could have passed for a sloppily prepared corpse, undergoing military funeral honors.

"How you feel?" Jack said.

Chase groaned. "Like I got shot in the neck, punched in the balls, and—"

Jack interrupted with wild laughter. Chase laughed, too. They kept laughing because it was genuine and wrong. Or because it was ironic and right. They laughed like stoners or like the suave retired rich men at the country club—the ones down the street from their father's house—who'd stopped counting time and lived for morning laughter on the grass. For a fleeting moment they were having fun. "Hey," said Jack, in a childish way, "you asked for it, man. It was either stomach or crotch, so I went low. But beyond that, how's it going up there?"

"Pretty shitty."

"Pretty shitty, how?"

"Like someone blowtorched the back of my head, on top of everything else."

That shut Jack up for a moment. "Let's put last night behind us, all of it," he said. "We have to figure this out, fast. You want some water?"

"No."

Wincing, Jack sat up, stretched, and enjoyed the sun—until a slow circling shadow broke his solace. The bird floated down like ash and landed on a mossy stone, staring at them with beady, dishonest eyes. "Buzzard's back," Jack said, running his hand across his arsenal of rocks. "I'm gonna kill this one."

In a fluid thrust Jack launched a rock sidearm at the vulture, which leapt off its perch, flapped, and landed again. The rock had merely clipped its talon, inflicting nothing; it seemed indignant now, spreading its hooked beak. Jack growled and forged his hands into claws. The bird watched him, jabbed its wings out, and took great beating hugs from the air, lifting higher, until it caught an updraft from the summit and gradually shrank into a leaden speck.

"There's a bit of sandwich left," Jack said. "I'll wet it down into a moist little ball. You're going to eat some. Whether you do it willingly or not is up to you." Again Jack wadded pills into a bit of bread and down they went.

"Jack, man, we have to talk."

Something in his brother's tone alarmed Jack. Instead of responding, he studied the sunrise. He imagined that a great bomb had dropped, like the explosion that ends the world in the movies, unfurling now in a slow sweep of total gamma death. "You see these *clouds*, man?" Jack said. "It's like doomsday, in slow motion."

Chase made an effort to lift his head, still fastened to the plank. Jack saw this struggle, unlatched the bungee cords, slipped the wood away, and let the head rest on soft dirt. In the process Chase focused on Jack's face and left his eyes there.

Jack could see that Chase was gritting, his jaws bulging against the pain of what he really wanted to say. "Well, shit, spit it out," Jack said. "I don't know what you're thinking, and I might not listen, but put it out there."

Chase said, "I want you to leave, Jack. I mean it. This morning."

Jack leapt up, distancing himself from his brother's request. "I'm not leaving you here. Forget it, buddy. End of discussion."

"If you try to run down and call for help," Chase said, "I'll smash my head against these rocks until it kills me."

"No, no, I don't think so," Jack said. "If I have to tape your mouth shut and drag you, you're coming with me. Sorry, but I won't be bitten again. I don't deserve that, and you're not getting off that easy. I'm cutting off your escape routes."

"Sit down, listen," Chase said, more softly, his eyes closed.

"I'll muzzle you."

"Sit."

Jack kicked a rock, a show of adolescent dissent, but then obliged. "Go on," he said. "You have me rapt, but I don't like where this is going."

Chase cleared his throat. "I hiked up here because I don't belong down there. Not anymore. Not ever again. I've become an awful person, a waste, and I can't be trusted. I got real fucked up, Jack, and put a gun in the sheriff's mouth. He'd found me on the highway, took me home. I was being difficult, resisting everything, and he was roughing me up in the front yard, as he damn well should have. I fought, he punched me, and everything was just red."

"And then what?"

"I just snapped. I can't explain it. Barely remember it."

Tossing hands above his head, Jack gave Chase a searing, disgusted glare. "That's just wonderful, really," he said. "I gave that sheriff an earful and ended up in shit creek myself. You have no idea what an asshole that makes me—"

"If it wasn't for the sheriff's time in the service," Chase interrupted, "I'd be in prison—for a decade, I'm sure." He paused to get his breath, to refocus. "It's like everything came to a sharp point, the culmination of all that's ever happened, and the choice was easy. This right here. Only this." His voice was clearer, less garbled, the work of either medicine, nourishment, or adrenalized desperation. To Jack, he sounded almost healthy again, which lifted his hopes. "I'll never walk," said Chase. "I'll never live like this. If I don't starve up here, I'll find a way to die down there, one way or another. So you can run down the mountain all you want, and tell the rescue party to go to hell because it ain't happening."

Chase's grave, inconsolable tone mortified Jack. "You think you're a doctor, but you're not," Jack said. "It's amazing what they do these days with neurons and shit, with vertebrae. You don't know anything; they *can* fix you. There's a computer, a machine, some robot, that'll rewire you, or at least get your arms working. You can have a good life in a wheelchair." That notion, Jack thought, was making his brother choke up. Then he saw that Chase was laughing. "Fuck off," said Jack. "This isn't your place to die. This isn't noble or cool or heroic. It's quitting, period."

"I'm rotting," Chase said. "See me? Smell me? It's over. I'm done."

"You're a quitter," Jack shouted. "You blame, blame, *blame* the world, and you always have. I screw up constantly, and I own it. You just wallow in what you say you can't do."

Ignoring that, Chase tried to sound authoritative: "I've seen guys shot through the spine. Even with immediate treatment, they still don't walk. I'll never hold anything again—no kid, no drink, nothing. I'll never be shit. And I'm not living without walking."

"Thinking like that, you're right, you won't."

"Let's be real ... if you're not leaving, you need to do me a favor."

"What?"

"You know what I'm getting at," Chase said. "You know what I want."

Jack stepped away. "Don't say that, don't even *think* that," he said. "That's the sickest idea you've ever had. And the worst thing anyone ever said."

Chase clenched his face and stared in the other direction, chewing the soft tissue of his cheek, stewing.

"You know, I think we have to be more creative with our incentives," Jack said, clapping for some reason. "So I have a proposition, okay? It could cost me what's left of my career, for sure, but it could be the funniest thing you've ever seen. You'll laugh until you're healed."

The battered head budged back around.

"I've got your attention—good. That's a start." Jack crouched low, to pitch his idea directly into Chase's face. "If you let me take you back to the cabin, back to town, back to life ... I swear to God, whenever we're able to roll back into Atlanta, day or night, I'll park the 'vette and run butt-ass naked down Peachtree Road. Like the time you dared me to streak that football game in high school, only I won't be wearing a gorilla mask, and this time I'll surely get caught. Okay? Sound like a plan? I'll park so you can see it all, prop you up on the passenger side. I don't care if it's forty degrees out. Don't care if it's the Peachtree Road Race, either. It's like the ultimate, stupidest boyhood dare. My white ass will blind you. I'll go to jail, but I don't care. You won't forget that. And you can't *miss* that. So how *about* that?"

Chase's eyes were distant. Nothing in his expression suggested he'd been listening. "You have to do me this favor," he said, in a rasp. "It's not immoral. Do it out of mercy, and it's not wrong. No worse than putting down a gimp dog."

Now Jack felt his skin move, a shiver up his back. "Be a man about this," he said. "Say what you mean, Chase."

"Put me *down*."

Jack stood up and turned away.

"Between the eyes, Jack. You don't have to watch. Just point. Pull. Hear. You'll know from the sound, and then get out. Wipe your prints off the gun and drop it near my hand. Don't look down."

Jack crouched again, dropping his arms and clutching his ankles for balance. "You think I could *live* with that? Even that sound?" he said. "What would that do to me? It would warp me—or anybody—that's what. You're my flesh and blood, you selfish prick."

Now Chase stared longingly at Jack, his eyes flaring. "I won't feel it," he said. "It'll just be over. Put me somewhere better."

The exhaustion, hunger, and maybe a slight fever caused Jack to tremor. To end his brother's nonsense, he grabbed the handgun and feigned throwing it, like a Hail Mary football pass, deep into the forest. "Here's your mercy," he said, repeating the motion but not letting go. As Jack looked up, he spotted the vulture wafting back down, and like the most unskilled and childlike shooting-range newbie, he took awkward aim at the bird. Shielding his eyes with one hand, reaching high with the other, and unleashing a great string of profanities, Jack opened fire. The shot missed the buzzard by ten feet, but a mix of poor technique and kickback launched the weapon into Jack's cheekbone, which sent him headfirst into the rocks behind him and knocked him unconscious.

Seconds later, Jack awoke in a miserable, twisted heap, as a trickle of warm blood ran from his split cheek into the corner of his right eye. Groaning, he rolled onto his back and watched the contrails vibrate and thicken above. He could feel his eyes bulging, his vision crosscut with flashes of bright green and specks of exploding black. In his concussed mind he heard a sharp but distant whistling. He felt woozy, sick, betrayed by Austrian firepower.

"See this? I'm bleeding for your sins," Jack said, standing up, kicking the gun aside. "You're going to live, Chase, whether you like it or not. I'll put this backpack over your head if I have to, then drag you down. Now let's get back to town, back to the city." He raised his arms in pretend triumph, looking for the cabin's roof. "You've been absent from our lives for too long," said Jack. "And you're not gonna miss your famous-ass brother running naked down Peachtree."

16

McLaren stopped, mid-step. Her right leg dangled in the air, her left planted on a mossy log. There was no mistaking the sound; it was the breathy report of gunfire, distant but pronounced, shot from somewhere near the rocks. She cocked her head up to the peak and squinted; the rocks were a steep but passable distance from where she stood, several hundred yards up, maybe a thousand yards.

Through her rifle site she hawked the massive cracks for movement. She saw the back of a man's head, a wavy-haired man with a pudgy neck, shaking wildly, as if exorcising bad thoughts. Before she could see the face the hair dipped away. "Hey, sir!" McLaren screamed toward the summit, before hunching, clasping her mouth, and clenching her chest against her own stupidity. There was no telling where the bullet had gone, or how many gunmen were involved in putting it there. No sense in announcing her approach.

McLaren reached for a shoulder radio that was not there. She stood still for a moment and put her eye to the gun site, and she wondered where a soft little radioman would have gotten his hands on a gun and how he'd known what to do with it. Having spoken with Jack, she couldn't imagine another person less likely to discharge a firearm—or to have climbed up through miles of thick mountain underbrush. Around the rocks nothing moved. McLaren stepped off the log, drew a breath, and started climbing, retracing her hurried footprints in the tide of leaves.

In all her years patrolling Cherokee, McLaren had unholstered her weapon only a dozen times, mostly after chasing the drunken drivers of pickup trucks that clearly contained gun racks. Only once, on a snow-dusted road in the night, did she confront an armed suspect.

Climbing with long strides, and with the crack of gunfire fresh in her mind, McLaren remembered the bleeding teenager. His name was Dusty Aaron, a favorite subject of Cherokee gossip, long rumored to have been schizophrenic. McLaren had seen Dusty speaking to himself on several occasions downtown, usually twitchy and disheveled. In her cruiser that night, McLaren spotted Dusty walking away from Cherokee, leaning into a mountain road, a chrome pistol in his right hand. The instant McLaren flashed her lights, Dusty spun around, winced in the headlights, and lifted the barrel of the pistol to his temple. McLaren put the cruiser in park, unholstered, and stepped out, the gun trained on the boy. "No! Not worth it," she'd said. "Put your hands on the hood and go easy." The boy smiled, said, "Nice tits," and aimed his pistol at the cruiser's windshield; he emptied the chamber, shattering glass, piercing the dash computer, and blowing holes through the upholstery. McLaren ignored her training and opted not to shoot the boy in his chest but in his thigh, and Dusty collapsed on the highway. McLaren kicked away the gun and called for medics. In the intervening minutes, the boy's tortured wailing did not cease, while in the road, beneath the headlight beams, the blood cut dark, snaking veins through the snow. Kneeling there, in the aftermath, McLaren wished she could have put the boy out of his misery.

A hundred yards uphill, McLaren peeked into her site. Still nothing. The canteen on her shoulder was unsettlingly light, but she tipped it back anyway. She didn't drink so much as lick moisture from the rim. Inside there were at least two swallows, enough to get her to the summit without lightheadedness. She charted a path through the trees that would flank around the rocks and put her at a vantage to see what was there before whatever was there saw her. The route appeared difficult but passible from a quarter mile away. She could cover that ground in thirty minutes or less.

Above the rocks McLaren saw what looked like black swirling snowflakes. Through her site she recognized the wings and circling flight patterns as a maelstrom of vultures. The birds flew high; she knew they were being timid. "What are you afraid of, friends?" she said. "What exactly do you see up there?"

She dropped the gun to her hip and watched a tiny copperhead slink out from a log, flash its tongue, and wave its arrowed head, searching. The snake seemed perplexed by human stink, writhing in spooked confusion, as its wicked chevrons popped against the wood. It wasn't like her to do it, and it would bother her later, but McLaren lifted her boot, swept up in her relative immensity and power, and she brought down the heel, crushing the skull, mincing shiny skin. She trekked upward as fast as she could.

***

Jack poked his finger into his right ear, shaking it: "The ringing won't quit. I think I have permanent damage. At least a ruptured drum."

After the errant shot, Chase had become catatonic. His eyelids were barely open, and the rest of his face sagged. Hope had drained from him. All traces of vitality were gone. Only occasional breaths suggested he hadn't slipped away. To Jack, his brother looked imprisoned, trapped, almost mummified within his sadness. He seemed on the brink of losing his life.

"Should we just hang here for a while, to see if it takes you?" Jack said. "I've been sitting here thinking. The thing is, I just don't know if I can haul you all the way down there, not without accidentally killing you that way."

A long sigh depressed Chase's stomach and chest. He laid his head to his left, to the cans of beer, which surprised him, being there. The lagers had rolled from Jack's backpack at some point and now lay in a uniform line, blatant in the sun. Seeing the cans, Chase inadvertently raised his forehead. Jack took the expression to be another sign, a request. His jowls wetted for a drink.

"Your eyebrows just told me what your mouth won't," Jack said. "Just relax, and I'll pour some Chuck's down your throat, a little ointment for the mind." Jack leapt back up, excited. "And I'll toss in a couple painkillers, for oomph. They're expired, but what the hell."

"Your tone's offensive," Chase said. "You sound like Mom ... fake chipper at the worst times."

Jack growled and cracked open two lagers. Tilting back his head, he took a long satisfactory pull and winced at the sting of carbonation. "It's warm, but not one bit skunked," he said. "A mountain miracle."

Chase closed his eyes. "No thanks."

"Don't *do* that, buddy," Jack said. "Don't leave me alone in this. Let's pretend this is your send-off brew." For better or worse, Jack had given Chase his first beer behind their grandpa's shed—prompting the boy to say he felt like a *dancer*—and he now thought of the warm Chuck's as the bookend to a notorious drinking career. "I'll be damned if you think I'm gulping these by myself," and with that Jack bent down, pulled back Chase's cheek, tossed in two narcotic pills, and poured a fizzy deluge. Chase swallowed and turned away.

"Whatever," Chase said, relaxing his face. "One beer."

Jack propped his brother onto an L-shaped ledge of warm stones. Chase's eyes tightened again.

"What is it?" Jack said.

"Up."

"Huh?"

"*Up*," Chase said. "A flock."

Squinting, Jack spun around and saw the vultures. "Maybe I'm overreacting," he said, "but I feel violated by these cocksuckers." He sat down next to Chase, tipped the open beer into his mouth, and then quickly tossed another pill—any pill—down the battered hatch. Chase winced and coughed and looked displeased, though he stared longingly at the can's label until Jack leaned over and served him several more gulps, before cracking open another. "I don't think I have enough rocks for all of them," Jack said. "I damn sure don't have enough bullets." He pulled from a can, too, and examined it in his hand, winching but satisfied.

"Taste good to you?" said Jack.

"Don't know. Can't tell. Can't taste."

"Just be patient. Chuck works wonders."

"No more beer," Chase said. "I think it's pulled something loose, on the roof of my mouth."

That irked Jack. He latched ahold of Chase's jaw and tipped the can over; the cheeks bulged with frothy beer, and the mouth overflowed. Chase tried to shake his head free, but a strange passion had consumed Jack, and he wasn't letting go until the can was empty. The suds bubbled down and streaked white stones gray. Chase relented and swallowed, then called his brother an asshole in the loudest, surest voice he'd used all morning. Jack responded by latching both hands over Chase's temples and squeezing the skull. Chase gritted against the pressure and pain but made no sound, hopeful the end might somehow come this way. In Jack's face he saw a man pummeled by emotion, by impulses he didn't understand. He'd never seen Jack so exhausted, so lost.

When Jack let go, winded by his efforts, his hands were shaking. "I can't believe you," he said. "I'm so fucked up by this." Jack folded his hands together, as if praying, squeezing the knuckles white. "Do you know how crushing this is, to everyone? Do you give a damn?"

"I'm sorry, Jack, but no sermons," Chase said. "It's just too late. And don't touch my face unless you plan to choke me out."

"Don't boss me."

"I'll boss you if I want."

"No, damn it," Jack said. "I'm the boss."

"Where'd you put the gun?"

"Can we *talk*, man?" Jack said. "There's stuff I want to know before you take it with you. And there's something you need to know." Jack opened another beer and drank half in a few seconds. He realized his original beer was not empty, and he set to quickly finishing that, racing himself. "First, please, just explain to me, in terms I'll remember, why we're here? You're city to the bone, and you choose to die up here in this godforsaken wilderness?"

Droplets of beer had settled on Chase's lips and cheeks; Jack leaned over and wiped them off with his jacket sleeve. Something in that gesture loosened Chase; his forehead and cheeks fell, his lips relaxed, and his defeated expression, to Jack, looked like the faces of crooks in old cop movies, the ones who knew they were cornered and might as well drop the dime. In a somber whisper Chase asked, "You ever wonder why we're so different?"

The question enthused Jack, indicating he was getting somewhere, tapping some real emotional vein, he thought. He gulped from the beer and set it down and cupped hands over his knees. But he had no sufficient answer. "It's just the way people are, even brothers, I think," said Jack. "We have the same blood, drink from the same teat, but we get into our own little grooves early, for better or worse. And that's life. I've seen bona fide saints and real assholes come out from under the same roof. It is strange, though, the way it works. The routes we've taken to get here."

Neither brother said anything for a while.

"It's dogged me forever," Chase finally said. "At least as far back as elementary. Call me a pessimist, but I do believe in God, by and large, and I guess He's moving us around in some kind of game, testing me and rewarding you, hurting me and exalting you. Nothing's fair. We roll along and tolerate the shit, or we step out, call it a night. Only it's not really our choice. In the end it's all His doing, right? So shouldn't we all get in? I'm thinking yes. Which makes life a gauntlet with no point, the way I see it. It's just a bunch of temporary nonsense. It's commotion without purpose, a long parade of nothing."

An avalanche of pebbles rolled away from Jack's boots as he jabbed them in the dirt. "What you just explained is called manic depression," Jack said. "You can be cured, though. I'm positive you can. It's just a matter of perspective. I think you have to lower your expectations. Almost nobody changes the world. You did the best you could." The beer beside Jack distracted him. He emptied it into his mouth. Only one can remained, shaded by the backpack.

"We agree on something: I was an awkward kid," Chase said. "You were fine."

"No," Chase said, "I wasn't. There were flaws, and real clinical problems that could have been addressed. My earliest memories are of me just sitting around, wanting to be you. Or wanting to run away, to do something drastic so everyone would care."

"Right," said Jack. "Believe me, I remember."

"And, man, we had it fine. Blessed, even. All we had to do was grow up and grab life by the throat." Chase felt that he was on a roll, his voice clearer, stronger than it had been for days. "I think this mental shit was born into me, though," he said. "I thought I could purge it out overseas—just shoot it through my gun. I wanted to be something bigger, to matter, you know. I could give a damn about the medals, but I'm telling you, I felt purpose at the beginning, once we moved into the base. Once I played soccer with those dusty kids with fucked-up teeth."

Rude memories drew Chase into himself, his face pruning. His open lips tightened. Jack watched them split against the teeth, blood droplets seeping from brown scabs. For the first time on the mountain, Jack reached over and touched his brother in a manner meant to mollify, to comfort, and not to fix.

"Spit it out," Jack said. "Don't hold back. Give me everything you've been holding on to. Swear to God, I'll take it with me, and keep it among us."

"No," said Chase. "No chance in hell."

"How about I go first?" said Jack. "And then you divulge your thing. Like a trade."

Chase whipped his face away. "I said no chance."

"Okay, well, brace yourself for this," Jack said, sitting up straight, forcing a prideful smile through his exhaustion. "I'm a father!"

"No."

"Yes."

"God no."

"Look, uncle, it's true."

"They tested?" Chase said.

"The blood is mine, man."

"Does Mom know?"

"Not yet," said Jack, shaking his head. "Almost nobody does. I can't bring myself to spread the news. I wasn't even told until the third trimester. The mother's dad forced her to contact me out of the blue and seek support. She interned at the station last fall. I hadn't seen her since."

"Girl or boy?"

"A little girl."

"Oh God," said Chase. "What's her name? Penance?"

Jack spouted a loud, offended laugh. "That's the thing that kills," he said. "The mom's so repulsed by me—and my 'toxic lifestyle' as she calls it—that she won't tell me the baby's real name. Three months old, and I don't know. In the court papers they refer to her as 'Rose.' That's what I call her, during her visits at the condo. But

I don't think it's correct, because it's always in quotes, like a code name."

"That's tough," Chase said. "Hate to hear it."

"If I'm wrong about the name, you can imagine how it must confuse the girl already."

"I'm sorry."

"It's enough to make me want to start over," said Jack. "I'm serious, man. To wipe the slate clean. To be somebody else, honestly."

"In that case, congratulations," Chase said. "I mean it, in every sense."

For a minute Jack said nothing, not until Chase's face again twisted against his thoughts. "I showed you mine ..." Jack said.

Chase composed himself, his breathing leveling out. "You won't think of me the same, but I want someone to know this, something about overseas," he said. "I want you to know everything."

"There you go," Jack said. "Bring it on. Air it out. I've been waiting for this for two years ... we all have."

"Right," said Chase. "It's just not easy to say."

Jack leaned in, rapt. "I need to know how you got hurt. If not, it'll always haunt me, not knowing." He backed away, allowing his brother space.

"We were sleeping in storage sheds, basically," said Chase. "Living this life of bazaars, turbans, death, bodies, shit. You have to try to put yourself there, mentally, right now."

"Absolutely," said Jack. "I'm there. Right there with you, in your hell. Keep going. Don't stop."

For a minute Chase closed his eyes and hummed, formulating the lie. "We called it pink mist," he said. "That's how we describe the poor fucks who get vaporized." Chase exhaled, turned his face to the rock wall. "I got shot, fell down, busted my head on a rock. A grenade launcher vaporized the fucker who shot me. ... So don't pity my ass."

"Jesus," said Jack. "Were you medevaced out of there, or whatever? And how'd this bastard shoot you exactly?"

The questions made Chase feel claustrophobic, pressured by what sounded like suspicion. "Look, it happens fast, these firefights, and they happen every day," Chase said. "I was trying to cross a creek behind my platoon sergeant, thinking about how uncomfortable my dick plate is when I'm running, and then I've got this snakebite on my thigh. I'm bleeding, like a spigot, and I can't walk, so the platoon sergeant drags me to the bank, where they pop me with morphine that doesn't work ..."

"And then?" Jack said.

"Then, man, nothing. No memory, no flashes of scenes, just a void. I wake up, and there's a man with a light on his head looking at me. I think it's the Taliban; I think they got me in some cave, running up their probes. So I try to throw a punch, but they've got me in soft restraints. I'm screaming and spitting and telling all these doctors who are just trying to save my life that I'll kill their families. It's horrible. I'm thrashing in this bed, like an idiot, and out pops the Purple Heart, tinkling on the hospital floor. Shit was in the sheets, I guess. I realize what it is, and I'm even more enraged then. I feel like an asshole saying this, but we don't *want* Purple Hearts. I don't want to be reminded what a good marksman the guy who shot me was. And I sure as hell don't want proof, pinned to my chest, that I'm a fuckup—"

"I don't know," said Jack.

"Don't know *what?*" Chase said.

"There's something about this ..." Jack studied the face in front of him, looking for telltale twitches of dishonesty. "Why do I feel like you're not telling me something?" he said. "Like you've skipped something crucial. Like you're lying to me at a time like this."

"Go to hell, Jack."

"I know you too well, man. You're ranting as a distraction. I believe that last bit, about the hospital, but what really put you there?"

Jack waited for a response. None came.

"And why would I think less of you for getting shot by the enemy, like you said? You're not making sense." Jack leaned in even closer, aggravated, worried. "No offense, but that's a pretty common story, awful as it is. You wouldn't be so bitter about taking some bullet like a damn hero—"

"I won't tell you the truth—I just can't," Chase said, a near whisper. "Can't have you thinking about me like that. Not family. No way. It all stays with me."

"You don't have to tell me," said Jack.

"What?"

"I know."

"You know what?"

"The sheriff told me, in his office," said Jack. "Goddamn it, I wish he was lying. Because I'm feeling pretty ashamed of you right now."

Again, Chase's face pruned with hideous memories, but now Jack made no attempt to intervene. The busted head tilted back, and the sockets flooded like swamps, tears spilling down to blood-caked hair. "All I can say," Chase huffed, "is that I probably saved several of my brothers by eliminating one—"

"*Enough,*" said Jack. "That's all yours, man. I don't want to carry any of that. And you better not say his fucking name." He crushed the beer can and herded all the empties into the backpack, mindful of his DNA on them. His stomach talked. He hadn't been this hungry in several years, having so rarely denied indulgences.

With the sun to his back Jack cast a shadow, which he pulled back and forth to shade and blind Chase at will. He blinded him now. "Just tell me one thing," Jack said. "Are they looking for you? Do the feds want to fry your ass? Is that it?"

"No," Chase said. "There was no suspicion. No one in the field that day said shit, to my knowledge. It happened, and he went home a hero, with a little parade."

"Jesus," Jack said, kicking rocks.

"Worst thing is knowing about his family," Chase said. "It was all online, covered by his local newspaper. They had that parade for him, and the mayor was crying with his folks. His mom is this sort of mother figure in the community. She spent weekends making food for charity, and the Rotary gave her an award for it. His dad's a volunteer fireman, some kind of Podunk big shot. It was goddamn crushing to read all that—"

"Stop!" said Jack. "I don't want to know more. I don't want it changing how I knew you."

Chase squeezed his eyelids together, bunching skin, as if grappling with a migraine. His breathing was stuttered gasps now. Then he opened his eyes again, silently begging.

They stared at each other, hardly breaking eye contact. Jack felt his muscles tightening, coiling against his next move. He was angry and disoriented, knocked far from his axis, and though he tried not to cry, because his brother had never seen it, he couldn't hold back. He whimpered and stammered and leaned over. Jack let go, and it came at once, a rush of pity, rage, guilt, confusion. The lackadaisical Jack was gone; he was rigid and serious now. He knew the freewheeling side of himself would never be so genuine as earlier that week. He stood there like a man who'd reached a dire conclusion. "This is on me," Jack said. "I'm guilty, too. I should have gotten here sooner, but I couldn't get out of my own way." He turned to Chase, his face smeared wet. "Why didn't you *call* me, knock on my door?" and Jack was screaming now. "Not just now but years ago. That's not weakness, man. It's family shit. I've got a city full of favors owed to me, and there's a thousand assholes out there that would've made good on them, a thousand jobs I could have set you up with. You could have lived, Chase. You could've been a fat happy fuck like the rest of us. You had no business over there in the sand. You weren't right for that kind of fighting, and I told you so. And look what it did to you—and to this poor kid. Two families, wrecked."

Chase relaxed again, quiet and demure. "Just go home," he said. "You can't stop it. Everything ends now, today. Whether I go out easy or awful, that's up to you."

Jack stomped around and cried some more. He brushed his shoulders across his cheeks, violently shook his face from side to side, and the gun again was heavy in his hand. "You're not going to get better, are you?" he said, clicking the safety off and on. "No matter what I do—no matter what counselors say, and the doctors fix—you're not going to try, are you?"

"There's no options," Chase said. "There never really was."

"If you won't accept them, like you haven't for two days, and for two years before that, you're right, there's no option," said Jack. "At this point, I think it's settled. I think you're unsalvageable. You're my blood, but you're scorched earth. We tried, but you are gone—"

"Not gone enough."

Jack shushed his brother. "Give me a minute, Chase. Just let me think a minute."

"Hey," Chase said, plaintively now, "take care of that kid, okay? Slow down, be good for her. You can, and you should. Beneath all the wild shit you've always wanted to do right. I think you're getting there, man. I see it. Be a man with this kid. And put in a good word about me when she's old enough to know."

"Just let me think a minute, Chase."

"Right? Okay? You listening?"

"Give me a damn minute."

"Yes, sir," he said. "Don't think of this as homicide or whatever. It's a reprieve, a gift."

"A gift?" Jack scoffed. "That's sadistic. That's fucking wrong."

"Then it's a rescue, and it's the last time you'll be called to save me. It's the best thing you've ever done for me."

"Man, maybe this is *sacred*, a genuinely sacred thing," said Jack. "It's an awful but sacred day, between us. Maybe even a foregone conclusion. That's what this is, I think. And that's the right word. Sacred. I really think that's what this is."

"I like it. Yes, sir," Chase said. "It's a sacred act, and you know it's necessary."

"It'd be better for you, wouldn't it?"

"It would, Jack."

"No, say it like you fucking *mean* it," Jack shouted. "Look at me and tell me it'll be better."

"It's a favor, Jack. A great one. The biggest one."

Jack stomped in frustration, waving the weapon over his head. "I'm not hearing what I need to hear," he said. "I need to feel like this is healing you, in a way. I'm not trying to erase you or dispose of you. But I think I'm okay with ending this, whatever we have, if you just let me know it's good."

"How else can I say it?"

"Tell me, like I said, that I can make things better, right now, with this. Tell me everything will be okay. Tell me that I'll get over this eventually. Tell me because you know—or maybe you don't. But tell me I'm right again, because I'm sure as hell not feeling that yet."

Chase huffed, shook his head. "Just pull back, man. Squeeze. Don't think of right or wrong. Come on ... *come on!*"

"Don't be nervous," said Jack.

"Oh, I'm not."

"You're talking like you're nervous."

"I'm ecstatic," said Chase. "It's ending. You're going to do it because you have the balls."

Again Jack stomped, grinding boots into the dust, fighting the gravity of Chase's request. "I don't think I can physically do it," he said. "It goes against everything—every fiber of me."

"You're thinking too much—mental paralysis," Chase said. "Don't think. Stop talking. Stop flipping out. No hesitation. No cold feet."

"I'm here because it's right, because it's in me to do this," said Jack. "Nothing that happened is your fault. That wasn't really you. But this is me. It's my own volition. I'm here because it's right. I'm here to take you home."

"To hell you're taking me home!"

"For the last time," said Jack, calmly, "give me a minute."

Chase's lips jutted out haggardly, unmoving, his eyes gone. He lifted his head to scream, his neck muscles like little canyons, and his wordless breath speckled phlegm across his chin—a nonsensical static, an animalistic whisper, a final crazed plea.

Extending the weapon, staring into Chase's face, Jack screamed back, full throat toward the ground, and in the midst of this primal contest, this strange cacophony, he flinched several times, before finding the strength to reach with his finger, feel the cryptic trigger, and squeeze back, his eyes open and aim true.

The death was instant and complete. The shot echoed, and a small red splotch swelled above the left eyebrow. Macabre confetti spat across stones and up into the wind as the head bounced and landed, the body still sitting upright. The last long breath seeped out wetly, and as the mouth fell open, Jack saw rows of perfect teeth around the brown wound. Trembling, Jack bent down, slowly reached out, and shut his brother's mouth. With two outspread fingers he closed the vacant eyes. Now everything mattered—every minute, every step in the woods. He would conduct a quick funeral, drag the body down a few yards, and be gone, all business, all survival. But still he watched the face and could not look away. A single red rivulet trickled down the forehead, toward the ear, forming a marsh in short hair at the temple. In death the kid was handsome, with hands at his hips and a dignified, straight-back posture. Jack stood over the body for a few moments, apologetic and solemn, his ears still ringing with the shot. Patient buzzards put shadows on the rocks.

He stepped back and bowed his head, but the moment of silence was broken by the hurried sound of boots thudding against the ground. Instinctively he pointed his weapon uphill, toward the summit and the sound.

McLaren aimed her rifle right through Jack, her forearms bulging with an intense grip, her eyes alive with something between indignation and panic. She was breathing heavy, her face wet with sweat. Together they stood in shock for a moment, Jack's mouth open. He felt a sickening, freefalling sensation, having not only committed murder, but likely doing so as the most credible kind of witness watched.

Jack let the weapon fall to his side. "I had to," he said.

Leaning into her aim, McLaren said, "Toss the gun behind you. On those leaves. Slow."

"I had to," Jack repleated.

"Do what I said."

"I had no choice. That's my brother."

"Drop the fucking—"

"Yes, ma'am."

Jack cautiously turned at his waist to toss the gun into a clump of pine straw. He took big breaths and steadied his hands, frightened enough by the circumstances to stop crying. McLaren kept Jack in her sites, and Jack shivered with thoughts of the rifle. He faced the summit again, lifted his hands, and shrugged his shoulders. "I tried for a day to drag him back down. Look at the forensics, or whatever. You'll see there was another shot to his head—"

"Get on the ground, hands on your head," McLaren said. "And shut up."

"Chase tried to off himself," said Jack, beginning to kneel, "but it only broke his neck."

"Keep your hands in front of you," said McLaren. "You want to get shot, too?"

The trickling blood again caught Jack's attention, and the orders didn't resonate. "That smell is human rot," he said. "It's from the first shot. And it's the only reason I found him, by way of these damn vultures." Jack looked skyward and then back to the rifle, which was still aimed at his sternum. The gun seemed fierce and daunting in the grip of such tight arms.

"Hell, my life's in shambles anyway," said Jack. "Cuff me. Fuck it."

"If I had 'em," said the deputy, "I would."

"If it wasn't for my mom," Jack said, "I'd beg you to just shoot me, too."

"Shut up."

"Sorry, ma'am. I'm—"

"Shut up a minute, Jack. Don't move. Let me process this, give it some thought."

McLaren told Jack to step back once, and then again. Still aiming her gun, she walked to the body and inspected the varied shades of blood, the sundried matter, touching nothing. She peered inquisitively into Jack's face and squinted, assessing. Then she jutted up and leapt back toward the summit, distancing herself from the scene, shaking her head.

"I can't condone this," said the deputy. "Frankly, I can't believe this."

Jack shook his head weakly.

"You understand the stakes here, right?"

"Yes," said Jack. "I do. But you have to understand these were horrible circumstances."

"The law isn't sympathetic."

"Is the law going to charge me?"

"I don't know."

"You really think this is criminal?" Jack said. "Tell me that, deputy."

"I don't know."

"Chase wanted this—he was already gone," Jack said. "I think it was right."

"Oh, it ain't right," McLaren said. "Nothing about this is right."

"No, you don't understand," said Jack. "This was like mercy."

"Look," said McLaren, "I won't say I blame you, so charging you doesn't seem just. But let's be clear: You'll be punished for this—for a long time. Everything here will fuck with your head. Trust me, it won't go away. Ever. Don't stare at him too long."

Jack turned halfway around, cringing. He bowed his head.

"This is what you're gonna do," McLaren said, clearing her throat and reverting back to her most authoritative tone. She squared her shoulders to Jack and aimed the rifle at the dirt. Not marching Jack to town and charging him with murder could cost McLaren her own freedom and her daughter a mother, but she also felt the mess in front of her was in some part her doing. Both of them would be imprisoned by regret for what they had or had not done, for their tardiness, and that seemed penance enough. If she'd arrived five minutes sooner, McLaren realized, she may have pulled the trigger herself, shouldering this curse instead of Jack. "You'll pull him into those trees, where the searchers and sightseers in planes can't spot him," McLaren ordered. "Put a pile of leaves around him. Blanket him good. Stack him under some of these flat stones, a few layers. Mark the place—the scene around the grave—with a bigger stone or two, because the pile won't last too long. But don't be obvious with the markers. You following me?"

Jack nodded.

"This won't be easy, okay, but you'll have to take every stitch of his clothing down this mountain with you, concealed in that backpack. Burn it all immediately, at the cabin, okay? Keep the fire small and don't let anyone see. As for what happens here, let nature take him. Don't concern yourself with this. Get your head someplace else and stay the hell out of Ash County through the winter."

Jack's mind filled with macabre images, and he broke down again, keeling over and then resting on one knee.

McLaren sighed in a way that was impatient but courteous. "This is key, man—the most crucial advice," she said. "It's going to hurt, and it's going to screw with your mind, but you'll come back in late spring, end of April, okay, and collect the bones, every piece you can find. Search this whole mountain face, a hundred-yard perimeter. And then put those bones at the bottom of Lake Lanier. At least a few hundred yards offshore—"

"What?" Jack shot back, sounding more vitriolic than he'd meant to.

"Listen, I'm risking a lot right now."

"Sorry," Jack said. "I'm not second-guessing you. But isn't this remote enough?"

"Nothing's remote anymore," McLaren said. "At the bottom of that lake, like I was saying, there's still an old-growth forest from before the dam. The calcified pines shoot sixty feet up from the mud. The lake keeps secrets. These mountains don't."

"All right," Jack said. "All right."

"On your way home tomorrow—and you *are* leaving tomorrow, at the latest—get to the lake, to a bridge, and put that gun in there, too. Deep as you can toss it."

Shaking his head, but intent to follow directions, Jack stood back up. "I can do all of that," he said. "If I did this, I can do that."

The deputy took a final glance at the body and carefully stepped back. "Flip over the bloody rocks, and dust them up, as natural-looking as possible. This time of year, it shouldn't be long before a soaking rain comes through."

"Listen," Jack said. "I don't know what you saw or heard, but I want you to know I had to. I'm not some monster. This was not the plan. I tried saving Chase every way I could. He begged for this over and over—"

"You've made your case, Jack. Stop reflecting, and start doing what I say. My life is on the line here, too."

Without meaning to, Jack stared for a moment at Chase, confirming again that hope was gone, before averting his eyes back to the lawwoman. He squatted to the ground and threw the bulk of his arms over the back of his head and neck. He screamed into the dust.

"Stop that crap," said the deputy. "Get a grip. There's time for that later."

Jack howled again.

"I said stop it. *Now.*"

Jack obeyed. He stood up slowly, sheepishly, a scorned child. "Sorry, ma'am."

"Get moving."

McLaren nodded once and hustled around a boulder, but she peeked back. "This goes without saying, but I wasn't here. I wasn't even on the mountain. You haven't seen me since town. No one will believe you if you say otherwise. And if you start talking—on the radio or anywhere else—I'll make sure you never leave jail. You understand, Jack?"

Jack nodded enthusiastically and saluted McLaren. "This goes to my grave," he said. "I don't know who you are."

McLaren bounded across rocks and vanished into the trees. The crunch of her footfalls grew distant, lower, faster, until there was no sound, save the hush of a knowing breeze.

17

To Jack the cabin seemed surreal, like a vestige of some disinfected world. It was late afternoon by the time he slouched into the backyard, dragging his boots and holding the backpack by the tips of his fingers. In the garage he found a can of gasoline, unzipped the backpack, and soaked Chase's fatigues, boots, and socks; he drenched the backpack until the straps and front pouch gleamed, holding it by a lone dry strap. Behind the shed he found a barrel. He placed the backpack at the bottom and buried it under brittle leaves, but his lighter was spent. He rummaged through the garage for another lighter or matches but found none. The kitchen would have something. He walked to the house and wanted to kick in the back door, but it was unlocked. For that he called himself a fool, though he knew he'd locked that door.

The sight of Carrie at the kitchen table paralyzed Jack. She looked intensely pure, if a little tired. She wore a blue hooded sweatshirt beneath a fleece vest, a magazine model for autumn outerwear. Her hands clutched an open beer. Next to her sat a ready cell phone.

"Jesus," she said.

Jack dropped his head. "Not quite."

She pushed the beer aside and held the phone. "I thought maybe you wouldn't make it back," she said. "None of the windows were locked, and I wanted to wait inside. Sorry if this is strange. I've been calling you. I'm not a stalker, I was just worried." She began to stand up but stopped at the sight of his face in the kitchen light. "Your cheek's swollen—and cut."

Jacked sighed and tried to smile for her, but his face felt weighted by lead, the gravity of regret. He rubbed his forehead, caught the stench of gasoline, and thrust his hands into his back pockets. "Had to spend the night up on some rocks," he said. "Most terrifying hours of my life, but nothing came of it. Big waste of time."

"I tried to report you missing," she said.

He rushed to the sink to scrub his hands. "Have the deputies been here? Or are they coming?"

"I had to tell them your real name."

"Of course."

"I told them your name, and they didn't sound too alarmed, Jack. They said they'd have to wait to launch a search. They were going to let you fend for yourself, and that's terrible." The way Carrie's lips fumbled out the last word suggested she'd been drinking beer for hours.

"It doesn't matter." He dried his hands, smelled them, and scrubbed with soap again. "Call them tomorrow, please, and tell them I'm safe. That we're safe. And that the Lumpkin boys went back to where they belong."

Carrie gasped again. "Are you hurt?"

"Just dirty."

"But you're bleeding."

"What?" Jack craned his neck for a glimpse of himself in the kitchen window. "A scratch," he said. "Got poked in the face by a branch."

Jack turned his back to Carrie, and now she shot up from her seat. "No, it's splattered across your back," she said. "And where the hell did you get that gun?"

The kitchen walls spun, and Jack's mind swam with delirious guilt. He'd thought the gun, tucked into the butt of his jeans, was covered by his jacket, but during his hurried descent it must have emerged. He didn't bother to make excuses, to concoct stories; he was exhausted, and not answering Carrie was not lying to her. In a drawer full of silverware and bug repellent he found a book of matches. Then he stripped into his boxer shorts and latched ahold of Carrie's wrist, pulling her out the door and through the yard. At the trash barrel she began to speak but closed her mouth, withholding her concerns. Jack tossed in his clothing and looked around, through the woods, down to the highway, and up toward the grave. "Please don't ask now," he said, "but I need you to pray. I don't know any real prayers."

Her face was fallen and blank.

"It's a noble thing, you waiting for me," he said. "If you're going to get fired from the bar, don't worry. You're better than that job."

Carrie nodded, but her eyes were confused. She leaned over the barrel but turned away quickly. Jack didn't ask—and would never ask—what she'd seen. He struck a match and tossed it in. From its base the barrel leapt to life. "Please," he said, "just bow your head and say something about God."

They prayed together in the reeking smoke, heads down, their faces dancing orange, until the leaves and cloth were ash, until the embers faintly heaved. Carrie dug into her pocket and pulled out a crinkled sheet of paper, which she'd neatly folded.

"Don't think I was snooping around the cabin," she said, "but I found this beside the couch, wadded into a ball. It was real dusty."

"I can't read another note," Jack said. "Not now."

"No," she said, "it's more of a letter. An unsent one. To you. And I think you should."

With trembling hands and fingernails like moldy crescents, Jack reached out, unfolded the letter, and held his breath:

> *Since you've been asking, Jack ...*
>> *I've never talked about this and probably never will, but they said the first guy I shot was named Farkard. I have no*

clue if that's how you spell it. We were on patrol, and we stopped by a bunch of these big jagged rocks. As I was getting out, I heard the ping of bullets on the opposite side of the Humvee. As that noise stopped, I crouched and set my sites on a pointy rock dusted with sand. Somehow I knew he'd picked that rock as cover. It was too easy. Any kid could have done what I did. He popped up like a mole and his nose was in the crosshairs. One squeeze. One second. And man that was it.

To be honest, I thought of Kennedy dying. I couldn't really move for a minute. When I got back to the truck, the guys were high fiving me. I hadn't been back for twenty minutes before I started grieving for the dead guy's mom. That was before they killed any of us, but still ...

Some nights I wondered, and still wonder, who Farkard was. I wonder if he loved to fight us or if he hated it. I wonder if all of them really hate us. This might sound psychotic, but I've been imagining Farkard and me in another place and time, a hypothetical summer that will never happen. We're not bound by religion or rules or any sort of indoctrinated hate. We're just fishing the Chattahoochee, up by Buford, pulling out brown trout and catfish by the dozen. We're plunging our fists in these icy coolers of beer, and Farkard actually likes it. There's music on a boom box, and we both know the words. Other people float by on rafts, wave to us, and everyone knows the words. We're all pretty young, and we've got that feeling that nothing is impossible, that we'll never run out of time.

Jack pressed the paper against his forehead and let it go, down into flames.

They went inside the cabin, drew a hot bath, and shed all of their clothes. Carrie said she'd bet a hundred dollars Jack had never been this filthy, not as a grown man. With a sponge and gritty soap she cleaned the back of his neck, careful with the bite mark, scrubbing off hard red patches and searching with her fingertips for other wounds she wouldn't find. She didn't ask, he didn't speak, and the secret began to bind them, albeit gently, as killer and accomplice. She trusted that his acts had been dignified, and in his hollow eyes she recognized a face she'd come to know on other men at the tavern: the gambler, fresh home from North Carolina casinos, trying to keep afloat in the wake of great loss. She rubbed the hardened ropes of his back and kissed his ears. Jack slumped over the lip of the tub and fell asleep.

***

The day brought strange country sounds, insect chirps and delirious birdsongs. Jack awoke and shot upright in bed, convinced he was still on the mountain. His shirt was damp with sweat from stormy dreams he could not recall. He tickled Carrie's ear until she groaned and smiled, luxuriating in the warmth of blankets. Jack said he would make breakfast.

"Breakfast?" she said, holding her watch. "It's one in the afternoon, Jack."

Jack snatched her watch to see for himself; he'd slept for sixteen hours. "Anyhow, we have to eat all the food left here," he said. "Because I'll never be back, and I don't want the animals or your hillbilly ilk coming in after it—ha!"

She acted offended and playfully slapped his arm.

"If you or your family want this place," he said, "we'll get the deed transferred. If they want to help sell it, you guys can have half."

"Stop talking like this," she said.

"No, really, I thought about it yesterday. I think it's fair."

She groaned again and rolled away from Jack, bothered by this business talk.

"I'm leaving this morning," he said. "My first priority is to accommodate you, though. I'd bring you to the city, but that'd require bringing you back, and I won't be crossing these county lines again. Not anytime soon."

In the kitchen, Jack emptied the perishable foods into a trash can and wheeled it to the highway, save four pieces of bread and one-fourth of a stick of butter. He locked all windows and the back door, turned off all lights. He felt rested and strong. They had their toast and coffee and loaded into the Corvette.

Through the windshield, Jack had a final long look at the cabin, and in a sudden furious burst he rolled down his window and screamed profanities until specks of saliva stuck to his door. Carrie yelled, "Baby, *baby*," until he put the car in reverse, revved backward onto the highway, screeched the tires, and pinned them back into their seats. He punched the car to fourth gear and slowed down, opting for neutral, gliding downhill for a couple of miles. They swept around a long curve, still in neutral, and Jack grinned. "Sorry. Where are we going?"

She positioned the rearview to see her face and fix her mascara and hair. "Just take me to the Lonesome," she said. "I need to make up for time lost yesterday."

"Lost?"

"Sorry," she said. "You know what I mean. But at least I closed your tab."

While passing the sheriff's department, Jack slunk down into his seat and looked the other way. He parked outside the tavern between two trucks, an effort to hide his car. "Give my best to the pastor," he said.

"Sure will," she said.

"And just chop up my card, please."

"Sure will."

"Cab fair's a kiss," he said, holding out his palm. Carrie gathered her things, her eyes darting around. Jack withdrew his hand and placed it on his heart, feigning palpitations. "Why so hurried?" he said.

She leaned outside the door. "Let's keep this hushed around here," she said. "And if you say a word about me on air, I won't answer your calls."

As she slid from her seat, her shoes crunching gravel, Jack whispered, "Just so you know, legally speaking, you have no reason to worry."

He fought his impulse to assist her and stayed in the car. Again, he felt the sting of her absence. She leaned down to the window. "Don't spit me out," she said.

"That's nothing you have to worry about, either," Jack said. "But I want to see you soon. Within the next few days, if possible. I'm going to need your help in the worst way, just to get up in the morning, just to be okay, because he didn't make it—"

"*Stop*," she said. "Not here. Don't tell me here."

Carrie eased the door shut and strutted to her job, gone without another word. Jack stole a glance at the sheriff's department, saw nobody, and backed into Main Street, creeping out of Cherokee below the speed limit. On the outskirts, a hokey wooden sign with a happy old Native American—"Cherokee Says: Come Back Soon, Y'all"—made him weep for twenty minutes, but by the next county, he'd stopped the racket and begun to feel like city Jack again. The mountains became hills, eternally rolling. The traffic thickened with vans and semis. The sky flashed with high, desperate billboards. The sun's long slant portended true winter night.

***

Jack exited the interstate for a two-lane highway, skirting the northernmost suburbs for the route that took him to Lake Lanier and its many bridges. He found what seemed the perfect location: a long bridge spanning dark water.

At the middle of the bridge he parked the car, stuffed the gun into his waistline, and walked to the rear quarter panel. He opened the trunk, found the tire iron, and faked an emergency, squatting beside a rear tire. He held the gun and examined it. In the black steel, under the barrel, Chase or someone else had carved: SORRY MOTHER. Jack reared back, rose over the barrier, and unleashed the weapon side-armed over the water, watching it sail and spin. The splash echoed, a slap and deep thump. He tossed the tire iron into his passenger seat and roared across the bridge, back into the woods, around vast subdivisions, until at last he found Interstate 85, southbound. He merged into a river of tail-lights, behind a milk truck. He'd never felt more invigorated by gridlock.

Closer to Atlanta, the interstate fattened, and Jack squirmed in his seat. The asphalt swept wide over ridges, under bunches of highways and surface streets, until it came to the hill Jack had been anticipating. He crested higher, to the apex, watching sky-rises heave up from the trees. At Peachtree Road he merged off the interstate three exits too late, on purpose, in order to approach his condo tower from the south. The setting sun would light the tower's blue glass pink, an effect that always made Jack feel like some kind of prince.

Two miles ahead he saw the great contemporary edifice, the tallest residential tower in the Southeast, but to Jack it seemed less like home than a pretentious sham, his temple of shitty priorities. Fighting the urge to stop, he passed bars he'd haunted for years. He saw national grocery stores and high-rise hotels where his favorite dives used to stand. The city, he thought, hadn't missed him. It went on. It would always go on. Somewhere Jack had read that life's only consistency is change, and he felt it was time to hasten the process, to begin anew and be, in a sense, reborn.

At the base of the Excellor building, Jack tossed his keys to the concierge and jogged to the oversized Peachtree side-walk, squinting into the sun. Men in suits were emptying out from some convention and filing to tavern patios. Jack had no idea what day it was; he was uninhibited, he thought, unlike the suits. He kicked off his boots, peeled away his shirt and socks, and dropped his jeans. He wadded the clothing and pushed it deep into a trash can. Drivers began to stare. In a single fluid motion Jack latched his thumbs around the waist of his boxer shorts, bent over to free himself from them, and began his fateful run on slapping feet. The wind behind him felt like cleansing water. At an outdoor café, women huddled next to fancy lamps and pointed. Some male voice at a shoe shop cheered for Jack by name. He couldn't help but laugh, lifting his arms as if breaking marathon tape. "Freedom!" he shouted, to nobody. "And Godspeed to idiots!" As commuters became truly stuck, mired in more and more commuters, they began to really notice Jack—the pale jiggle of belly, the gyrating lumps behind—and when a woman blared her horn, it incited the whole unmoving mass to follow suit. In the logjam Jack saw an opportunity: He cut left off the sidewalk and wove through cars, until he reached the yellow-lined center of Peachtree, headed south like a snowbird, fueled by this cacophony of honking and his own laughter, the kind that bubbles up from the gut, the soundtrack of a maniac.

Acknowledgements

A decade in the making, this book wouldn't exist without the help of so many people. Chief among them are the U.S. servicemembers I've worked with on journalism projects since 2003, beginning when I was a greenhorn reporter in rural Indiana. The intent here was to shape the stories and thoughts they shared—alongside other sources of inspiration—into a novel that sheds light on their experiences in a fresh and profound way.

First and foremost is U.S. Army Cpl. Samuel Walley, whose intelligence, wild spirit, and strength in overcoming catastrophic injury and mental torment astounds me to this day. (Samuel had reached a too-common low point when we met; he's since graduated college with honors, gotten married, become a public speaker, and as of this writing was recently promoted to assistant manager for the PTSD Foundation of America's Georgia Chapter.) The same goes for U.S. Marine Corps Cpl. Charles Leak. And a long list of other incredibly resilient men and women.

Thanks to my former literary agent, Damian McNicholl, for always believing in this story and taking it into the trenches with me. Thanks to publisher Mike Sager of The Sager Group for writing the *Esquire* story that set this all in motion—and for ultimately bringing the book into the world.

Friends and great writers who've shared thoughts on this book and encouraged me to keep going include Charles McNair, Thomas Mullen, Charles Bethea, Thomas Lake, and

Bret Witter. Thanks to Harvey Klinger, Jarel Portman, Matt Fullerty, and my astute, wonderful mom for close reads and encouragement. I'm indebted forever to professors Matthew Brennan, Tom Noyes, Robert Rebein, and Dan Bowlman.

Thanks as always to my beloved band of ATL coconspirators—Lori, Lola, and Marley Green—for putting up with Daddy through thousands of late nights and so many setbacks in this quest.

About the Author

Josh Green is an award-winning journalist, fiction author, and editor whose work has appeared in *Atlanta, Garden & Gun, Indianapolis Monthly, The Atlanta Journal-Constitution, The Los Angeles Review, The Baltimore Review,* and several anthologies. His first book, *Dirtyville Rhapsodies*, was hailed by *Men's Health* as a "Best Book for the Beach" and was named a top 10 book of the year by *Atlanta*. He lives with his wife and daughters in Atlanta.

About the Publisher

The Sager Group was founded in 1984. In 2012 it was chartered as a multimedia content brand, with the intent of empowering those who create art—an umbrella beneath which makers can pursue, and profit from, their craft directly, without gatekeepers. TSG publishes books; ministers to artists and provides modest grants; and produces documentary, feature, and commercial films. By harnessing the means of production, The Sager Group helps artists help themselves. For more information, please see www.TheSagerGroup.net.

More Books from The Sager Group

The Swamp: Deceit and Corruption in the CIA
An Elizabeth Petrov Thriller (Book 1)
by Jeff Grant

Chains of Nobility: Brotherhood of the Mamluks (Book 1-3)
by Brad Graft

Meeting Mozart: A Novel Drawn from the Secret Diaries of Lorenzo Da Ponte
by Howard Jay Smith

Death Came Swiftly: Novel About the Tay Bridge Disaster of 1879 by Bill Abrams

A Boy and His Dog in Hell: And Other Stories
by Mike Sager

Miss Havilland: A Novel
by Gay Daly

The Orphan's Daughter: A Novel
by Jan Cherubin

Lifeboat No. 8: Surviving the Titanic
by Elizabeth Kaye

Into the River of Angels: A Novel by George R. Wolfe

See our entire library at TheSagerGroup.net

THE SAGER GROUP

Artifex Te Adiuva

Made in United States
North Haven, CT
24 May 2024